UNDER A SPELL?

Mac stood in the doorway of the hotel suite, quiet, motionless, and watched the auburn-haired beauty. She still wore the skintight dress that showed every curve, curves he wanted to explore. In the back of his mind a voice told him he'd already touched her, but he didn't remember a thing. Surely he would remember touching something that looked so good. She leaned over the table sampling with her fingers bits and pieces of everything on the trays, obviously unaware that he was watching her.

"Looks good," he said, totally beguiled by the schoolmarm-turned-goddess. "May I join you?"

She swung around, her hair flying about her head, as if in slow motion. She smiled—she always smiled. "Of course. Sit here and I'll fix you a plate."

Kathleen knelt on the floor in front of him, and held out a plate of food to Mac. He touched her fingers when he took the plate. His senses tingled, his legs weakened. She had to be a witch. He found no other explanation for what she did to him. God, he thought, first I'm confronted by a little old woman straight from Santa's Workshop, and now a sorceress, bewitching me with her spell . . .

Enchanted

Patti Berg

JOVE BOOKS, NEW YORK

ENCHANTED

A Jove Book / published by arrangement with
the author

PRINTING HISTORY
Jove edition / November 1994

ISBN: 0-515-11512-6

A JOVE BOOK®
Jove Books are published by The Berkley Publishing Group,
200 Madison Avenue, New York, New York 10016.
JOVE and the "J" design are trademarks
belonging to Jove Publications, Inc.

PRINTED IN THE UNITED STATES OF AMERICA

10 9 8 7 6 5 4 3 2 1

PROLOGUE

Merry Nicholas shuffled through Central Park toting two candy-cane–striped carpetbags. Her voluminous red dress and starched white apron rustled in the faint summery breeze as she maneuvered through Frisbee throwers, barking dogs, and baby carriages. When she reached Fifth Avenue she stopped, tilted her head skyward, and squinted into the sun. The bright light gave way to a cloudy vision—a woman; a man; another woman. Merry's eyes twinkled over the top of rectangular spectacles. "Ah, yes, yes, yes." She nodded. "I know just what's needed here. Don't worry, Nicky. I'll take care of everything."

The vision disappeared as Merry scurried on her way, singing, "Fa la la la la, la la, la, la."

CHAPTER

ONE

Eleven pairs of eyes looked in awe at the man seated at the head of the conference table. No one made a sound. No one breathed until Mr. O'Brien turned a page.

They watched him, impressed with the way he scrutinized the contents of the magazine mock-up. He scanned one page, then the next, his expressionless face never changing. He didn't spend time analyzing individual portions of the document, but they knew he wouldn't overlook even the smallest detail. McKenna O'Brien liked things perfect—*t*'s crossed, *i*'s dotted—and heaven help those who misspelled a word.

McKenna O'Brien—Mac to his friends, *Mr.* O'Brien to his staff—garnered respect from all who knew him. He took crazy, half-baked schemes and made them successes; hired people for their talent rather than their education. He had a commanding, powerful personality, and no one disputed his authority. He had the rare gift of making millions on everything he touched; in fact, the whispers around town said McKenna O'Brien could spin straw into gold, and a lot of people believed it.

Mac hesitated when he reached the final page. He turned the magazine over and gave the cover one more look. His fingers drummed on the table as he inventoried the faces of his editorial staff. He hated to see them squirm while they waited for his verdict on the latest periodical developed by his publishing empire, but he didn't let even a thread of emotion show on his face. Not a scowl, not a smile. Nothing to hint at his approval or dislike, until his gaze met Kathleen Flannigan's. That's when his sun-bleached, strawberry blond brows knit together over his frowning, smoky blue eyes.

"Would you care to explain *where* you got the idea for *this* magazine?"

Kathleen looked him straight in the eyes. "It's called *Success*, and I took your basic idea and ran with it. The topics are hot. We have excellent writers, and our surveys show the circulation will be larger than anything else we publish."

"I don't recognize *any* of my basic ideas, *Ms*. Flannigan."

"You wanted a new and innovative magazine for women and that's what I've put together."

Mac looked down at the mock-up, thumbing through its pages. "No. What I wanted was a magazine for successful businesswomen, the ones who've reached the top. They want to read about investments and finances and . . ." He raised his eyes and quickly scanned Kathleen's outdated navy suit, amused at her taste in fashion, then lowered his eyes again to the mock-up. ". . . and fashions for work."

"You're wrong."

Mac's head shot up. No one ever told him he was wrong, least of all his staff. But Kathleen Flannigan bucked him at every turn and had done so since the day he hired her. "Then tell me," he said, "what do successful women want?"

"To be considered a success no matter what their station in life, be it housewife or president. To not be looked down at for being a maid or secretary, or in some other career that others might not consider the pinnacle of success."

Kathleen took a deep breath, aimed her gaze directly at Mac. She grinned, then looking at her shoulder, very carefully, very dramatically, brushed an invisible piece of lint off her jacket.

Mac came close to laughing at Kathleen's theatrics, but didn't. Instead, he leaned back in his chair, folded his arms across his chest, and contemplated her words. All the others around the conference table seemed to disappear as he directed his attention to Kathleen, searching her eyes, those azure eyes that had driven him crazy six years before, the same eyes he had ignored for the last five. He saw her determination, that strong-willed drive that wouldn't give up.

The sun's rays glinted off the glossy, brightly colored cover of the magazine, and he forced his thoughts away from Kathleen and back to the issue at hand. It didn't really matter what he thought of *Success*. It looked good. It would probably garner a lot of attention on the magazine racks. What did he know about the contents of a woman's magazine? He hired people like Kathleen because they knew and loved the business, and Kathleen, in particular, had the uncanny knack of knowing just what the public would like.

Kathleen. He didn't want to think about her. For the past five years he had stayed away from meetings such as this just so he wouldn't have to see her. Why had he attended today? Why had he put himself through the torture of seeing the woman he had forced himself to forget?

He pushed back the massive black leather executive chair, took the mock-up, and walked to the window, staring out at the high-rises that surrounded his building. He noticed with sadness that only a trace of blue sky could be seen overhead. Twenty years ago he could see the world from this room; now he saw nothing but skyscrapers. When had New York swallowed him? he wondered. He had long ago tired of it, so why couldn't he walk away and leave it all behind? Because walking away was never easy. Hadn't he proved that when he walked away from Kathleen?

When he looked back at his staff, all eyes focused on him, each person involved with the magazine waiting for his decision on whether or not to go ahead. He could easily quash the concept now. He could drop six months' worth of work in the trash can at his feet. But, in reality, the only thing he had against the magazine was that Kathleen was at its helm, and he knew he couldn't throw away what promised to be a big moneymaker for his company, simply because he wanted to stay away from the magazine's creator.

His eyes rested on Kathleen's, and hers bore a hole straight to his soul. Ignoring the lump in his throat, he gritted his teeth, took four long strides across the room, and stopped at her side. He dropped the mock-up on the table in front of her. Bending his large, six-foot-five-inch frame, he leaned over, his face so close to Kathleen's that he could see each individual pore on her makeup-free face.

"If you say it will work, you've got my blessing. However"—he stood up straight, looming over Kathleen—"this is your baby." His voice lowered, almost to a whisper. "Don't expect any help from me."

"Damn it, Mac. Why do you always let that woman get to you?" That's what his father would have said if he'd been in the boardroom and seen Mac's lack of warmth and charm. But his dad hadn't been in the boardroom in over five years, and the words Mac heard were the ones filling his head as he stared at his surroundings—his dad's old office, filled with cherished mementos, worn but comfortable chairs, floor-to-ceiling bookcases overstuffed with reference books, Zane Greys, and Louis L'Amours, and the old oak desk Mac had carved his name in as a boy.

He reached across the desk and picked up the photo of his father, staring into the warm gray eyes of the elderly gentleman. "I turned forty-nine yesterday, Dad," he whispered. "Nearly half a century of living and what have I accomplished? I've doubled your empire. I socialize with presidents and kings. But I'm lonely." He shook off his sadness and set the photo back in its usual spot on the left side of his desk.

He shuffled through a pile of papers, wishing the work, the company, and everything else demanding his attention would disappear. He pinched the bridge of his nose, attempting to drive away the headache that had plagued him since early morning. Forcing himself to relax, he leaned back in his chair, dug his fingers into his neck, and kneaded the taut muscles. Stolen moments of relaxation rarely occurred, but today he didn't care. Today he started reflecting on his life, and he didn't like what he saw.

"Excuse me, Mr. O'Brien."

He didn't even see Grace, his secretary since time began, walk into the room, carrying another pile of dreaded paper.

"I hate to bother you, but I have something important to discuss."

"Oh, God. Whatever you do, don't tell me you're quitting." He leaned on the desk, resting his chin on the heels of his hands, pressing fingers into his temples.

"No"—Grace chuckled—"but you just might fire me."

"Why?"

"I want to talk about the Christmas party."

He looked from the slightly built woman with a head of tightly permed grayish brown hair to the calendar on his desk. "It's June."

"Yes, I know it's June," Grace said, "but in order to get the best location, we have to reserve early. Now—"

"You know I don't celebrate Christmas."

"You used to—"

"Those are the key words, Grace," he interrupted again. "I *used to*. But not anymore."

"But the parties were a tradition when your father was alive. Remember how he loved dressing up like Santa for the kids?"

"That was a long time ago. People don't have time for office Christmas parties anymore. They're too busy."

"That's just an excuse."

"Okay, then. Let's just say *I'm* too busy for a Christmas party, and I'm too busy to continue this conversation."

"Very well, sir," Grace huffed. "I'll try again next month." She dropped a stack of folders on his desk and walked to the door, turning back for one parting remark. "By the way. I hope you don't mind if I change your signature block to Scrooge O'Brien."

Mac frowned as he watched the door close behind Grace, an institution around McKenna Publishing. More like a mother than a secretary, Grace was one of the few people who could get away with back-talking the boss. But her dedication and loyalty never failed, and Mac was positive she'd die at her desk.

He quickly dismissed all thoughts of Grace and Christmas parties, and tried to forget the headache. But other thoughts crept into his mind, and soon the wording of the contract blurred as his eyes moved from the legalese to the photo of his father, and then to the sterling silver frame at the right side of his desk. It held the picture of an older woman, white-haired and plump, with bright red cheeks and a loving smile. People who saw the photo assumed she was Mac's grandmother. In truth, he liked the frame—and the picture that had come with it. He never considered replacing it with a photo of someone he knew. He cherished the frame and the memory of his father who had given it to him one Christmas morning, just a few hours before he died.

There was a story behind the gift, something he never quite believed. Remembering his father's words made Mac laugh and brought back sentimental thoughts of the man who never had a harsh word to say and found good in everything that surrounded him.

"There's something special about this," his father told him, running his fingers over the dulled silver. "I was in an antique store the other night, looking for something unique for your mother. There were a bunch of old frames sitting on a shelf, mostly wood and brass. I found this one hidden behind the others. It was tarnished and covered with dust, but when I picked it up, it shimmered a bit. Maybe it wasn't actually a shimmer, because the silver needed polishing. I wiped off some of the dust with my finger to see the picture and, now don't think I'm losing my mind, but I could have sworn the lady in that picture winked at me."

Mac smiled as he remembered the story. So like his dad to find something magical about a tarnished silver frame and a picture of an old woman. But he never forgot the words, nor the love in his father's eyes when he gave his son that last Christmas hug. The day after his father's funeral, Mac polished the silver, buffed it until it glowed, and put it on his desk, a constant reminder of the man he deeply missed.

Christmas hadn't been the same since that day. A big part of him had died along with his dad—the part that laughed and cried and found good in everyone and everything—and he wanted it back. He just didn't know how to bring it to life.

He stared into the eyes of the woman in the photo. *I wish I could believe in magic the way my father did. I wish you could wink and bring me happiness.* He laughed, shook his head, and returned to the contract before him.

Kathleen didn't knock timidly. Timidity wasn't a word in Kathleen Flannigan's vocabulary. She didn't even wait for Mac to invite her in, but pushed open the door, slammed it behind her, tossed the mock-up on his desk, then took a seat across from the giant she called boss.

Mac's head didn't move; only his eyes looked up from his work. Don't look into her eyes, he told himself. Her eyes had mesmerized him ten years ago when she was only twenty-two. Find something else to focus on. Not the lips. No, definitely not the lips. Ah, the lapel of that boring navy jacket. "Do you have an appointment?" he asked, emotionless.

"No, sir. But we need to talk."

"I'm listening." He looked down at the papers on his desk, away from her startling blue eyes, away from her lips.

"Why do you find it so difficult to like my work?" She leaned back in the chair, crossed her legs, and waited for an explanation.

He raised his head, let his eyes stray to her one exposed knee. He remembered the old days when her knees were covered with faded blue jeans, skintight, and looking much too tempting to a man who wanted desperately to ignore his desire for a much younger woman. Get a grip, Mac, he chastised himself.

Kathleen followed his eyes and uncomfortably adjusted her skirt over the bare expanse of skin.

He crossed his arms over his chest, drumming the fingers of his left hand on the opposite arm, a posture that frightened most people. His overwhelming size intimidated others. But Kathleen Flannigan didn't look threatened.

Their eyes met.

The battle began.

"I don't dislike your work. If I did, you wouldn't be in my employ." His eyes narrowed, and he stole another quick glance at her legs. "The only thing I dislike is how you go out of your way to do things contrary to my wishes."

"What you wish for and what's best for you and the company aren't necessarily the same things. You want a profitable magazine—that's what I plan to give you."

Unfolding his arms, he braced his hands on the edge of the desk and leaned forward. "I suppose if anyone can do it, you can. You've always been rather lucky."

"Not lucky. I'm good. Damn good."

One eyebrow rose at her statement. "I won't dispute that. I've known it for years."

"Then why do you ignore me?"

Silence. He turned away from Kathleen and stared out the window. How could he answer that question? In five long years he hadn't been able to bring himself to ask her about the rumor he'd heard about her and his father. Not that he wanted to believe the rumor, but he'd never had a chance to question his dad, and it was much easier to ignore Kathleen than confront her with his fears.

Just as he had ignored her for five years, he ignored her question. Instead of answering, he picked up his pen and scribbled a just-remembered thought on a piece of paper— *Housekeeper*. Then he looked up, but not at Kathleen. "Tell me about *Success*," he said, looking over her shoulder, focusing on the bookcases behind her.

"It's going to be great." Pride rang out in her words. "It's not directed at any particular group, but for successful women and women who want to be successful. It's full of ideas to make their lives easier, help them achieve greater success. It's for women who know how to handle men, and for women who need a little help in that department."

Try as he might, Mac couldn't keep his eyes from Kathleen's face, nor a smile from his lips as he looked at the animation in her expression while she spoke about the magazine she so obviously loved. One of the many things Mac hadn't forgotten about Kathleen was that she never lacked emotion, strong emotion.

"Did I say something wrong?" she asked.

"No. I was just wondering. You aren't aiming this magazine toward feminists, are you?"

"And if I was?"

Mac shrugged his shoulders. "That would make it too much like other magazines on the stand."

"You're right. But like I said, it's not aimed at any one group. In fact"—Kathleen focused on the silver-framed photo on Mac's desk—"I think even your grandmother could benefit from the advice in my magazine."

Suppressing his laughter, Mac realized that, just like everyone else, Kathleen assumed the woman in the photograph was his grandmother. If she only knew that his ninety-eight-year-old grandmother had been the ultimate feminist in her day, and even now refused to take anyone's advice.

"What about advertising?" he asked, turning his thoughts back to the magazine and the things he knew would make it or break it. "What about marketing? What about writers?"

"It's all under control. We're working on the advertising, but we've got the best articles from the best writers. You'll be pleased when you see the final copy."

"So, you plan on letting me see the finished product? I thought you might try to evade my critical eye."

"I've always valued your opinion. I've missed your input over the years." She stood and walked slowly, thoughtfully, to the window and looked out at the New York skyline. "We used to be friends, Mac. What happened? Why did things change?"

Ask her now, Mac, an inner voice told him. Ask her about what went on between her and your dad. Ask her about her daughter. His teeth clenched at his thoughts. His eyes narrowed, and the headache that had nearly faded reappeared with a vengeance. Taking time to massage his temples and think of something to say, he stared at her back, at the strands of auburn hair escaping from the bun at the nape of her neck, at the shapeless navy blue suit that hid from view most of her feminine delights. What had happened to the pretty young girl with a head full of ideas, who laughed at his jokes, and made him feel twenty all over again?

He looked from her back to the skyline, then into her eyes when she turned around, the look in her eyes that told him she needed an answer. "Things didn't change," he said. "You changed."

"No," she stated flatly. "I just got older, and wiser."

"That's not all. I've watched you with your staff, with the others in the office. You're a lot tougher than you used to be."

"A woman has to be tough to get ahead. I have a big goal to achieve, and I won't get there by being weak."

Mac searched her eyes, her face, looking for just a trace of the Kathleen he had known a long time ago, but the vulnerability and the innocence were gone. "So, what's your goal?"

She went back to the chair, took the mock-up from his desk, and sat down. "First, I plan to make this magazine a success. A huge success. Second, I plan on running McKenna Publishing."

He didn't see any laughter in her eyes, only the sincerity with which she made the statement. "Have you already hired a hit man to get rid of me?" He hoped a touch of humor would enter his voice, but years of training kept his poker face and nonemotional voice in check.

"I don't need a hit man," she said, staring hard into his eyes. "You'll be the cause of your own demise."

He thanked his lucky stars he didn't have a mouth full of beer, or he would have spat it across the room at her outrageous statement. Yet, he had heard her words and clearly understood her meaning. Publishing made him rich. It didn't make him happy. And that fact, alone, would surely drive him to an early grave.

"You don't believe me, do you?" she added.

"I have no intention of giving up my hold on this company."

"You don't love the publishing business, not the way you should. So why not let someone like me, someone who does love it, take over?"

"Because you haven't got what it takes."

She leaned forward in her chair, giving Mac a better view of her haughty expression. "My balls are just as big as yours, *Mr. O'Brien*. I just wear them in a different place."

That did it. God, the woman was driving him mad. Why not give her McKenna Publishing right now? That would be more desirable than listening to her boastful remarks.

"I'll make you a deal," he said, keeping his voice calm in spite of the anger building inside. "We'll talk about a promotion if this magazine lives up to all your projections."

"Why don't we talk about it now? I've been here a long time. You know my work, and this magazine *will* succeed. I deserve a promotion. A sizable one."

He took a moment to ponder her words. He left his comfortable chair and stood where Kathleen had been moments before, the hot sunlight beaming down upon him through the window. Everything she said rang true. He had grown tired of the publishing world, but that had happened a long time ago. About the same time he realized Kathleen Flannigan had gotten under his skin. The same time he realized she was too young. The same time he went to Europe to clear his mind.

A year away had done the trick. He saw everything in a different light when he returned—especially Kathleen. Gone were the faded blue jeans and bouncing ponytail, replaced by those awful blue suits and that horrible bun. But the biggest change of all was the presence of a newborn baby, and no husband in sight. And those rumors. Those horrible rumors.

He remembered those days in Europe, and how he had wanted to come home and see her again. He had missed her—oh, how he had missed her. But all those feelings diminished the moment he saw the baby, the moment his father died. He refused to confront her, refused to find out the truth. It was easier to form his own opinions and avoid her. So he kept his distance, forcing Kathleen from his mind, but not completely from his heart. And now she was creeping back into his brain. Why, after so many years, did all those earlier desires have to reappear? He didn't want her in his thoughts. He didn't want her anywhere near. And the closer she got to the top at McKenna Publishing, the closer she got to him. But she was good. Damn good. Just as she had said. McKenna Publishing needed her, even if he didn't.

His thoughts disturbed him. The quiet disturbed him. He felt her eyes boring into his back. He left the window and went to the marble-topped wet bar, opened the refrigerator, and took out a bottle of Molson. Turning to Kathleen, he twisted off the top, took a sip, and stared into her frowning eyes.

"I might need someone to head up New Ventures."

She didn't waste a minute in responding. "That's a start."

"And what if you don't succeed?"

"I will."

She smiled.

He scowled.

CHAPTER
TWO

Mac adjusted the thermostat one more time, trying without success to bring a hint of cool air into his exercise room. The oppressive heat and humidity didn't keep him from his daily routine—no matter what, he never failed to put in an hour each day.

He wiped his brow with the back of his hand, climbed on the stationary bike, increased the tension, and immediately had the speed up to twenty-five miles an hour, where he would keep it for at least fifteen minutes. Sweat glistened on his naked chest and back while he pumped the pedals at a furious pace. He shoved all thoughts of work completely out of his head. Work had its own time and place—the exercise room was off limits. Here he relieved his stress, regained his sanity, and kept his body in perfect condition, kept himself looking as he had twenty years before.

For the past half hour he'd been attempting to meditate, to clear his mind of everything but his straining muscles and the flow of tension out of his body. That's how it usually worked when he entered the exercise room. But not today.

He'd been awake most of the night thinking about Kathleen, about her eyes, her smile, her legs, her child, and about her ridiculous goal. My God, he thought. A woman running McKenna Publishing. Preposterous. His grandmother may have run the company once upon a time, but a woman wouldn't run it again. Besides, he had every intention of passing McKenna Publishing down to his firstborn son. Unfortunately, he didn't have an heir, and at the rate he was going, his prospects of producing one were nil. He felt obligated to get married first, and that prospect, too, seemed extremely remote. But marriage and an heir had been uppermost in his mind of late. Of course, some people, like Kathleen Flannigan, didn't let things like tradition keep them from producing an heir outside of marriage. That thought had been nagging him all day, too.

Kathleen didn't do things in the conventional way. What had he ever seen in her? His tastes ran to the soft, feminine, sexy types—blonde hair, petite, and sophisticated. Like Ashley Tate, the woman who'd been his significant other for ten long years, and the biggest reason he'd run away from Kathleen.

No. That wasn't the reason he'd run. Kathleen wasn't his type. She was much too tall. And even though she kept her hair hidden in that prissy bun, he knew it was much too long, too curly, and too auburn. If he didn't know better, he'd swear the woman had been educated at the FBI academy. She certainly dressed like a federal agent—didn't she own anything besides navy and gray? Didn't she know short skirts were fashionable again? The woman had legs—his eyes and brain zoomed to her legs whenever she entered a room. Long, slender legs. The best-looking legs he'd ever seen. There were a lot of things about Kathleen Flannigan that bothered him, but her legs disturbed him the most.

Again he tightened the tension on the bike and attempted to shove all thoughts of Kathleen completely out of his head.

But he couldn't get her out of his thoughts. She had been just one of many things that had gone wrong yesterday. Even his housekeeper had quit. She gave him no reason, just said she'd gotten a sudden urge to travel. She didn't know where. She didn't even know why. She just felt compelled to pack up and leave. A *premonition*, she called it. *Insanity*, was Mac's conclusion. Hell, he told her he'd increase her salary, give her a bonus. She still wanted to leave. He asked her to stick around until he could get hold of the agency. In the end, though, he couldn't talk her into staying. Now he had no one. To make matters worse, he'd been so upset by his conversation with Kathleen, he'd forgotten to have Grace arrange for a new housekeeper. He needed someone. It didn't matter about references, he just wanted someone who could cook, clean, and iron. Any woman would do.

He looked at the Rolex on his wrist. Thirty seconds longer. Time to pour on speed. He stood on the pedals, leaned against the handlebars, and pumped with all his might. All thoughts but the increasing speed left his brain. He concentrated totally on pushing the speedometer to the farthest point. Just a little faster. Just a little more sweat.

Buzz!

"Get the door," he gasped.

Buzz!

"Hell!" He'd forgotten about the housekeeper, or his lack of one.

He stopped pedaling right before reaching the ultimate speed, grabbed a towel to wipe the perspiration from his face, hands, and arms, dropped it over the handlebars, then stormed to the front door, clad only in sweaty gray exercise shorts.

The buzz sounded again just as his fingers reached the knob. He yanked open the door and startled the delivery boy who stood before him, eyes wide, clutching a long white box with a big blue bow.

"Are you Mr. O'Brien?"

He scowled. "Yes?"

"These are for you." The boy gulped, thrust the box into Mac's hands, and beat a hasty retreat, not even waiting for a tip.

Must be some mistake, Mac thought, closing the door and setting the box on the foyer table. He noticed the vase that usually sat on that table was empty. Fresh flowers always filled that vase, but not today. He had no one to fill the vase, no one to arrange the flowers, no one to answer the door, no one to take care of all the things he took for granted.

He pulled the blue ribbon off the box, removed the lid, and smelled the sweet aroma of the long-stemmed red roses inside. He took them and the heavy crystal vase into the kitchen, filled the vase with water, and clumsily arranged the flowers. He searched the box for a card but found nothing. He assumed Ashley had sent them, then wondered why. She must want something.

Tonight they were going to the Pallenbergs'. She'd been trying for weeks to talk him into taking her to the social event of the summer. He hated going out on weeknights, but he'd finally relented, knowing she would hound him until he accepted. Ashley Tate—beautiful, sophisticated, and, to Mac's dismay, a snob. He gave her everything money could buy. That's all she wanted. At forty-two, she still didn't want a husband. She definitely didn't want children. If truth be told, she probably didn't want him, either—just his money.

So why did he stick with her? Because he didn't know what he wanted, or what he needed. Because he knew how to handle sophisticated people. He'd grown up with them, he socialized with them, he didn't know anything else. And the thought of bringing a stranger into his world, or the thought of living in any other world, scared the hell out of him. He knew what to expect from Ashley, and, after ten years, it would be hard to start over with someone new.

The loud buzz of the doorbell startled him out of his thoughts. He carried the vase to the entryway, set it down on the table, and opened the door.

"I'm sorry, sir," the delivery boy muttered. "I forgot to give you the card."

"Thanks." Mac stared at the unfamiliar writing, then at the boy's retreat. "Hold on a moment," Mac called after him.

"Yes, sir," the boy said, turning around, fear written on his face.

Mac smiled. "You forgot your tip."

The boy's expression eased as he watched Mac fumble around in the drawer of the foyer table, the place where he always kept spare change for just such occasions. He pressed the money into the boy's hand, then closed the door.

His brow furrowed at the words *Mr. O'Brien* scrawled on the envelope. Obviously not from Ashley, he surmised, tearing open the flap.

Thanks for the promotion.

The furrowed brow turned to a frown, then to a throbbing headache. Kathleen Flannigan had entered his brain, and it looked like she meant to stay.

Mac stuck his hand into the shower, testing the hot, hard-pounding spray. He dropped the towel he wore around his hips and stepped into the ebony-tiled enclosure. He started to close the door when he heard the doorbell's buzz—again.

"Damn!"

He shut off the nozzle, grabbed the towel from the floor, wrapped it around his waist, and headed to the door. How many more interruptions could he expect today?

Leaving a puddle of water on the bathroom floor, and damp footprints trailing across the thick cream-colored carpeting, he had made it only to the bedroom door when the buzz sounded again. "Hold your horses," he mumbled. The towel slipped twice as he marched down the long hallway and through the massive living room, his anger building as he carefully struggled to secure his attire. The buzz sounded again.

"I'm coming!" he yelled. This had better be important, he thought, while inventing a barrage of swear words to use as assault weapons against the person or persons disrupting his shower.

Turning the knob, he stood behind the slightly opened door, and peered around the edge to speak to the caller, but the woman before him didn't wait for his greeting.

"Ah, Mr. O'Brien. I'm so glad you're home." She was short, round, with fluffy white hair she wore piled on top of her head. She spoke with an accent he couldn't quite place, but he didn't have time to make any further observations before she scurried inside and shoved the door closed behind her.

Mac shivered at the sudden drop of temperature. Did he imagine it, or had an icy gust of wind just blown into the room?

The stranger dropped two large, candy-cane–striped carpetbags, put her hands on her hips, and stared at Mac, who looked quite befuddled. "No, no, no," she said, shaking a finger at Mac's bare chest. "You'll catch your death of cold walking around half-naked like that."

Mac clutched the cold, damp towel to his body. "Look, lady. I don't know who you are, but no one has the right to barge into my house."

"I didn't barge. You opened the door for me."

"I opened the door to see who was there."

"That's right. You saw who was there and I came in. I'm your new housekeeper, and I really would appreciate it if you'd get out of that wet towel and put something more respectable on. My word, young man, you leave *nothing* to the imagination."

He frowned and, in an absentminded gesture, crossed his hands over the front of the towel. "It's my house and I'll dress any way I want." Actually, he wanted to be dressed in something warmer. God, he was freezing.

And then her words registered. *Housekeeper?*

"Wait a minute. How can you be the new housekeeper? I haven't called the agency yet."

"Good. Then I've saved you all that time and trouble." She fidgeted with the roses, arranging them to perfection.

Maybe he needed to try another tactic to get her out of his house. Then, again, he did need a housekeeper, and she wasn't the least bit threatening. In fact, she looked rather familiar, but he couldn't remember where he'd seen her before. "Do I know you?"

"So to speak." She opened one of the carpetbags and pulled out a feather duster, busying herself around the room.

"What's that supposed to mean?"

She stopped her dusting and turned to stare at Mac. "Haven't you put any clothes on yet?"

"I'm not moving one inch until you tell me who the hell you are."

"Is that all you're waiting for?"

"Yes."

"Name's Mrs. Nicholas, but you can call me Merry. That's Merry—spelled M-E-R-R-Y."

"Okay, Merry—spelled M-E-R-R-Y. Who the hell are you?"

"I told you. Your new housekeeper. Now, please stop swearing."

"I don't swear." He followed her into the living room, where she delicately dusted the glass and chrome, and the black-and-white leather furniture.

"My, my, my. This furniture won't do at all."

"What?"

"Don't worry. I've got a few things in my bags to make this place look a bit more homey."

He stepped in front of the rosy-cheeked lady, whose eyes leveled at his hairy chest. "Do you expect me to let you barge in here and take over?"

"Of course I do, young man. Now, run along and finish your shower, or whatever it was you were doing when I arrived. I'll talk to you when you're decent."

He'd been dismissed—by a total stranger.

Mac came out of his bedroom half an hour later dressed in corduroy slacks and a winter-weight sweater. He'd checked the thermostat. It was set at seventy-two degrees, but the temperature had dropped to sixty. He couldn't fool around with it now, though. He wanted to learn more about Merry Nicholas.

He found her in the kitchen, humming a tune while she arranged a vase of red and white carnations.

"Oh, hello, Mr. O'Brien. Don't you look handsome all dressed up like that." She bustled over to the table and pulled out a chair. "Here. I've made you a nice warm lunch, and I've got cookies baking in the oven."

"I don't eat lunch."

"Of course you do. Mine, anyway. Now sit down and eat."

He wasn't about to argue with her. Besides, the soup and sandwich looked and smelled delicious. And was that hot chocolate in the mug, with miniature marshmallows floating on top?

He bit into the sliced turkey on white bread and savored the taste of thickly spread mayonnaise. When had he last allowed himself the luxury of high-cholesterol mayonnaise?

"Mrs. Nicholas?"

"Merry. Please."

"Merry? How did you know I needed a housekeeper?" Since taking his shower he had regained some of his senses. He couldn't let this little old lady take the upper hand with him. But, against his better judgment, he realized there was something about her he rather enjoyed, something kind of cherubic.

She shrugged her shoulders and pulled open the oven door to take out a tray of sugar cookies. "Oh, I just have a way of knowing when someone needs me."

"Like a premonition?" He remembered his other house-keeper's word that morning.

"*Premonition?* No, no, no. That's a warning something bad is going to happen. Nothing bad happens when I'm around."

"Nothing?"

"Of course not, child."

Mac took another bite and forced himself to smile. He hadn't been a child to anyone in well over thirty years. He liked the feeling. In fact, he liked Merry, in spite of her uniquely forceful personality. Somehow, whether it was the tone of her voice or the matter-of-fact things she said, she made him happy. God, he hadn't been really happy in ages.

"Are you from New York, Merry?" he asked, peering over the top of his turkey sandwich.

"Oh, no, no, no. I just came here for the summer." She sat down at the table across from him with a cup of the steaming hot chocolate and a plate full of freshly baked sugar cookies.

When she sat down, he noticed the potted plant on the table. *Poinsettias?* Weren't they available only at Christmas?

Her small, rectangular-lensed glasses settled on the end of her nose, perched so precariously close to the edge he thought they would topple off. She gazed over their shiny gold rims while talking to Mac. "I always go away for the summer. Nicky, that's my husband, likes to tinker in his workshop all summer long. He just loves making things for the kids."

"The kids?"

"Oh, you know," she said with a wink.

He shook his head. No, he didn't know. Why couldn't she give him a straight answer? If he didn't know better, he could swear Mrs. Claus had just winked at him. Of course! That's where he had seen her before. The photo on his desk. The photo of the woman his dad swore had winked at him.

"I just remembered where I've seen you before."

"Oh, I knew you'd remember. How many years ago was it you got that frame for Christmas? Five? Six?"

"Five, but how did you know about the frame?"

She shrugged her shoulders. "Like I said, I just know these things."

"But . . . it *is* you in the picture?"

"Oh, I've been in a picture or two in my time."

"You're not going to answer me, are you?"

She glanced at the clock, then jumped up from the table. "Look at the time, Mr. O'Brien. Don't you have work to do and a party to go to tonight? Do you need me to iron your shirt? I'm really good at ironing, you know. Not all women can do that well, but I've got the knack."

She *can* read my thoughts. This little old lady has just walked into my life, appears to know everything about me, and I'm allowing it to continue. I must be losing my mind.

Mac spent most of the afternoon at his desk, catching up on a stack of correspondence that needed his personal reply. Although Merry never bothered him, he could hear her humming Christmas carols in the living room which adjoined his office. It sounded as though she was pushing furniture around, but he didn't want to look, afraid of what the strange lady might be doing. She seemed harmless enough, maybe a bit eccentric, but he didn't think she was casing the place or pocketing away valuables.

At six o'clock he walked into the living room, tall, handsome, and dapper, totally unprepared for the scene that greeted him.

Merry sat in an ancient maple rocker before a blazing fire, a lacy white afghan draped around her shoulders. Before he could ask where the rocker came from, she looked up from her knitting. "Oh, my dear. You look absolutely splendid in that tuxedo. My Nicky, now, he's partial to flannel shirts and suspenders. I just can't imagine him in anything quite so fancy."

"I don't suppose you'd like to take one of my old tuxes home to him?"

"No, no, no. Nicky's not nearly as tall as you. Actually, he's a bit on the short side. And his belly, oh, you know that old saying about a bowlful of jelly. Well, that fits my Nicky to a tee."

"Somehow that doesn't surprise me," Mac mumbled under his breath.

"What was that you said?"

"Oh, nothing." Mac stood by the door, contemplating the mysterious rocker, the husband named Nicky, the bowlful of jelly. It was all too unbelievable, too crazy to even consider. No, she couldn't be Mrs. Claus. After all, he quit believing in Santa forty years ago—Santa was a childish myth—and Mac lived in the real world.

"I'll be home late," he said, dreading the thought of leaving his nice, rather chilly apartment for the heat and humidity of the hot June night.

"You mean early—as in near morning?"

"Okay. Very late. Don't wait up for me."

"Now, now, now, Mr. O'Brien. I have every intention of waiting up. Besides, I have a few things to discuss with you."

"Such as?"

"Such as you'll never find a wife at this Pallenberg shindig you're going to tonight."

"Who said I'm looking for a wife?"

She didn't answer, just glared at him over those funny little glasses in that defiant stance she seemed to have taken all day, her arms folded under her ample bosom.

"I'm not looking for a wife at the Pallenbergs'."

"I should hope not. Those society types aren't right for you at all."

"And you know who is right for me?"

"I've got a few ideas. Run along now, child, and enjoy your party. We'll talk later."

Mac disliked parties. He preferred quiet, intimate affairs, just himself and a beautiful woman. But his position in society demanded that he attend and make his presence known. Since the day he turned two and his mother put him in his first tuxedo, short pants and all, he'd been attending grand functions like this one. At two he kicked and screamed, until his mother took him aside, wiped away his tears, and told him to straighten up and act like a fine young man. He bore the O'Brien name, and O'Briens always put their best foot forward, even when they hated the task.

Tonight, as always, he did as expected, hobnobbing with the crème de la crème, the jet-setters whose lives revolved around parties, basking in the sun, and enjoying a steady stream of old money that never seemed to run dry. He could be just like them. He could let someone else operate McKenna Publishing, and all the other entities that made up the McKenna empire. But he'd never be able to live with himself if he didn't earn his way in this world. Mac had never wanted anything handed to him on a silver platter, although many people forced the plate in front of his face.

He stood before a six-foot ice carving of embracing swans, sipped a delicate glass of champagne, and wished he held a cold bottle of beer. The frigid air around the icy sculpture was the only invigorating thing about this party, with the possible exception of the woman he had accompanied.

Ashley stood with Mrs. Pallenberg, looking beautiful, graceful, and serene, with her blond hair swept off her back to reveal a slender, perfectly straight neck. Even in the heat she appeared cool, as though the night's warmth were air-conditioned just for her.

His eyes trailed down her spine, slender, straight, to her narrow waist, where the silk of her gown began. When had he last caressed that spine, slipped Ashley's gown from her shoulders to savor the satiny smooth skin of her breasts? One year? Two? He lost count a long time ago. Instead of making love, they shopped for jewels and furs. Instead of indulging in rich desserts, they ate rabbit food. Instead of sweating together in a passionate embrace, he exercised to keep in shape, in case someday someone might want to see what he looked like out of his fancy suits.

Oh, Ashley. How did we ever get together? Mac watched her animation as she flitted from one person to another, kissing a hand here, a cheek there. Ten years ago he asked her to marry him, but marriage didn't appear on her agenda, especially when he mentioned children. They turned her off completely. But he still stuck with her, year in and year out. She laughed, she looked beautiful, she kept him from being lonely on business trips. At one point their life together had been good. When did it end? He couldn't remember why or when the passion died. It just happened, and he blamed no one but himself.

He dated others on occasion, but nothing serious. Ashley didn't seem to mind as long as no one found out. The other women shared a common bond with Ashley—rich, pampered, spoiled. He had a knack for attracting the wrong type of women, the ones who flocked around him and his wealth. He'd been born into money and found it very hard to get out of the rut.

"You look rather bored this evening," Ashley whispered, slipping her hand around his arm.

"*Bored?* What makes you think I'm bored?"

"I haven't seen a smile on your face even once this evening. Come on now. Don't you have a smile, even for me?"

He looked down at the blonde, the top of her head not even reaching his shoulders. His forced smile didn't touch his eyes. "How much longer do we have to stay here?"

"It wouldn't be proper to leave so soon. I've watched you, darling. You haven't moved from this spot or talked to your friends all evening." She kissed her index and middle fingers and pressed them against his lips as a photographer snapped their picture. "You're embarrassing me in front of our friends, Mac. And looking miserable ruins your appearance."

"I am miserable."

"Have another drink. You'll feel better."

"It's not a drink I want." He took her small hand in his larger one, set the champagne glass down on the table, and nearly dragged her across the patio to the inside of the house.

"Come on. We're getting out of here."

"But I'm not ready to leave."

"Do you want to stay here by yourself?"

Her lips turned into a pout. "No. Please, Mac. Won't you stay just a little bit longer?"

"Why don't we go back to my place . . ." He stopped, remembering Merry Nicholas had taken up residence. He couldn't take Ashley home with him tonight. "Why don't we get a room at the Plaza, order a million things from room service, and, well, you know, enjoy the evening?"

"That's not my idea of a good evening and you know it."

Mac put his hands on her shoulders and held her in front of him. He stared into her lifeless brown eyes. He had no feelings left. Somehow, in the last twenty-four hours, his eyes had opened, and he realized he no longer wanted to continue this farce of a relationship. "You're right. I've known it for a long time, and, God help me, I've put up with it. But not any longer."

"What do you mean?"

"It's over. No more you and me."

"You can't possibly mean that."

"It's been over for years. I don't know why we've hung on to each other."

"But you love me."

"I do?"

"Of course you do. You've always loved me."

"Maybe once upon a time. But we're not in a fairy tale and we're not going to live happily ever after."

"Don't do it, Mac. I won't let you dump me."

"I don't consider it dumping, just, well, sort of a parting of the ways."

"You've lost your mind."

"No. I think I've finally found it." He leaned over and kissed the top of her head. "I'll take you home."

She jerked away from him. "I'll get home on my own. Don't worry about me. I'll be perfectly fine."

He walked to the doorway, a heaviness pressing against his chest. Ten years of his life down the drain. Could he start over? Did he want to start over? He turned back to look at Ashley. Her eyes narrowed, her lips pursed. And then he heard her parting words.

"Damn you, Mac. I'll get even. Just you wait."

CHAPTER

THREE

Mac smelled the pine the moment he stepped through the door. The fresh-baked apple pie, heavily spiced with cinnamon, assailed his senses and made him think of his childhood, and Christmas mornings long ago forgotten.

Merry, still awake as she had promised, sat in her rocker and looked up from her knitting, peering over the top of her glasses. A broad smile appeared on her rosy-cheeked face. "My, my, my. You're home much earlier than I expected."

"It's late, Merry. You shouldn't have stayed up."

"I said I would."

He pulled a straight-backed chair close to Merry, straddled the seat, and folded his arms atop its back. He watched her nimble fingers skillfully maneuvering needles and yarn into a lacy pattern. Never before had he watched a woman knit, and it amazed him that she could look at him and talk and not miss a stitch.

"Are you ready to talk?" she asked.

"If you want to discuss my personal life, I think I'd rather pass. It's in shambles at the moment."

"Then now's the time to talk, young man." She pushed her ball of red knitting yarn and her needles into the carpetbag next to her chair, then offered Mac a cookie from the plate on the table beside her.

"No, thanks," he said, but found himself plucking one off the plate. He inspected the cookie, turning it around and around in his fingers. It looked like an angel coated in white icing with silver sprinkles on the tips of the wings.

"Bit early for Christmas, isn't it?"

"Oh, my gracious, no. I prefer to think of it as Christmas all year long. Puts me in a most wonderful mood."

"I told my secretary that I didn't like Christmas. Are you trying to change my mind?"

"Oh, my, my, my. I plan to change much more than your mind, Mr. O'Brien."

"Such as?"

"Why, your life, of course."

Mac shook his head and laughed. "I like you, Merry."

"I like you, too," she said with a wink. "But I believe we have something important to discuss."

He stole another cookie and waited for Merry to begin.

"I've come to the conclusion since I got here this afternoon that you need a wife. Makes a man so much happier. Someday you'll have to ask my Nicky about that. Bless my soul, I don't know what he'd do without me."

"I just ended a ten-year relationship. The last thing I need is a wife. Besides, I'm not the marrying kind."

"Nonsense, young man. Every man needs a wife. You just haven't found the right woman."

"And how do you propose I find one?"

"Oh, it's very simple."

"If it's so simple, how come I'm forty-nine years old and still unmarried? Believe me, I've tried just about everything."

"Not everything. Seems to me you've been looking for a wife from the meager pickings at those parties you attend. Now, I'm not saying there aren't quality women in your crowd, but I just don't think any of them are quite right for you."

"Do *you* know what's right for me?"

"I know, but I'm sure somewhere in your mind is a vision of what you want. Why don't you tell me?"

While Mac was thinking, he looked around the room at the personal touches Merry had added. Doilies on the arms and backs of chairs, gilded picture frames filled with colorful photos of children and babies. The cozy room seemed to suit him. The crackling of the fire warmed his soul, sending the bitter feelings and hateful words of his evening with Ashley out of his brain. He couldn't remember ever feeling such peace and serenity. If this was a dream, he didn't want it to end.

He left his chair to stoke the fire. How could he tell Merry what he wanted in a wife? "I'm not quite sure where to begin."

"I find the beginning is always the best."

"You mean what she should look like?"

"I had something more, well, enduring in mind."

"Oh. Do you mind if I get a beer?"

Merry got up from her chair and pulled her knitted shawl tight around her shoulders. "You drink too much beer. I'll get you a nice warm glass of milk. While I'm gone, think about the enduring part for a moment or two."

Mac pulled the rocker close to the fireplace and shoved a couch around so he could relax in front of the blaze. He slipped off his shoes before sitting down and putting his feet on the sofa, closed his eyes for a moment, and thought about the woman of his dreams. He couldn't see a face. What he saw was a feeling. Warmth. Laughter. Intelligence. A strong sense of family. He saw what his father had—a woman who cared, loved, gave her life to her husband and son. And for one fleeting moment he thought he saw long, auburn hair.

"Here you go," Merry said as she put the glass of milk into his outstretched hand. Settling down, cozy and snug in the rocker, she looked into Mac's face, lit by the light of the fire.

"So, young man, what type of woman can I help you find?"

"She doesn't exist, Merry."

"My, my, my, Mr. O'Brien."

Mac laughed at the way Merry muttered her expletives in threes.

"What you truly want *does* exist. Sometimes you just have to believe in miracles."

Mac considered her words. He didn't believe in miracles, but he believed in Merry, believed she had some strange, mystical powers. He didn't know why he believed that, but he did. "It will take a miracle to find what I'm looking for, but what's your plan?"

"Run an ad in the personals column of a newspaper."

He nearly choked. He'd never heard such an insane idea. Desperate people, sick and deranged people, ran ads in the personals column. The idea was utterly preposterous. "Absolutely not."

"And your suggestion is better?"

"What suggestion?"

"That's just it. You have no other idea, so you'll have to go with mine."

Merry pushed out of the rocker, picked up the half-full glass and plate of cookie crumbs. She turned when she reached the kitchen door. "Now, Mr. O'Brien. I believe it's way past your bedtime. Get your pajamas on, brush your teeth, and hop into bed. I'll wake you bright and early so you can call the newspaper. The sooner that ad appears, the better off all of us will be."

"But I don't know what to put in a personal ad."

"I know. Count on me, young man. I'll write the words, and before you know it, the woman of your dreams will pop into your life."

He eyed her skeptically. He hated the idea, but Merry had made up her mind and, apparently, his too. Tomorrow morning he'd place the ad.

Kathleen sat at the conference table surrounded by advertising copy, holding one particular piece which she had stared at for nearly five minutes.

Her advertising and art managers, Jon and Wayne, sat on either side of the table, taking notes and hastily sketching ideas that might please the perfectionist who perused their work.

"What is it about that piece that you don't like?" Jon asked.

"It just isn't right."

"It's what you asked for. A businesswoman sitting in the back of her limo reading a copy of *Success*."

"But . . ." Kathleen stopped abruptly when she heard the door open. A lump formed in her throat as Mac walked into the room. Why on earth does he have to be so drop-dead gorgeous? she wondered, trying to regain her composure.

"May I have a word with you, Ms. Flannigan?"

She looked at Jon and Wayne and the mess of papers strewn across the table. Be assertive, she told herself. "I won't be much longer. I'll come to your office when we're through."

He smiled. She hadn't seen that entrancing smile in years, not since he came back from Europe.

"I'll wait." He walked to the far end of the conference table, sat down, crossed his legs and arms, leaned back in the chair, and stared at Kathleen.

How in the hell am I supposed to work with him watching me like that? She looked again at the copy before her, lifted it up to shield her face from Mac's glare. She tried to concentrate but couldn't. She peered over the top. He hadn't stopped staring. She took a deep breath, studied the picture, and finally realized what she disliked.

"Jon. Wayne. Look at the woman. She's all wrong."

Jon and Wayne shared a perplexed look. "She looks good to me," Wayne said with a sigh, thumping his chest to imitate a wildly beating heart.

"Great legs," Jon added.

"That's the problem. She shouldn't have great legs. She shouldn't look . . . *good*." Kathleen pounded her chest, mimicking Wayne.

"Why?" Both men asked in unison.

"Because I don't want this magazine to have the reputation of being for *beautiful* successful women. I want it to be for *any* woman who is or wants to be successful."

She heard the footsteps approaching. Avoiding Mac's eyes, she continued to stare at the woman in the picture. She felt his hands clutch the back of her chair, could almost hear his breathing as he leaned over her shoulder to look at the copy.

"There's nothing wrong with a successful woman looking beautiful."

She felt his breath near her ear. Warm—no, hot. His cologne an almost intoxicating smell. Why does he have to stand so close?

"Thank you for your input, Mr. O'Brien. But, as you'll recall, this is *my* magazine and you said you wouldn't offer any help. I believe that should apply to your interpretation of how a successful woman should look."

"Just offering a personal opinion, Ms. Flannigan. It has no reflection on your magazine at all."

"Good." Kathleen turned her head and glared into his eyes. "May I finish my meeting without any more interruptions?"

"Please do." He continued to lean over her chair.

"The woman is okay," she said to Wayne and Jon. "But couldn't you change her hairstyle? Her clothes?"

"How about a bun, support hose, and orthopedic shoes?" Mac laughed.

Kathleen slammed the copy down on the table. "Enough. What did you want to see me about?"

He grinned and strolled to the door. "Thanks for the roses."

As he walked from the room, Kathleen wanted to hurl something heavy at the insufferable man. But then, again, she realized she hadn't seen this much warmth radiating from him in years. And she liked it.

Kathleen ran into the overcrowded, disheveled, two-bedroom apartment and grabbed for the ringing phone. She kicked off her navy pumps and sent them sailing across the room to land near her bedroom door. "Hello."

"Hello, kiddo." She heard her dad's voice and she instantly smiled.

"Hi, Daddy. Is everything okay? Julie's not driving you and Mom crazy, is she?"

"We're having a great time. You know your mother always wanted more children."

Kathleen laughed. "You're not too old to give it another try."

"I think we'll stick with grandchildren. Your daughter's begging me to give her the phone. Talk to you later, hon."

Kathleen listened to the crash, assuming the phone at the other end had fallen on the floor. Then she heard Julie's voice, and tears instantly appeared at the corners of her eyes.

"Hi, Mommy. Guess what?"

"What?"

"Grandpa let me ride Scotty today."

"Scotty? I don't remember that name. Did he get a new horse?"

"No, Mommy. That's the one Grandpa used to call Randolph Scott. But I think that's a silly name for a horse."

"I think it's silly, too." Kathleen would never admit to her daughter that she'd been the one to put the name on that particular gelding, or that she'd been the one to convince her dad to give the others names like John Wayne and Roy Rogers. At the time they sounded a whole lot better than Fury and Flicka and Thunder.

"Grandma and I made chocolate chip cookies today."

"Mmm. Sounds delicious."

"I wrote you a letter, too. And I put chocolate fingerprints on the paper so you wouldn't forget me."

"I won't forget you, honey."

"But you won't see me for a long, long time."

"The time will fly by," Kathleen lied, already feeling miserable, and Julie had been gone less than a week.

"Grandma says I have to go now. She said it costs lots of money to call you on the phone."

Kathleen laughed. Her mother had always been frugal, and Kathleen followed in her footsteps. "Be a good girl for Grandma and Grandpa?"

"I will, Mommy. I love you."

"I love you, too, honey."

Kathleen listened to the click, then the dial tone. So much for a long conversation.

She hung up the receiver. Then she noticed the quiet. No Big Bird or Cookie Monster on the TV; no five-year-old asking "why, why, why"; nothing but peace and solitude. God, she hated it.

Julie gave Kathleen the family life she'd missed since leaving Montana. Adopting Julie, apart from the job she loved, had been the best thing to happen to her. She never regretted it for a moment, even though her friends thought she had lost her mind. "Adoption. My God, Kathleen. A brat will only tie you down." That's what they said. But she laughed at them then, and she laughed at them now. The little girl lit up her life in a way no one else ever had.

She slipped off her pin-striped jacket. Like most everything she wore to the office, it was navy and white, a little too big, and probably in need of cleaning and pressing. She draped it over the back of a battered old chair, piling on top of it the white silk blouse and the just-below-knee-length skirt. She made a mental note to take time to clean the disaster she called an apartment. Maybe she should consider getting a housekeeper, but hated the idea of spending her money on something so frivolous, when she could do it herself. But she hated cleaning. She wasn't fond of cooking, either. She'd rather curl up with pen and paper in her spare time and write, or develop innovative ideas for new magazines she knew would never see the light of day.

Stripped to just her delicate silk-and-lace panties and bra, one of the few luxuries she allowed herself, she turned the dial on the thermostat and hoped she could cool her apartment without having to take out a loan to pay her electric bill. In the kitchen she took a Diet Coke from the refrigerator, popped open the top, and stuck a flex straw into the can. She searched through an already open cabinet for something to eat and ended up in her dad's old hand-me-down recliner with a spoon, a jar of Jif, and a bag of Hershey's Kisses for dessert. Savoring the taste of the creamy peanut butter, she gave thanks to the good Lord that she had never had a weight problem. Eating junk food was her one and only vice, and she refused to give it up.

She popped a Kiss between her lips, letting it melt in her mouth, and thought about McKenna O'Brien, the most elusive, frustrating man she'd ever encountered. Maybe she shouldn't have sent the roses, but she wanted to plant herself firmly in his brain. It had been a long time since they'd had a civil conversation. Oh, how she wished they could return to those days when they had talked for hours, laughed, and he had listened intently to all her crazy schemes. Back then, Mac was a big man with a big heart. But he went away, and when he returned, his father died, and everything seemed to change, especially their relationship.

Of course, Ashley had been the woman in his life back then, just as she was now, and Kathleen had been just a friend. She never understood how Mac could be blinded by the wicked witch of Manhattan society, but he never discussed Ashley with her, and she never asked. In ten years of working at McKenna Publishing, Kathleen had never seen anyone but Ashley with Mac. At social functions, at office parties, she clung to Mac, and behind her smiling mask, Ashley's expression said, *Hands off, this man is mine.* And when she looked at Kathleen, daggers of hate flew from her eyes. Had Ashley ever said more than six words to Kathleen? *Hello. How are you? Drop dead.*

Kathleen laughed to herself. That woman has Mac wrapped up so tight I'm surprised he can breathe. Ashley's cold, calculated manner, along with his father's death, had turned the big-hearted man into a power-driven mogul. But in spite of all that, Kathleen still loved him. She knew, deep inside, the man she had admired and dreamed of was still there, hidden beneath that cool exterior. Hadn't she seen just a touch of his warmth when he thanked her for the roses?

She picked up the newspaper, scanning the world news, the nation's political scene, even the society pages. And then she saw the photo. Mac and Ashley standing like lovers before an ice-sculpted swan, her fingers pressed to his lips.

She stared at the picture. Quit dreaming, she told herself. Get on with your life. Mac wasn't yours then, he isn't yours now. And from the looks of this picture, he'll never be yours.

She let out a long, deep sigh, licked clean another spoonful of peanut butter, and tried to push Mac from her mind, but it didn't work. Instead, she imagined his bare stomach, wondering if his chest was hairy or smooth, if he looked as good naked as he did in his expensive suits. She even wondered if he did push-ups to keep in shape, thinking how much fun it would be to help him during his exercise routine.

She remembered his picture on the cover of *Fortune* magazine. She had only been eighteen, but after reading the article about the heir apparent to the McKenna empire, she was smitten. Smart, sexy—she loved reading his quotes about running a big business, and she made it her goal to someday work for him. He was her hero. He still was, even though they were exact opposites. He was conservative; she was liberal. He was forty-nine; she was thirty-two. He was sophisticated; she was Montana middle class. And never the twain shall meet.

He had a love life, she had a dream. And it was time to put the dream to sleep and get on with her life. She tossed aside all but the classifieds and immediately searched for the personals. *WSM seeks WSF. Must be great-looking gal for a great-looking guy.* What a crock!

This is crazy. I'll never find a man in the personals. I must be sick, deranged. But I'm not going to pine over Mac any longer.

CHAPTER
FOUR

Kathleen didn't waste any time Saturday morning worrying about housecleaning or grocery shopping. She hadn't seen or heard from Mac since their encounter on Wednesday, and she was more determined than ever to wipe him out of her heart and mind.

Dressed in jogging shorts and a T-shirt, she ran down five flights of stairs, her daily exercise. She hated it, but she wanted to keep her legs in shape. On top of that, she figured her heart needed all the exercise it could get since she had a tendency to clog her vessels with fatty foods.

"Good morning, Sam." Her face brightened for the elderly man who stood on the corner selling papers. She grabbed a copy of the paper from the top of the stack, handed Sam a five and jogged in place while she patiently waited for his arthritic fingers to produce the correct amount of change.

"Sure is a pretty day," he said, tipping his hat to Kathleen, who thought Sam's internal clock must have stopped sometime in the 1950s. A sweet, gentle man, they exchanged very few words when she picked up her paper each day, but the words were always pleasant, and such a nice way to start the day.

"It's a *beautiful* day, Sam." Kathleen blew the old man a kiss and flashed him a generous smile as she began the jog back to her apartment, anxious to sift through the weekend personal ads. She had sworn last night to find a man if it killed her. Then again, she thought, if she found someone in the personals, she just *might* end up dead. She tossed the fleeting thought aside and ran back to her building.

She climbed the steps two at a time, entering the apartment just as the teakettle started to whistle. She poured boiling milk into a large earthenware mug and doctored it with a few generous squirts of chocolate syrup.

With the newspaper under her arm, the cup of hot chocolate and a day-old slice of cold pepperoni pizza for breakfast, she headed for the living room and the recliner. She spread the paper before her on the coffee table—or, rather, the beat-up old black steamer trunk that served as a coffee table—and flipped through page after page of world events and the dullest headlines imaginable. At last she reached the classifieds.

Her finger ran down column after column, finding nothing that jumped out at her, just the same old stuff. Doesn't anyone have an imagination? And then she found it. She sat up straighter, circled the ad with a thick, red marker.

Are you the Christmas present I've been longing to have under my tree? Only small, perfectly wrapped gifts need apply. Late 40ish gentleman desires feminine, 30ish gifts only—no antiques.

She laughed at the ad. Well, I'm not small, and I'm probably not what he wants, but I think I'd like to meet the man who had the nerve to write such utter nonsense. She scribbled down the box where she needed to send her reply, grabbed her tablet, and stuck a well-chewed pen in her mouth while she dreamed up the perfect words.

Merry walked into Mac's study carrying the letters she had picked up at the newspaper office. She read as she walked, not paying the least bit of attention to anything around her, but somehow managed to avoid a collision with chairs and tables.

Mac watched her pull up a chair and sit at the desk beside him. She wore the same clothes every day, but looked as crisp and fresh as she had the first moment she'd walked through his door. A red dress, a white apron, black laced-up leather shoes, and white stockings. He had given up wondering about her. Now he just accepted her as the sweetest, most endearing lady he'd ever encountered.

"Not nearly as many letters as I was expecting," she said, grabbing the scissors to slice off the tops of the envelopes.

"How many did you expect? That ad was awful. I must have been crazy to let you talk me into this."

"Nonsense. I'm sure the right woman is in this pile." One by one she pulled out the letters and read them out loud to Mac, who made copious notes of things that struck his fancy.

"Read that part again," he said, intrigued by something written in the fourth letter.

"Let me see. Oh, yes. Here it is. 'If you're looking for the perfect present, look no further. I'm five foot two, eyes of blue, and oh, what those five feet can do!' " Merry muttered something unintelligible under her breath, and Mac laughed at her obvious disgust with the letter.

In spite of Merry, he thought the words were a breath of fresh air in a pile of stale letters. "That one's a definite."

"Whatever you say."

Why had she given in so easily? Mac wondered. She picked up the next envelope, a big, Christmas red one, and pulled out an old-fashioned card with an old-fashioned Santa on the front. He watched Merry's eyes light up at the vision before her. If he wasn't mistaken, her eyes misted just the slightest bit.

"Now, this is more like it," she said. Beautifully scripted words, written in gold ink, formed the shape of a Christmas tree on expensive, watermarked green stationery. The woman obviously had put a lot of time and thought into her reply.

"No matter what this one says, I think she's a definite," she said, wiping a tear away from her cheek.

"You're too sentimental."

"Not in the least. I just know this one's perfect."

"What about the others?"

"Oh, I have no problem with you checking out several, but I'll place my money on this lovely lady right here."

Mac took the card and paper out of Merry's hands and stared at the writing. It took him a minute before he digested what it said. "So, you think this one's perfect?"

"Of course."

"Did you read it?"

"No. That's not necessary."

Mac pushed away from the desk, headed for the kitchen, and a snack of the ever-present Christmas cookies or some other confection Merry kept stocked for his recently ravenous appetite.

When he reached the kitchen table, with Merry following close behind, he popped a piece of fudge in his mouth, took a few bites, then swallowed the dark, creamy chocolate. He washed the sweetness down with a swig of milk, then waved the green paper in front of Merry's face. "Let me read this to you.

" 'My tree has splendid ornaments, with rather fine limbs, and my trunk consists of thirty-two rings. Enduring, quality gifts come from the heart—gifts under my branches not necessary, but a mature, finely aged tree may grow by my side.' "

"See. I told you she's perfect."

"You've got to be out of your mind. She doesn't make sense."

Merry grabbed the piece of paper out of his hand. "Here, let me decipher this for you."

Mac pulled the paper back. "That's not necessary. You'll embarrass both of us."

"I say she's a definite."

He took another drink of milk, grabbed a napkin, piled on several pieces of fudge, then stomped to his study, alone, to contemplate the reply he held in his hands.

He studied the note, interpreting each line:

Splendid ornaments? Umm. Great breasts.

Rather fine limbs? Legs. Great legs.

32 rings? Thirty-two. She'll probably think I'm too old.

Well, Mac thought, she does have a few possibilities.

He tossed the green paper on top of the other "keeper," then went on to read the rest of the letters. Two out of eight wasn't bad. His gut feeling told him to throw out the green paper on top of the pile, but Merry would never forgive him. Deep down inside, he was curious.

The letter came less than a week after Kathleen sent her reply. It was short, to the point. If interested, she needed to meet him in the lounge at the Plaza, eight P.M. Monday night. He'd be wearing a sprig of holly in his lapel. Holly? How strange. Well, there'd be no mistaking him for anyone else. She, in turn, should wear white gloves. She liked the idea of the Plaza, although she didn't frequent such rich surroundings. There would be a crowd, it would be easy to find, and even easier to escape should there be a need to run.

What, she wondered, had she gotten herself into that she had to think about an escape route? Worse yet, what on earth would she wear? Business attire? White gloves would look atrocious with navy blue pinstripes. She didn't own a cocktail dress. Besides what she wore to work, her wardrobe consisted of jeans and T-shirts, a few sweaters, but definitely nothing she could wear to the Plaza.

She looked at her watch. Eight o'clock. Too late to go shopping tonight. That left Sunday. She hated shopping because she hated the clothes. Things had a tendency to be too fancy for her tastes. She preferred the clothes she used to buy in the dress shops at home in Montana. Unassuming, never calling attention to the body she wanted to hide.

She struck out on her shopping expedition at noon on Sunday. Macy's had nothing. Bloomingdale's. Saks. Nothing she looked at really stuck out. Too many sequins. Too little fabric. As late Sunday afternoon approached, her arms laden with bags of toys and clothing for Julie, but nothing for herself, she began to feel desperate. Her feet ached so badly she didn't think she could walk another step. And then she saw it—Holly's. How appropriate, she thought. But it did seem strange that she'd walked by these storefronts hundreds of times before and hadn't noticed this shop. Surely she would have remembered it—a store all decked out for Christmas—at the end of June?

Holly's sparkled with glittering snowflakes painted on the windows bordered with garlands of holly. A pine-cone wreath hung on the door, a polished brass bell hung in its center. A Christmas tree glistened with ornaments illuminated by thousands of colored lights. But Kathleen's eyes zoomed to the white velvet strapless and form-fitting dress in the window. To her amazement, the mannequin looked strangely like her, and on her hands she wore long white gloves. She had seen herself in a dress like this in those recurring dreams when she danced with Mac.

Once inside she smelled the pine, the peppermint, the cinnamon, and hot apple cider. Mesmerized by the sights and scents, Kathleen found herself surrounded by attendants—four tiny men, barely reaching her elbows.

They took her bags, offered her cider, removed her shoes, and slipped soft, white satin heels onto her feet. They felt like comfortable bedroom slippers—she could even wiggle her toes. Measuring tapes slipped around her waist, her thighs, her bust. They measured her height and removed the rubber band pulling her hair into a ponytail. Behind a midnight blue screen, painted with hundreds of delicate white snowflakes, she removed her jeans and T-shirt and slipped into the gown. It felt heavenly against her skin. She stepped out of the dressing area to see four brightly lit smiles. She turned to the mirror. Could that beautiful woman staring back at her really be Kathleen Flannigan?

Caught up in the excitement, the thrill of finding such a wonderful dress, she couldn't even remember if money exchanged hands. But with packages tucked under her arm, she walked out the door at five o'clock. The lights went off, and Holly's lost its magical glow. Had it really existed? If it hadn't, how could she be standing here holding the green-and-red foil box—the one containing the white dress, the white gloves?

It wasn't worth speculating about what could and couldn't be. She'd found what she had wanted—just in the nick of time.

Kathleen hadn't slept. Instead, she'd lain awake thinking about the man she would meet on Monday. In spite of her sleepless night, she entered her office in a good mood, a smile on her face, and ready to face the world. Mondays always meant rushes; staff meeting at nine, piles of reading, articles to edit, layouts to approve, calls to return. Lunch with a writer at one, meetings with the advertising and art execs, and then a dreaded appointment with Mac at five. She didn't have time to meet with him, but she couldn't find an excuse not to. Why on earth did he want to see her?

At precisely one minute until the hour, she entered Mac's office. He looked ready. She wasn't.

He walked around the desk, looking wonderful, like a model in *GQ*, clad in a charcoal gray suit, crisp white shirt, dark red tie. His jacket was unbuttoned and his left hand was tucked into his pants pocket. She'd never noticed his shoes before, but today he wore cowboy boots. They weren't scuffed and marred like her friends' at home, but dark gray leather, spit-polished and shined. Her eyes roamed from the top of his head to the tips of his boots, then meandered up again to his eyes. She was speechless.

He stuck out his right hand to shake hers. "Would you like something to drink? Coffee? Tea? A beer?"

"No. Nothing, thank you."

He pulled the chair out, holding it while she sat. He took his place in the massive chair on the other side of the desk, folded his hands in front of him, and leaned forward.

"I was wondering how you're doing on *your* magazine. My spies haven't been able to tell me a thing."

"I don't see any need for spies. I'd be happy to tell you anything you want to know."

"Okay." He smiled. "Did the woman executive change from beautiful to frumpy?"

It took a moment for her to realize he meant the woman in the advertisement. "Not frumpy. Just more businesslike."

"And what is your definition of *businesslike*?"

She stared at her watch. "I'm sorry, Mr. O'Brien. I have a date tonight and unless you have some important business to discuss, I really must hurry."

"It's important to me. But it's not the magazine I want to discuss," he said, picking up a pencil and drumming it on the desk.

"No?" She frowned.

"No. It was a comment you made at our last meeting."

Kathleen looked at him, puzzled. What comment had she made?

"I see you don't remember," he said.

"Can you refresh my memory?"

"Gladly. It was about us being friends once upon a time, and what happened."

"We *were* friends," Kathleen said. She looked across the desk into his eyes, but she saw only a trace of their former warmth. She turned her focus to the window, but saw nothing, only a blur, and the memory of she and Mac the way they had been so many years ago, locking horns during one of their sparring matches. Back then, not unlike today, they both believed they were right, no matter what the topic, and neither wanted to give in. But in those sparring matches they laughed over their disagreements. The laughter stopped when he went to Europe, and when he came back, everything had changed. He no longer wanted to talk, he refused to talk, and eventually she gave up trying. She had retreated into her work and her daughter, and he disappeared from her life, except on those rare occasions when they met at work. Maybe now he was ready to talk, and she was ready to listen.

Once again she looked at the man she had never stopped admiring, in spite of everything. Did she see a trace of regret in his face for all those lost years? "I've waited a long time to find out what went wrong. Do you want to talk about it now?"

"There's not much to talk about, Kath. You changed. I changed. We can't go back, so why don't we forget what happened back then, and just go on from today?"

"If that's what you want." Those weren't the words she wanted to hear, but she'd ignore the past for now. However, she had every intention of bringing the subject up again. "Did you ask me here just to say that, or was there something else you wanted to discuss?"

"How about the friendship you had with my dad?" The words rushed from his mouth. "I understand you kept him company while I was in Europe."

"We saw each other occasionally." What on earth could she possibly tell Mac about his father that he didn't already know? Could she tell him that Patrick O'Brien had worshipped his son and was devastated when he left the country with Ashley Tate? "Did you want to know something specific?"

Mac shook his head. "I missed out on the last year of his life. You didn't." He left his desk and went to the bookcases. There was a sculpted bronze Remington horse and rider on one of the shelves, one of his father's favorite possessions. He touched it as though contact would bring his father closer. "I guess I just wanted to know what he did, if he was happy."

"He missed you terribly."

"Is that why you became friends?"

What a strange question. Kathleen tried to remember their first meeting, the first time they were alone, and not together at a meeting or company function. "Somebody told him I grew up in Montana. It really surprised me when he came to my office one day, just to talk about life in the West."

Kathleen joined Mac at the bookcases, scanning the titles of bound leather classics, some obviously first editions, and an array of paperbacks, some tattered and torn. She had spent many hours with Patrick O'Brien in this room, and she fondly remembered how much they had shared when Mac went away. She pulled one of the worn paperbacks from the shelf. "Your father loved reading Louis L'Amour," she said, fanning through the pages. "What about you?"

"Afraid I don't have time."

Kathleen shoved the book back into its slot and walked over to a massive buckskin leather armchair, where Mac's dad used to sit, where he had spent many hours talking about his son, mostly about how he wished Mac had never met Ashley, how he wished he'd settle down with a woman the O'Brien family could love. She lightly ran her hands over the back of the chair. "He liked hearing stories about the ranch I grew up on. He talked about hunting and fishing, things he enjoyed but rarely got to do. We talked about old Western movies, and our heroes—I liked Randolph Scott, and he liked John Wayne." Kathleen smiled at the memories. "I liked your dad. We had a good time together."

Mac went back to his desk, sat on the edge and picked up the framed photo of his father. "There were so many things I wanted to tell him when I got back from Europe, but my timing was pretty bad. It was Christmas Eve, and the house was full of guests. Dad and I didn't have much of a chance to talk." Mac looked at Kathleen. "You know he died on Christmas Day, don't you?"

Kathleen nodded.

"All those things I wanted to tell him—none of it mattered after he died. Everything would have been different if I hadn't gone away."

"Nothing would have been different, Mac." Kathleen walked to his side and placed a hand on his shoulder. She hadn't touched him in six years, but that electrifying feeling she had experienced back then only increased. With all her heart she wanted to put her arms around him and give him comfort, but she was afraid he'd only pull away.

And he did. He put the frame back on the desk, went to his chair, and sat down. "It wasn't my intention to bring up my dad. Hell! I don't even know why I wanted to see you."

"There was a time when we used to sit in your office and just keep each other company. We didn't talk. You did your work and I did mine. Do you remember?"

"I remember. But that was a long time ago, and we can't go back."

Time for reminiscing ended. The concrete barrier Mac had erected between them returned.

"You still haven't answered my question about the magazine," he stated. "Is everything going well?"

I suppose if he wants to talk about business, Kathleen thought, we'll talk about business. At least that's better than not talking at all. At least it's a start. "We're having a tough time with the advertising, but we'll get it worked out."

His expression softened. "I know I said I wouldn't help, but if you need anything, I hope you'll ask."

"Thanks, but I can make it work, Mac. I know you don't believe that, but it's true."

"If you think I gave you the go-ahead believing you might fail, you're wrong. I have no doubt whatsoever that you'll succeed." He leaned back in his chair, resuming his look of control. "I don't play hunches in this business, Kath. I want to make money on this project. I want you to get your promotion. There's no hidden motive. Strictly business, that's all."

"Okay. Strictly business." Damn him! She had hoped they'd resolve that unknown problem between them, that they'd once again be friends. Just a few moments ago, she thought they had been on the verge of renewing their old friendship. She couldn't have been more wrong. But she gave it one more attempt. What they had shared was much too special, much too valuable to give up easily. "I take it a return to our old friendship is out of the question?"

Mac opened a drawer, thumbed through some file folders, and pulled one out. Putting it on his desk, he opened it up and started reading the contents. A moment later he looked up at

Kathleen, his face an expressionless mask. "Just business, Kathleen. That's all there is."

"Okay." She gritted her teeth at his cold harsh words, rose from her chair and made a calculated attempt to calmly walk to the door. She put her fingers to the knob, then turned around, hoping to catch a glimpse of the old Mac, but he appeared deep in thought, his eyes trained on his papers. What the hell could he be thinking? Why did he open up to her one moment, then clam up the next? He was the most infuriating man she'd ever met.

He looked up from his papers. "Did you need something else?"

That did it! She couldn't contain her anger and frustration any longer. She yanked open the door and slammed it behind her. When she reached her office, she slammed that door too, fell into her chair, and exhaled all her pent-up emotion. What the hell had she done to deserve this treatment from Mac? He'd grown too darn moody over the years, too serious. She must be crazy to care so much, to let his behavior ruin her frame of mind and, quite possibly, her evening. No. She wouldn't let his sour humor put a damper on her date tonight. She planned to enjoy herself, in spite of him.

She grabbed her briefcase and opened a desk drawer to retrieve her purse, and hidden below it was that newspaper photo of Mac and Ashley at the Pallenbergs'. Her humor plummeted.

Damn that man, she swore to herself. How could she possibly be in love with such an insufferable pig?

CHAPTER

FIVE

The Plaza's lounge overflowed with people, more than Mac had expected. With luck, he wouldn't run into anyone he knew. Not that it mattered, but he didn't want to answer any questions. He felt ridiculous sitting alone at a table waiting for a blind date. Forty-nine years old and placing an ad in the Personals. He really had gone insane.

Seven o'clock on the dot. Mac thrived on punctuality—but what about the ladies he expected? What if they showed up at the same time? Why did he send letters to two women? Why did he even send one?

He stared at his beer, deep in thought, not paying attention to the people entering the lounge. Then he heard it. A low, raspy voice. "Are you expecting me?"

She wore short white gloves and stood about five feet two. Her eyes were big, blue.

"Hello." Mac could barely get a word out of his constricted throat as he stood up and tried not to gape at the petite, dark-haired woman at his side. Somehow he managed to pull out the chair for the creature whose generous breasts nearly spilled out of the extremely low-cut red spandex tank dress she wore.

She slipped off her gloves and offered a hand to Mac in greeting. "I'm Hillary."

"Mac," he croaked, then took her hand in his, holding it

a second longer than necessary. Hers was warm. His was clammy.

"Pleased to meet you," she said, raking his palm with long red fingernails as she pulled her hand away.

Mac returned to his chair, nodding for the waiter.

"What may I bring you?" The man addressed Hillary, his eyes straying to her cleavage.

"Jack Daniel's, straight up."

Mac nearly gasped.

"And you, sir?"

"Another Molson. No, on second thought, I'll have the same as the lady." Mac smiled weakly. He couldn't afford to look like a wimp. If Hillary could drink whiskey straight up, he could too.

"Tell me about yourself," Mac said, unable to think of anything more creative as he fought to keep his gaze on her face. Sitting with a stranger was more than uncomfortable; it was downright miserable. To make matters worse, he looked at Hillary like a display piece—a commodity whose purchase he was contemplating.

"Well," she said, then appeared to lose her train of thought as she opened the small white purse she held in her lap. She fumbled through the contents and pulled out a pack of Marlboros.

The waiter appeared with their drinks the moment the cigarette touched Hillary's lips. "I'm sorry, ma'am. You can't smoke in here."

Hillary grinned and put her index finger to the waiter's lips. "Just one quick puff, please?" she purred.

The waiter's eyes dropped to the rose tattoo on her left breast, and when he looked up again, his face flushed, he removed the lighter from Hillary's fingers and laid it on the table next to her gloves. "Sorry." He winked and left Mac to deal with any further problems.

"No sweat," Hillary said, waving the unlit cigarette in Mac's face. "Nasty habit, but I hate to give it up."

Mac watched Hillary open her purse and drop the lipstick-stained cigarette inside, fought back his disdain, and attempted to start a conversation. "You were about to tell me about yourself."

"Oh, right." She took a sip of her whiskey then ran her tongue over her dark red lips. "I'm not from New York, but I bet you already guessed that from my accent."

He hadn't guessed. He'd been too busy trying to overlook Hillary's offensive mannerisms, trying instead to concentrate on her tiny, turned-up nose. Long, thick, dark eyelashes. Liza Minnelli black hair. And that rose tattoo that increased in size every time Hillary took a breath.

"I want to be an actress," she said, forcing Mac's attention back to her face. "But I'm just not having any luck. Danny, he's my agent, says I really got lots of potential."

"Is that so?" Mac yawned.

"Oh, yeah. I went on an audition just the other day. The director said I could be a real star, with my looks and all."

"I see." He took a good look at Hillary. At first glance, in the dim light, she looked great, but on closer inspection he could see the pucker lines around her lips, the caked makeup at her hairline, the heavy buildup of mascara at the corners of her eyes. He swallowed the last of his beer, and started on the whiskey.

"Yeah, well, to be honest, it's some kind of really low-budget movie. You know, the kind nice girls shouldn't be in. I like the idea of being a star, but the guy sort of gave me the creeps."

"Sounds like the kind of guy you should stay away from."

"Well, Danny wasn't too crazy about me telling the producer I wasn't interested."

"Have you thought about finding a different agent?"

"Nah. Danny's okay."

Hillary downed the rest of her whiskey. Mac followed suit. He needed it to dull his senses and to get through the conversation with Hillary.

"Hey! What about you?" Hillary asked. "Why'd you put that ad in the columns?"

"Somebody dared me to," he lied. If he admitted his plan had been to find the perfect wife, she'd think he was crazy, and she'd probably be right. Just look what a disaster Hillary had turned out to be.

"Yeah, I thought it was something like that. I mean, all that talk about trees and gifts. Did you like my line, the 'five foot two, eyes of blue' bit?"

"Pretty clever."

"Well, yeah. I've used it a few times before." She picked up her gloves and purse. "Look, Mac. Thanks for the drink, but I'm really not interested. You know, you're a little too old for me, and, well, gosh, I got to go."

Mac stood. He didn't have time to pull out Hillary's chair. She departed in a flash. He wished he could run out too. Disappear before the next woman arrived.

He drank another Molson and checked his watch, over and over. He didn't expect the next lady until eight, but when she walked in at seven-thirty he wasn't surprised. She had flaming red hair and a short, tight black dress. Every man in the room followed her with gaping eyes. She sauntered across the room and took a seat at the bar, stuffing the white gloves into her purse.

Mac cautiously approached the bar, his beer clutched tightly in his fingers. He stood next to her and raised one boot to the foot rail. "I think you were expecting me."

She stared Mac straight in the eyes. "I beg your pardon. Are you speaking to me?"

Mac had an inkling he'd made a mistake. "I'm the guy with the holly." He fingered his lapel.

She frowned.

His smile disappeared. "Maybe I've made a mistake."

"I'm sure you have," she said, tilting her head and her eyes until she found the top of his head. "For starters, you're too big. I don't like big men. And I hate holly." She swung the strap of her purse over her shoulder and walked away, ignoring the drink the bartender had just poured.

"You paying for this?" the bartender asked.

Mac dug into his pocket, dropped a five on the bar, and didn't bother waiting for change.

He went back to his table, hating to look around. The eyes that had been staring at the redhead now stared at him. Merry would never hear the end of this. How could he have let her talk him into this fiasco? What more could go wrong?

He glanced at his watch: 7:35. Twenty-five minutes to wait. If she didn't show up by 8:05, he would leave.

The waiter set another beer in front of Mac. "Meeting any more women tonight?" he questioned.

"One." Mac stared at his drink and held up an index finger.

"Would you like me to have another beer ready when she arrives?"

Mac thought about it for only a moment, then nodded. "Might be a good idea."

Kathleen stared at the clock. 7:35. Oh, my God. I'm late, she thought. How could she possibly have taken so long to get ready when all she'd done was shower, dress, brush her teeth, apply a light spray of cologne, then add a few brush strokes of mascara to her already dark lashes?

When she pulled her hair out of the bun it hung in long, unruly auburn waves that cascaded down her back. She stood before the full-length mirror and gasped. How on God's green earth could she go out looking like this? The dress was too short; too low; too tight; too—too wrong. But she didn't have time to change, and she didn't have anything else to wear.

She slipped into the three-inch heels, praying the man from the Personals would be well over six feet tall. Searching through the pile of discarded clothing on her bed, she grabbed her purse, threw in a lipstick, a brush, her wallet, then made the ultimate decision to spend money on a cab. She'd never make it on time if she took the bus. Taking one quick look in the mirror, she stuck out her tongue and made an ugly face, picked up the gloves, and ran out the door, opting for the elevator instead of the stairs.

A horrendous number of cars, buses, and taxis jammed the streets. She had to hurry. She didn't want to be late and miss her date. If she did, she'd never forgive herself. She'd also feel like a fool standing in the lounge dressed in such a conspicuous way without anyone to meet. The hotel management might get the wrong idea.

The Plaza came into view. She applied another coating of lipstick, checked for any loose mascara under her eyes, paid the driver, took a deep breath, and rushed into the hotel.

She stood in the lobby looking beautiful and bewildered, until the bell captain came to her rescue, ushering her to the lounge.

8:05. The place buzzed with activity. How could she ever find a man with a sprig of holly in his lapel? Then, at a distant table, she saw McKenna O'Brien. Damn! What's he doing here? How could she look for the man with the holly? What would Mac say if he saw her? How could she explain? And, oh, why couldn't he be the man she was meeting, instead of some stranger?

Maybe he didn't see her. How could he? Too many people

crowded around in the darkness, and he sat at the far end of the room. She squinted, trying to get a better look at her boss. Her shoulders slumped. Oh, God! He had holly in his lapel.

"Excuse me, sir," the waiter said, "but I think your next date just walked in."

Mac gulped down the beer, turned to the entry, and saw only a throng of faceless people. "Where?"

"The tall one in the white dress. She's wearing white gloves, just like the others."

Mac saw only the woman's back. She appeared to be leaving.

"Nice legs," Mac said with a sly smile.

"That's not all, sir. You missed seeing the best part."

"Bring me another beer. I'll be right back." Mac wobbled, almost pushing over the chair as he stood up.

The woman seemed desperate to leave, weaving her way through the crowd. But Mac hadn't waited all evening just to have her disappear before they could meet. Shoving between bodies, he reached out, wrapped his big hand around her slender upper arm. "Don't leave."

She tried to pull away, but his hand stayed clutched around her arm. He could feel her muscles tense, then felt them relax. She did not turn around, not then, giving him a leisurely moment to peruse her body in the white dress that hugged every curve—her slim waist, slightly rounded hips, and long, long legs.

Mac's eyes reached her three-inch heels when she finally turned his way. He took his time finding her eyes, slowly studying the body of the woman before him.

His ad had said *small packages*, but what he saw before him made him instantly reconsider. He liked every inch of her legs, the high heels that made them look even better and must have made her over six feet tall. He liked the long, slender arms and envisioned himself captured in their embrace. Oh, this woman could possibly be all and more than he had ever dreamed of.

Another second passed while he carefully considered her fine proportions. He sensed her staring at him, knew he had to look at her in return. Auburn hair fell over her bare left shoulder in one long curl. She wore just a trace of cologne, something light, inexpensive. Blue eyes. Azure eyes—warm, questioning. Familiar.

"Hello, Mr. O'Brien."

Slowly, ever so slowly, recognition dawned. His eyes widened. His fingers tightened around her arm.

"Damn!" He scowled, released his grip, and turned away. Of all people, why did Kathleen Flannigan have to answer his ad? He should have known. Should have sensed it from the words she'd written.

She touched him. He felt the heat of her hand, the burning of his skin through his jacket, through his shirtsleeve.

"Wait. Please." She spoke softly, almost a plea.

He turned back and studied her face. Her eyes twinkled. God, how he loved her eyes.

Mac gripped the hand resting on his arm and maneuvered her through the crowd to his table. The waiter stood at attention, holding a chair out for Kathleen. Mac sat down across from her. He took a quick swallow from the cold bottle of beer and stared into her innocent yet devilish eyes. His brain and heart battled each other. Seeing Kathleen again made him happy, in spite of those ugly rumors, in spite of the fact she had slammed a door in his face just a few hours earlier. But how could he look at her when she knew he had to resort to the Personal ads to get a date? His pride bristled.

"What the hell are you doing here?"

"It's eight o'clock. We had a date."

"No—I had a date with . . ." He paused to think before uttering another word. She had an infectious smile. He laughed at himself. Kathleen resorted to personal ads too. "I had a date with a beautiful woman. I'm glad she could make it."

"Thank you."

Again his eyes left Kathleen's, traveling to where he could watch the rise and fall of soft, slightly tanned skin above the white fabric that hugged her so well. Propriety told him not to stare; the beer told him otherwise.

"Why were you running out?" he asked.

"This whole situation is rather embarrassing. My God, Mac, we can't be together for five minutes without fighting, yet we meet each other through the personals."

"It is rather funny."

"Funny? It's humiliating."

"But we're the only ones who know. We don't have to tell a soul."

She thought about his statement. "I suppose you're right. Besides, we may end up hating each other before the evening's over."

"Or, we could find we're mutually attracted. I have to admit, I'm a sucker for splendid ornaments and rather fine limbs." His grin turned into laughter. He wanted to concentrate on her face, her smile, but his eyes roamed. Kathleen had so many attributes worth watching.

"But your ad asked for small packages only?"

"Just a passing fancy."

"You've had a change of heart?"

"I don't think the heart was ever that concerned. Let's just say I've had a change of mind."

"I'm glad you've changed," she said, slowly pulling off one of her gloves, her eyes never leaving his. "Three hours ago I thought you were an insufferable pig."

"Me?" He smiled. "I might be insufferable. But a pig? No."

His eyes traversed the length of her arm as the glove slid away, baring her slender wrist and long, jewelry-free fingers. He couldn't believe the seductive power of such a simple gesture. Again, he met her eyes. "You look beautiful tonight. I hardly recognized you."

"You've never looked at me before."

"Oh, but you're wrong. There was a time when I looked a lot. All those times when we'd work late into the evening on one of your crazy ideas. I've never forgotten the image of you in blue jeans."

She shook her head. "That was a long time ago."

"Maybe. But I've been thinking about you a lot the last few weeks."

"Why? Why now, after all these years?"

"I'm not sure. I turned forty-nine a few weeks ago and something clicked. I realized I'd wasted a lot of years with Ashley, and I finally got the nerve to call it quits."

Kathleen's eyes widened, her smile grew. "You did?"

"I decided I wanted more, and suddenly I remembered the times we spent together. They were good times, Kath."

She nodded in agreement. "We were all a little surprised when you showed up at our staff meeting. You've kept yourself hidden away for so many years, I think some people forgot you existed."

"What about you?" he asked, hoping to hear that she hadn't forgotten him any more than he had forgotten her. But she remained silent, staring at his fingers wrapped around the bottle of beer.

He raised the bottle to his lips and Kathleen's eyes followed. "I've never forgotten you," she said, and the beer came close to sticking in his constricted throat upon hearing her words. It's what he had wanted her to say, but he didn't think the words could have sounded so wonderful.

"I didn't forget you either," he said, remembering the good times, trying to disregard the rumors that had turned sweet memories sour. "Forgetting you would be pretty impossible."

Kathleen's chest rose, he heard her breath catch and hold, and he thought he saw tears forming at the corners of her eyes. But that wasn't possible. Kathleen didn't cry.

Change the subject quickly, he told himself. "You know, you were right when you said I didn't love the publishing business. That's part of the reason I've concentrated my efforts on real-estate transactions." That, and the fact that I wanted to avoid you, that I was afraid of seeing you again. "Traveling around, buying property—it's a hell of a lot more exciting than working behind a desk, and it gets me out of the city."

"Isn't it funny?" She laughed. "I grew up in the country, but I love New York. You've lived here all your life, but you can't wait to escape."

"I guess we can add that to our long list of differences. Let's see how many I can count." He drew a line with his finger through the circular puddle of water on the table where his beer bottle had been set. "One. I'm conservative, you're liberal. . . ."

"Two," she interrupted. "I'm a woman, you're a man." She drew a line right next to his, then looked up and smiled. "Differences aren't always bad, you know."

Damn! Does she have to have such a beautiful smile? He pulled his gaze from her magnetic eyes and mouth and looked at her hands resting on the table, the finger that had drawn the line now drawing circles in the moisture at the base of his beer. He wanted to touch her, but instead touched the delicate silk of the gloves that lay near her hands, hands that were so close he could almost feel their heat. Slowly he raised his eyes. Her smile hadn't disappeared. "Flirting can be dangerous, Kath," he whispered. "It could lead to something you'll regret."

Kathleen slowly shook her head in disagreement. "I've regretted very few things in my life. I've never regretted one moment I've spent with you."

Mac frowned and took another swallow of beer. "This is crazy. You can't possibly think the two of us, together, would work. We'd argue. We'd fight. You'd drive me crazy."

"I hope so." She moved her finger from the bottle to his thumb and lightly, somewhat unsure, covered his hand with hers. "That's what makes life exciting."

Mac pulled his hand away and waved for the waiter. "I need another beer. How about you?"

"Some things are easy to forget in six years. I don't drink."

"What would you . . ." Mac put up his hand to stop her answer just as the waiter appeared. "A Diet Coke for the lady, and I'll take another Molson." He easily remembered Kathleen's ever-present Diet Coke, but his memory failed when he tried to remember how much liquor he'd had this evening. When the first wave of dizziness hit, he realized if he'd kept count, the number would be way too high.

Hopefully Kathleen didn't notice his discomfort. He loosened his tie and unfastened the top button of his shirt. Again, he raised the bottle to his lips but Kathleen caught his hand and took the bottle from his grasp. "I think you've had too much to drink."

So, she had noticed after all. "You're right." He sighed and shook his head, totally disgusted with himself and with what was happening. "I'm sorry, Kath. I was in college the last time I drank too much. I thought I'd learned my lesson."

"Tonight hasn't been easy," she said, and he appreciated the way she seemed to make amends for his behavior.

"I don't usually sit in bars waiting for women."

"What about placing personal ads?"

"No, this was the first, and the last. But what about you? Why did you answer?"

Kathleen looked at the holly in his lapel, then back into his eyes. "I had to know what kind of arrogant, insecure man could write such an ad."

"Arrogant? Insecure? Not me."

"Yes, Mac. You."

He laughed. "You know, I haven't laughed, I mean really laughed, in a very long time. It feels pretty good." And then he realized that was the only thing that felt good. His head ached. His stomach churned. When had he last eaten? Early that morning? He rubbed the back of his neck. It was cold and damp.

"Is something wrong? You look ill." Kathleen's concern sounded in her voice.

"I'm fine. Just fine." He tried to look alert, in control. Never in his life had he passed out and he'd be damned if he'd pass out in front of Kathleen.

Beads of perspiration formed on his brow. How could he wipe them away without calling attention to his distress? The room was insufferably hot. He unfastened another button on his shirt. A gust of cool air blew out of the air conditioning vents and across his face. It revived him, if only for a moment.

"It's too hot in here. Would you like to go somewhere else? I'm starving. Maybe we could get some dinner?"

"So, you intend to make this a real date?"

He nodded slightly, afraid if he did anything else he'd fall out of his chair.

He caught the waiter's attention, calling him to the table. "Thanks for all your help tonight," Mac said, his words slow, almost slurred.

"It's been a pleasure serving you, sir."

Mac stood, reaching into his pocket for his money clip.

He pulled off a hundred-dollar bill. "Keep the change."

"Thank you." The waiter examined the bill with a satisfied smile. "I hope to serve you again, sir."

Mac took Kathleen's hand. "Come on. Let's get out of here." He had every intention of escorting her, but he had the uncanny feeling she held him more than he held her. The oppressive warmth of the June evening stifled him. Exhaustion and drink took hold of his legs, his arms, the neck that tried to hold up his head. A dizzying wave of nausea seemed to overpower him, a feeling he couldn't shake.

"You were right. I'm not feeling well. Do you think we could get a room here? Maybe order room service?"

Kathleen stopped abruptly. "A room here? What kind of date are you proposing?"

"I swear, Kath, my intentions are completely virtuous."

"Okay, but don't get any ideas."

Mac leaned against the desk while the clerk obtained the key to one of the penthouse suites. He felt as if he had been riding on a merry-go-round for hours at a dizzying rate of speed and had just stepped off. His mouth felt as if it had been stuffed with cotton.

"Your key, sir."

Why did the desk clerk look at him so strangely? Why did Kathleen have her arm wrapped so tightly around him? Why did he feel people staring at him?

Alone in the elevator, he thought they would never reach the top. He took off his coat, pulled off his tie. Warm air blew out of the elevator's ventilation system. Stuffy; very, very stuffy. He pulled his shirt loose from his trousers and unfastened the buttons. He needed cool air. He needed to lie down.

He heard the bell; felt the elevator stop, the doors open. "I think it's the door on the right," he said, but felt Kathleen steering him to the left.

"What did you do with the key?"

He heard her voice, soft, sultry. He wanted to sleep, but he wanted her with him. When he woke up, would she be in his bed?

"I think it's in my pocket." His head pounded. He dug his fingers into his temples, trying to push away the pain. If both of his hands were busy rubbing his head, why could he feel a hand in his pocket? Why did it feel so good?

Kathleen opened the door and led him inside. He dropped the coat, the tie. Warm arms surrounded him. He felt the softness of her breasts against his chest. She led him to the bedroom, to the bed. She pulled back the covers. He sat on the edge of the bed and pulled her into his arms. Then everything became blurry.

CHAPTER

SIX

"Come on, Mac. Let me take you to bed." Kathleen felt his dead weight come alive at her words, felt him moving under his own power rather than hanging so heavily on her shoulder, as they went to the bedroom.

"Oh, Kathy. Oh, Kathy," he mumbled, the nonsensical words issuing from his mouth as he wrapped his strong muscular arms around her.

Oh, Kathy, my eye! Kathleen thought he was out of his mind—and if she had been a blackmail aficionado, after this night she'd be able to get anything she wanted from Mr. McKenna O'Brien.

She tried to push him away, hoping his stupor would shove him into sleep. Instead, a moment of lust prevailed upon his senses. His fingers traced the length of her spine, his hands reaching lower to caress the roundness of her bottom.

All the while he fondled, she skillfully led him to the bed, trying to escape his hold. She found herself caught in his embrace, and as they plummeted to the bed, he rolled her beneath him. His fingers ran through her hair, pulling, tugging, pushing it away from her neck so his warm, moist lips could explore the sensitive spot below her ear.

Did she really want to get away? At first her hands pushed, then they touched, her fingers hesitant, wanting to know every inch of the body that pressed against her, but unsure of the rights and wrongs of her emotions.

She tossed all uncertainty out of her mind and let her fingers roam. Sliding her hands under his shirt, she kneaded the muscles of his broad shoulders, reveling in his strength.

Shivers ran through her, not from the cool, air-conditioned room, but from the warmth of his mouth moving slowly from her ear, down her neck, to her shoulder blades.

"God, you're beautiful," he whispered and skillfully balanced the huge length of his body above her. She grazed her fingers through the light sprinkling of hair on his chest, over the rippling muscles of his flat, hard stomach.

He lowered himself until their bodies met—their legs, their hips, their chests. Every possible sensation coursed through her body. Lust, desire, need.

His lips, which had tasted for one brief moment the valley between her breasts, eased their way toward her lips. His eyes opened, those smoky blue eyes that had stared at her for years but had never been so close. They closed, his lips lightly brushed her cheek, her ear. She felt his head on her shoulder, the nuzzling of her neck, and then the heaviness of his body pressed hard against hers.

His breathing grew deep, resonant. His mouth fell open and he snored.

How in bloody hell could he have the nerve to pass out now? Kathleen swore to herself.

She pushed against him, wiggling her body out from under his. She wanted to pound his chest, yell and scream. He had excited her, and she damned him for falling asleep just as her senses skyrocketed.

Kathleen stretched out on the sofa with the room-service menu, contemplating what she should order. Mac *had* invited her to dinner. Did it really matter that he had passed out on the bed, snoring loud enough to wake the dead *and* the living?

She looked at the crystal clock on the coffee table, realizing she had half an hour before room service closed. She'd give Mac a few more minutes, and if he didn't awaken, she'd order and eat without him, or find some way to revive the slumbering giant.

From the moment she sat on the couch, she relived every second of the escapade that took them from lounge, to lobby, to elevator, to bed. When had she felt the first sensation? Perhaps it had been when she stuck her hand in his pocket to retrieve the room key. Putting her hand in a man's pants pocket seemed such a personal, intimate thing. Warm. Tight. Close. Perhaps it had been ten years before when she had seen him on the cover of *Fortune*. Had there ever been a time when her senses hadn't been aroused by a mere look, a word, a smile from Mac?

Did he mean it when he said she was beautiful? Yes, he had been drunk. Yes, he had made advances he might not have made at any other time. The great McKenna O'Brien had lost his control. It bothered her, but not in a negative way. She liked seeing his vulnerability. It made him human. But she suspected not everyone would see it that way.

How had the people reacted who saw them in the lobby, Mac's arm slung over her shoulder for support? Had she really seen Reginald Morgan, the "Prince of Porn," walking by? And what about Annabella Adams, the syndicated gossip columnist? Would she soon be reading about McKenna O'Brien's exploits at the Plaza, with a mysterious woman, in all the tabloids—legitimate ones and the not-so-newsworthy?

Enough musing. Her stomach growled and she wanted to eat. She picked up the receiver and punched in the number for room service. It rang only twice before being answered.

"I'd like to place an order." She listened to the helpful voice at the other end of the line.

"Let's see." She ran her finger down the menu. "The tray of chilled lobster, crab, and shrimp sounds good. And . . . no, that's not all. We'll have fettuccine Alfredo. Hot rolls and butter. A tray of pastries. I prefer chocolate. What? Oh, just the two of us. We'll also need a pot of hot coffee, milk, and how about a few Diet Cokes, and a bucket of ice. I guess that ought to do it. Yes. Thank you. You have a nice evening too."

Now to wake Mac.

She hadn't closed the bedroom door just in case he called out in his sleep. She didn't hear his snoring as she approached the room. The dim light of a lamp lit the bed. Mac sat, his head resting on his arms, which were folded across bent knees. His hair was mussed, his shirt discarded.

"Hello." She leaned against the doorjamb, smiling at the man whose touch still burned her skin.

"Dinner sounds interesting." A faint amusement tinged his voice. He attempted to smile.

"I wasn't sure what you'd like so I ordered a little of everything."

"Did you think I'd feel like eating?"

"I wasn't sure. I hoped I wouldn't have to eat it all by myself." Kathleen crossed the room and sat on the end of the bed. She wanted to stay out of his reach, even though she knew he wouldn't try anything now. He probably didn't remember the earlier episode.

"Do you feel any better?" she asked, running her fingers through her hair, pushing it behind her ears, only to have it fall right back against her cheeks.

"Not really. I feel like an ass." He swung his legs to the side of the bed and stood, cautiously. His legs wobbled, but only for a moment. "I didn't do anything stupid, did I?"

Kathleen hesitated a second too long.

"What did I do?"

"Nothing worth mentioning." She didn't want to discuss it, didn't want him to pry an answer out of her. She'd never let him know what he'd done and how much she had enjoyed it, right up to the point where it ended all too soon.

Kathleen's eyes followed Mac to the bathroom. "God. I hope there's a toothbrush in here," he said, sorting through a basket full of odds and ends until he found the items he wanted.

Turning around, he smiled at Kathleen through the doorway, holding his treasures in the air for her to see. "I'll be out in a moment. If the food comes, don't eat it all without me." He kicked closed the door, and Kathleen retreated to the living room, just in time to answer the knock at the door.

"Room service."

Mac stared at his eyes in the mirror. Bloodshot. He looked awful. His muscles ached, his brain pounded against his skull. And Kathleen asked if he felt better. Better than what? Better than a rodeo rider who'd just been thrown and kicked? That's how he felt. How could he hold his head up high when he walked out of the bathroom to face her again? What did she mean by he'd done nothing worth mentioning? What had he done? He wouldn't find out by standing in the bathroom talking to himself for the rest of the night. He had to face her sometime. It might as well be now.

He stood in the doorway, quiet, motionless, and watched the auburn-haired beauty. She still wore the skintight dress that showed every curve, curves he wanted to explore. In the back of his mind a voice told him he'd already touched her, but he didn't remember a thing. Surely he would remember touching something that looked so good. She leaned over the table sampling with her fingers bits and pieces of everything on the trays. She looked wonderful, especially her bare feet and longer-than-long legs. Obviously she wasn't aware that he stood in the doorway. She licked her fingers, humming with the soft, piped-in music playing throughout the suite. Her hips swayed, her foot tapped, and a lump the size of a golf ball formed in his throat.

"Looks good," he said, totally beguiled by the schoolmarm-turned-goddess.

She swung around, her hair flying about her head, as if in slow motion. She smiled—she always smiled. Her eyes sparkled. "You look a little better." She laughed.

He had thought the room was cold, but she was all the warmth he needed.

"May I join you?" He waited for her invitation. He didn't need one, but he waited just the same.

"Of course." He watched her eyes leave his for a moment and travel to his chest, to his unbuttoned shirt. She fluffed the pillows on the couch. "Sit here and I'll fix you a plate."

"I'm not sure I can eat," he said, relaxing in the soft comfort of the sofa, his eyes never leaving the splendid curve of her back and bottom while she filled his plate.

"This stuff's wonderful. As soon as your stomach's full, you'll feel good as new."

"I hope you're right."

Kathleen knelt on the floor in front of him, holding a plate in each hand. She held one out to Mac. He touched her fingers when he took the plate. His senses tingled, his legs weakened. She had to be a witch. He found no other explanation for what she did to him. God, he thought, first I'm confronted by a little old woman straight from Santa's workshop, and now a sorceress, bewitching me with her spell.

He shook his head to rid himself of thoughts of witches and rosy-cheeked women.

Kathleen watched his every move. "I thought you were feeling better."

She dipped a piece of lobster into a silver cup of drawn butter, then slowly, leisurely, bit into the dripping morsel. Not giving a thought to the outcome of his action, he reached out with his thumb and wiped a drop of butter from her lower lip. He lingered a moment, then brought his thumb to his mouth and licked it clean. "I'm feeling better all the time."

He watched the rise and fall of Kathleen's breasts. Her breathing deep, slow.

What the hell am I doing? What is she doing? He turned away from the power of her eyes. A few hours ago they were yelling at each other, and now all he wanted to do was pull her into his arms and kiss away all those doubts and fears that had been haunting him.

"You should try the fettuccine," she said, invading his thoughts, breaking her spell.

"Do you always eat so much?" he asked.

"Yes, but my tastes and pocketbook usually opt for peanut butter and hot dogs. I could get used to this, though. Here, give it a try." She held a fork full of shrimp and crab up to Mac's mouth, and he pulled it off with his teeth. She may not have been trying to be sensual, but she was doing a damned good job.

Mac pushed up from the couch and added more food to his plate. He stared down at the lady curled up on the floor. Did he dare join her?

He moved the drinks and trays of food to the coffee table. "No need to keep jumping up and down," he said, then went to the fireplace. He thought about lighting a fire, then realized they didn't need any more heat in the room.

He could sense her watching him, but she didn't say a word. What should he do next? He could leave. He could sit next to her on the floor. He could return to the couch.

He opted to sit in the chair on the opposite side of the coffee table. He couldn't think of a safer option.

"I make you nervous, don't I?" she asked.

"Yes."

"You're not nervous at work."

"That's different."

"Why? Because you feel you're in control?"

"I'm always in control—in business anyway."

"I prefer you this way," she whispered, soft, sultry.

Why did he find everything about her so sensual? Her voice, her movements, the way she licked her lips? He set his plate on the table and got up from the chair. He went to the thermostat and turned the dial, lowering the temperature. The fan came on instantly. Cool air blew out of the vents.

He picked up the phone and started to dial room service for beer, but the lingering throb in his head made him reconsider. Damn! She made him feel sixteen instead of forty-nine, young and insecure, wanting to cop a feel but afraid of the repercussions. Hell! Isn't that what he wanted? A change in his routine? A chance to start over? To be young and impulsive again?

He paced the floor, attempting to regain just a speck of composure. When he stopped in front of Kathleen, he looked down into the face of contentment. Oh, Kath, he inwardly sighed. What am I getting us into? He wanted to touch her, but didn't. He wanted to smile, but couldn't. It took what little courage he had left just so speak. "We need to talk."

"What would you like to talk about?"

Her smile deepened. His throat constricted.

He took a deep breath. "I think if we're going to have any kind of relationship we should get to know each other better."

"Are we going to have a relationship?" Her question seemed innocent enough, but Mac knew Kathleen was anything but innocent. She knew what she wanted, and she seemed to know just how to get it.

"There's something going on between us, but I sure as hell don't know what it is."

"Mutual attraction?" she asked and reached across the coffee table for her glass. When she tugged at the top of her strapless dress, Mac nearly lost what little remained of his composure.

"Are you attracted to me?" he asked.

She bit her lower lip and again let her eyes travel up and down the length of his body. "Yes."

"How could you possibly be attracted to me? I'm older than you—"

"Wait a minute," she interrupted. "So what if you're older? You're also richer and bigger. You're also the opposite sex and very good looking."

"I suppose you say these things to every older man you date."

"I haven't dated in years."

"Why?"

"The truth?"

"The truth."

"Because I've been waiting for you to open your eyes and look at me."

Her words stabbed at his heart. Six long years wasted because he'd been afraid of his feelings, afraid he was too old for her. He'd been such a fool.

"I've closed my eyes to lots of things in the last few years."

"They weren't always closed, were they?"

He knelt down beside her, taking a strand of her hair, feeling its texture, letting the curl wrap around his finger. "No."

"Then I didn't imagine it all those years ago? You did feel something for me?"

He trailed his fingers along her cheek, touched the bottom of her chin, and tilted her face toward him. "Yes, I felt something, something I felt would be better to run away from."

The smile left her face, replaced by a myriad of emotions—anger, grief, confusion. "Why did you run away?"

Mac avoided her eyes, just as he avoided her question. It was easier to reach for an éclair than to give her an honest answer. "I don't want to talk about that."

"Okay," she whispered, then took another sip of soda, sadly staring at Mac over the rim of her glass. Within seconds, her smile returned. "If you don't want to talk about *that*, then tell me how a cultured gentleman like you ended up drinking so much beer? And why is it that you have to pepper all your sentences with *damn* or *hell*?"

He chewed thoughtfully on her question and on the cream-filled pastry. He grinned, glad she didn't pursue the previous topic. "Because women like you have a tendency to anger me."

"Oh, come on. I don't believe that for one moment. If you don't like a woman, or a man for that matter, you just give them one of your death stares and ignore them. That has nothing whatsoever to do with the beer, the *damn*s, the *hell*s, or me." She reached over and grabbed a dish of chocolate mousse from the dessert tray.

Mac groaned. "Would you stop doing that?"

Kathleen eyed him, puzzled. "Doing what?"

"Bending over like that. Every time you do I can see all the way down your dress."

"Then quit looking."

"I like looking."

Kathleen jumped up from the couch and went to the closet.

"Where do you think you're going?" Mac bellowed, following her to the closet, afraid she was going to leave.

She pulled his coat off the hanger and slipped it on over her dress. The sleeves extended beyond the tips of her fingers. She felt tiny inside the coat that nearly swallowed her, but she found it to be the perfect attire for hiding her body. "Now you don't have to look," she barked, stomping back to the couch and her chocolate mousse.

Looking at Kathleen made his loins ache. Looking at Kathleen and not touching her was the hardest thing he'd ever done. A million thoughts filled his head—good ones, bad ones—but in the end, propriety won.

He followed her back to the couch and sat on the floor at her feet. He leaned back against the sofa and sighed. "Okay. I'll admit it. You're driving me crazy." Turning around to look at the woman sitting above him, he smiled with warmth and affection. "Maybe it's time to talk."

Five hours later they hadn't run out of words. Kathleen listened to Mac open his heart about the not-so-poor little rich boy's life. He'd grown up with everything, including love from both his mother and father. He wasn't ignored. He wasn't sent off to boarding schools. He was a very bright child who wanted to know everything about his father's business, and at the early age of twelve started working in the mail room, doing odds and ends, learning every aspect of the empire that would someday be his.

He lay on the couch, his head in Kathleen's lap. She played with his hair. At times she wanted to kiss his brow, stroke his cheek, touch his chest—but that wouldn't happen tonight. She knew the magical spell would be broken if anything physical happened. Tonight they would talk, and talk only.

"You'll never guess what I wanted to be when I grew up," Mac said with a laugh.

"What?"

"A cowboy."

"What's funny about that? Most little boys want to be cowboys."

"The funny thing is, I haven't gotten it out of my system."

"Neither did your dad," Kathleen added. "Unfortunately, the closest he got to being a cowboy was having all those Remingtons and Russells in his office."

Why did she have to mention his dad once again? Why did she have to know him so well, know of his dad's love for the West and its culture? Hell! He had to force those ridiculous rumors out of his head. His father wouldn't have had an affair—not with Kathleen, not with anyone.

"You're right, Kath," he said, absently stroking her hand which rested on his chest. "I'm just like my dad. Both way too busy to give in to a foolish whim like becoming a cowboy."

"It's not too late to change careers."

"I'm forty-nine years old, Kath. At my age I can't start over. At thirty-two you see things differently than you do when you're nearly fifty." He sat up, and only inches separated them. "Do you realize I'm old enough to be your father?"

"Or lover," she tossed back without thinking.

Again he felt the stirring in his loins. "Is that a possibility?" He stretched his arm out along the back of the couch behind her head.

"Not tonight."

"But it *is* a possibility."

"If you really think a thirty-two-year-old woman could be interested *that* way in a forty-nine-year-old man." She laughed at him. Why did he think his age made a difference? Didn't he realize the bond between them went beyond age, went beyond physical attraction—that age was secondary to everything else?

"Are you interested *that way*?" he asked.

"Are you really so unsure that you have to ask?"

"I'm unsure of everything when I'm around you."

Kathleen didn't comment, afraid if she said anything more, they'd end up in the bedroom. Although that's where her heart wanted to be, her brain told her to wait. She glanced at the clock, yawned, and stretched. "Do you realize I have to be at work in less than three hours?"

"Call in sick," he teased.

"No. My boss would know I'm lying."

His hand touched her neck and lightly caressed the bare skin. He wrapped a strand of hair around his finger. "I don't want tonight to end."

"It has to. I've eaten too much junk food, and I haven't had a wink of sleep."

"Can we have dinner tonight, after work?"

She hesitated. "I can't. I have too much work to do."

"Tomorrow night?"

She shook her head. "I'm sorry. I've got so much to do on the magazine that I can't take a moment off. Maybe Saturday?"

"How about lunch during the week?"

"I can't. Too many meetings."

He removed his hand from her shoulder and stood, pulling her up from the couch. "Are you trying to avoid me already?"

"No. I'm trying to get a promotion."

"Is it that important?"

"It's the second most important thing in my life."

"And the first is?"

"Julie."

"Oh. Your daughter." His low voice sounded disappointed. "I'm glad she's first on your list."

"She'll always come first. Now, are you going to take me home?"

He didn't answer, just went to the phone and requested a taxi while Kathleen slipped on her shoes.

He found his tie slung over a chair and hung it around his neck. He stepped into his shoes, then went back to Kathleen, debating what to do next.

She started to take off his jacket, but he pulled her hands away. He didn't release them.

"Keep it on. I might have second thoughts about leaving if you're not wearing it."

She smiled, pulling her hands away from his before he could draw them to his lips.

"And I might not want to leave if you do that."

They walked to the door, both of them taking one last look at the room they had shared, the dirty glasses and plates, the leftover food. She'd never forget this night. She hoped Mac felt the same.

They rode down in an empty elevator. The door opened, but Mac pulled Kathleen close, keeping her inside as the door closed, and the elevator stood still on the lobby level.

"I know you don't want me to kiss you, but I've never let a woman give me orders and I'm not going to start now."

She didn't resist when he opened the coat and put his hands inside, slowly, tenderly letting them slip under the light wool of his jacket and around her silky-smooth back. He pulled her close, lowering his head to her upturned face.

"God, you're beautiful." Their lips met, gently, carefully exploring newfound territory. For Kathleen the kiss became the finishing touch to what had started hours earlier in the bed of a penthouse suite at the Plaza. For Mac, it became the fulfillment of a desire he had shoved to the back of his mind six long years before.

The door opened again. "Excuse me, sir." The bellboy cleared his throat and blushed at the sight before him. "Your taxi's waiting."

At five-thirty in the morning, very few people littered the lobby, only the bellboy and a desk clerk. Mac tightened his coat around Kathleen to keep out the morning's chill, draped his arm over her shoulder, and pulled her close. They walked out of the Plaza into the pinkish gray dawn. The taxi waited at the curb, the driver standing beside the opened door.

Again, Mac slid his hands down Kathleen's back, cupping her bottom and pulling her close. That's when the first light flashed, and the photographer ran up for a closer shot. Another flash.

Mac pushed Kathleen into the cab, turned to yell at the photographer, and raised his hand to cover his face as the next flash went off. He climbed into the car and the driver shut the door behind him.

"Damn those photographers," Mac cursed. "God only knows what they'll print in the paper."

CHAPTER

SEVEN

Kathleen wanted to die. She propped her chin up with her hand, hoping and praying no one would walk in and see that she was half-asleep. She could kill Mac for keeping her out all night. Yet, the magic of the evening played over and over in her brain and heart, and she wouldn't trade the exhaustion she now suffered for even one moment of her night with the man of her dreams.

She checked her schedule. No staff meetings, no lunches, no chance of yawning or nodding off to sleep in front of strangers or colleagues. Her desk overflowed with copy, artwork, pressures, and deadlines. Half a dozen phone messages had been affixed to her phone so they wouldn't get lost in the shuffle. She laughed. Where do I begin?

In front of her lay the beginnings of an article she had hastily scribbled about "The Arrogant Male." Words had been crossed out with new ones written above, added lines cascaded down the side margins, and arrows moved text from one spot to another. With a red felt-tip pen she doodled in the blank spaces, drawing nothing but squares, rectangles, and circles, daydreaming of her evening with Mac, wondering when she would see him again.

She found it hard to concentrate on the article. She had originally penned it with Mac in mind. She even planned to add a paragraph or two about the arrogant man she had met from the ad in the personals. Funny they should turn out to be one and the same. Mac definitely had an arrogant streak, but he could also be generous and kind, and she found something endearing in each of his characteristics—the good and the not-so-good.

She jumped at a knock on her door. Obviously, even the DO NOT DISTURB sign posted outside wasn't good enough to keep some people from barging in.

Before she could say "Come in," the door opened and Ashley Tate breezed into the room. Kathleen didn't move, just raised her eyes from the paper and inwardly groaned. *What could she possibly want, and why is she intruding on my wonderful thoughts?*

Ashley snatched the scribbled article off the desk, scanned the contents, then tossed it back amongst the clutter.

"I suppose that's for your new magazine?" Ashley scoffed. "Mac told me all about it. He hates the concept, you know. For the life of me I don't understand why he's letting you continue with it."

Kathleen rubbed her eyes, then found a sickeningly sweet smile to plaster on her face. "It's such a pleasure having you drop by my office, especially with such fond words for my work. I've rarely had the pleasure of your company. Is there something you need? Something I can help you with?"

"No, nothing at all. I was on my way to see Mac and thought I'd drop in."

"How kind of you."

"By the way. Did you receive your invitation to McKenna's anniversary ball?"

Kathleen opened her top drawer, took out the gold embossed envelope, and waved it in the air with a grin.

"Oh, I'm so glad they didn't forget you. You do have a date, don't you?"

Kathleen bristled at the catty tone of Ashley's voice. "I've been too busy to think about a date. But please, don't worry about me."

"I do hope you'll be able to find someone. One of the janitors maybe?" Ashley grinned, obviously content that her claws were sinking so deep into Kathleen's skin. "It's not much fun being alone at an affair like this. I'm sure all the other guests will be couples. You know, like Mac and me."

Kathleen seethed. Mac will find himself in one hell of a mess if he parades Ashley on his arm in front of me. She gritted her teeth and responded. "Thank you for being so concerned about my welfare. I'll be sure to let you know if I can't find a date." Now leave, she wanted to add, but didn't.

Ashley started for the door, then turned around, a questioning frown on her face. "I know you had a meeting with Mac yesterday. I do hope nothing is wrong."

So that's the reason she's in here, Kathleen thought. Her curiosity is eating away at her. Kathleen smiled. "Everything's fine."

"I was terribly concerned. I heard how upset Mac was about the new magazine."

"And who told you he was upset?"

"Oh, the word gets around. I have friends here who love to keep me informed. I hope you weren't too upset when you stormed out of his office yesterday."

"It's nothing you should be concerned with. Besides, Mac and I managed to work things out quite nicely, thank you."

Ashley raised an eyebrow. "Yes, he can be quite sweet, even to you, I suppose."

Ashley pulled out a chair and sat, gracefully crossing her legs. She leaned forward and whispered, as if in deepest confidence. "May I tell you something, my dear?"

Kathleen said nothing, only acknowledged her with a questioning nod.

"This isn't easy to say, but, to be perfectly honest, you look dreadful today. You really shouldn't burn the candle at both ends. A good night's sleep does wonders for your appearance."

"It really is sweet of you to express your concern." Kathleen bit her tongue to keep from telling Ashley she spent the night with Mac just to see her reaction. She absently pushed a stray strand of hair back behind her ear. It definitely had a mind of its own this morning, and she knew she looked a sight. But she didn't need Ashley to clue her in, and she found it quite easy to adopt Ashley's venomous tone. "But honestly, Ashley. Surely you must know how difficult it is to look your best when you've been out all night."

"No." Ashley looked bemused. "I always get at least eight hours of sleep."

"You're so very fortunate."

Ashley grinned, then aimed her eyes at the article she had scanned earlier. "I do hope you weren't working on *that*." She frowned just the slightest bit, as though her face might permanently wrinkle if she used too much expression.

Kathleen thought about what she had written, deciding her evening with Mac had been too special to trivialize in a magazine article. She looked at the paper, then back at Ashley, who stared, curiously, at Kathleen's quiet, pensive face. "This," she said, wadding up the paper and tossing it in the trash can, "was just a fleeting thought, one that wasn't going anywhere."

"Mac wouldn't be pleased if he knew you were wasting your time."

"I rarely waste my time, or anything else, Ms. Tate, except when people barge into my office, unannounced, with absolutely nothing constructive to say."

Ashley stood in a huff. "Everything I've said to you, Ms. Flannigan, has been constructive. And I think you should remember that my words should be accepted as though they were coming from Mac himself."

"And when did McKenna O'Brien appoint you as his spokesperson?"

"I've always spoken on Mac's behalf. I know he's not happy with the magazine, I know he's not happy with you, and I think you know it."

Kathleen gripped the edge of her desk and leaned forward. "No, I don't, Ms. Tate. Mac and I had a long discussion about this magazine and my position at McKenna Publishing. It was a private discussion, one I don't believe he would discuss with staff, or anyone else for that matter."

"He discusses everything with me."

"Is that so? I was under the impression your relationship was over."

"You're mistaken. Mac's in love with me, and he always will be."

Kathleen chose not to believe Ashley's words, and she wanted her out of her office. "I don't care what your relationship is, but I doubt even you know Mac's true feelings about this magazine, this company, or anything else."

Ashley stuck her chin high in the air, looking down her nose at Kathleen. "You seem terribly edgy this morning. Perhaps you should start sleeping at night instead of gallivanting around till all hours."

"What I do with my personal time is none of your business, Ms. Tate. Now, if you'll excuse me, I have work to do."

Ashley slammed the door and smacked into several staff members clustered outside Kathleen's office, apparently listening to the boisterous exchange that had gone on inside.

She pushed them aside and stormed down the hall, taking the elevator to the penthouse offices Mac occupied.

Grace looked up from the paperwork on her desk. "I'm sorry, Miss Tate, but Mr. O'Brien isn't in today."

"Good," Ashley retorted, walking past Grace's desk and pushing open the door to Mac's office. "I need some privacy. I'm sure he won't mind me using his office." She closed the door and locked it before Grace could do or say anything else.

She hated this room with its dark oak paneling and bookshelves, buckskin leather upholstery, and the big, ugly, ancient oak desk. She had managed to decorate Mac's home, but he wouldn't let her touch a thing in his office.

She sat in the executive chair, almost swallowed in its immensity. She thought about Kathleen, that frumpy old maid who had had to resort to adopting a child for companionship. She laughed. Mac had been so gullible when she told him that story about Kathleen's affair with his dad. Whether he believed it or not, those words had been enough to end his silly crush on a girl who didn't fit into his class. But what could she do this time to get him back? She didn't even know what had gone wrong.

It had to be a mistake. After ten years together, how could he possibly want anyone else? She tried to think what his reason could be. She knew she hadn't done anything different, so the fault must be his. She had tried to see him every day for the past two weeks, but his new housekeeper wouldn't even open the door, and his secretary continually said he couldn't be disturbed. Why, then, had Kathleen been granted admittance? And to think she had stormed out of his office. Ashley wouldn't dream of slamming Mac's door. He wouldn't put up with it. Ashley knew how to handle Mac—with kid gloves, a little pout, a few tears, but never,

never slam the door. That made him mad—and when Mac got mad, she stayed out of his way.

Toying with the ugly bronze sculpted cowboy on his desk, she thought about their relationship, about her status in society. She liked being known as McKenna O'Brien's lady friend. He lavished her with presents, took her on trips, and he asked nothing in return, except sex every now and then. She could put up with that on occasion.

She looked at her watch. Nine-thirty. Too early for lunch. Maybe she should go to her club anyway. At least there would be someone interesting to talk to. People loved to listen to her. She had so much to say, and they always looked happy to see her.

She opened the office door and overheard Mac's secretary ordering flowers. She smiled. He wants to make up. How nice. Well, I won't let him back too easily. I'll make him suffer for a while. Maybe a diamond bracelet would be a nice getting-back-together present. She smiled at Grace and disappeared into the elevator.

Kathleen's stomach growled with hunger as she paced the floor. Jon followed her with his eyes.

"Look, Kathy. Maybe the timing just isn't right."

She stopped and glared. "No. The timing is right. We just have to look for a different angle."

"I've thought of everything."

"There must be something else."

"I told you. There's already a glut of women's magazines on the market. The economy's in a slump and the big spenders don't want to invest in anything new right now. I can't pull advertising dollars out of my pocket."

"Maybe the press conference will help."

"The press conference won't help unless you have some good news to give them."

"Then find some good news," Kathleen ordered and started for the door. She turned back to look at Jon buried in paperwork, shaking his head at the figures before him.

She put her hand on his shoulder. "I'll put some ideas on paper and see what I can come up with. Why don't you call it quits, go home, and spend the afternoon with your kids."

He nodded his head, but Kathleen felt his shoulders slump, sensed his defeat.

Walking out of Jon's office toward her own, she ignored the whispers as she walked by the desks lined up like dominoes down the main corridor of the floor. She had too much on her mind. The problem with the advertisers was serious. She knew the press conference would help, but she didn't want to be overly optimistic. She needed to sit down at her desk, in the quiet of her office, and think up new strategies to attract the advertisers. Jon had talent, but she couldn't leave everything up to him. If she had to work twenty-four hours a day she would. This magazine had to succeed.

When Kathleen entered her office, the scent of a hundred fragrant roses overpowered her. She smiled and thought the most pleasant of thoughts—Mac.

Vases stood on two corners of her desk, one on her credenza, another on top of her bookcase. She went to each arrangement, touching the cold crystal vases while inhaling deeply to capture the memory of the multicolored roses, their aroma, their beauty. She found the card lying on her desk. It had only one word written on it, *Mac*, but that one word spoke volumes.

The phone rang. "Kathleen Flannigan," she answered in her brisk, businesslike manner.

"Good morning."

She fell into her chair, swinging around to stare out the window at the high-rises surrounding her. "Good afternoon."

"I hope you're not too tired. I kept you out rather late."

"I've never felt better. Thank you for the roses. They're beautiful."

"I thought they might perk up your day."

"They did," she whispered.

"Will you change your mind and have lunch with me?" he asked.

"I wish I could, but—"

"But you're too busy," he interrupted.

"You do understand, don't you?"

"No. No one should ever be too busy for the boss."

Kathleen laughed. "If the boss wanted to discuss business, I wouldn't be too busy."

"What if the boss wanted to discuss something other than business?"

"I hate to mix business with pleasure."

"Oh? Which one am I—business or pleasure?" He sounded sexy, and extremely seductive.

"Both. And I need to keep the two separate."

"God, you're difficult."

"I'm a single parent. I have to work for a living."

She heard nothing at the other end of the line. What could he be thinking? Anytime she mentioned Julie, he grew silent.

"I take it you're not going out to lunch?" he asked, sounding disappointed.

"No."

"You always work straight through, don't you?"

"Most of the time."

"Maybe I should issue a directive saying all employees *will* take a lunch."

"You have a lot of dedicated employees. They'd probably ignore your directive."

"I'm being selfish. I want to see you."

She twisted the phone's cord around her finger. "Next Saturday's still open."

He sighed. "Next Saturday's a long way away."

"I know, but—"

"Please don't say any more. I already know your excuses by heart."

"I might change my mind."

"No, you won't, and I won't ask you to."

"Thank you. I won't ask you to change, either. I rather like you just the way you are."

He laughed. "You mean opinionated and stubborn?"

"That, too."

"What else?"

"Tall, handsome . . ."

"Forty-nine," he interjected.

It annoyed Kathleen that he kept dredging up the subject of age. "Your age doesn't bother me and it shouldn't bother you. As a matter of fact, I like my men older."

"You've had others?"

"My father is older," she stammered, then let out a deep sigh, wondering why those words escaped from her mouth.

"Don't worry, Kath. I know you're not comparing me with your dad."

"He's a wonderful man. I could make worse comparisons."

"There's no one I can compare you with," he said. "No one at all."

"Is that a compliment?" she asked.

"Yes."

She savored his words "Thank you," she whispered.

"I should let you get back to work."

Kathleen thought about how little she'd accomplished that morning between Ashley's interruption, her meeting with Jon, and her thoughts about the previous night. "It hasn't been easy to concentrate today."

"You were thinking about me?"

"Part of the time."

"Good. Keep thinking about me, but try to get some work done. I won't make money if your head's in the clouds." The laughter in his voice was infectious, and Kathleen caught herself smiling.

"Thank you, Mac. For everything."

"Any time."

The knock came at one-thirty. Kathleen's head rested in her hands as she looked over the art department's cost estimates for the magazine, trying her hardest not to fall asleep. The numbers didn't look good. Nothing looked good, except the roses that surrounded her.

"Come in," she said, looking up from the paper to see two men in tuxedos push a cart laden with sterling-silver-covered platters into her crowded office. She didn't have to ask. Her face lit up like a child's on Christmas morning. Mac must have decided not to listen to her refusal to have lunch—and she was delighted.

"Please don't let us disturb you, madam. We'll only be a moment."

She watched with intrigue as they assembled a small round table, covering it with a white linen cloth, silverware, crystal goblets, and fine bone china.

They carried in two Chippendale chairs upholstered in white damask, and set them on either side of the table. One of the waiters came to Kathleen, bowed, and took her hand, escorting her to a chair. He unfolded the red linen napkin and laid it across her lap.

"If there's anything else we can get for you, ma'am, we'll be just outside the door. The gentleman will be here momentarily."

She watched them depart just as Mac sauntered in, breathtakingly handsome, and exceedingly dapper.

"Ah, lunch. One of the finest meals of the day." He leaned over and placed a soft, lingering kiss on Kathleen's cheek, brushed a strand of hair from behind her ear so it hung in a ringlet along the side of her face, then took the chair across from her.

"You said you don't go out to lunch, so I thought I'd have it brought to you."

"It's nearly two o'clock."

"And you probably haven't eaten since last night. Correct?"

She smiled into eyes that glimmered with hope, and anticipation. "I'm starving."

"Good. Just what I wanted to hear you say." He lifted the lid from the first platter, and Kathleen couldn't help but laugh when she saw two Big Macs sitting on the tray, surrounded by french fries and hot apple pies.

"Now, this is what I call a meal," he said, surveying the feast before him. "God, I love junk food."

Kathleen licked her lips. "Mmm, this looks divine." She ripped the top off a packet of catsup, squeezed it onto her plate, stuck in a french fry, and popped it into her mouth. "How did you know I have a penchant for the finer things in life?"

"I'm psychic. And I, too, have a penchant for the finer things in life. You're one of them."

"You're much too kind," she said, sticking a salty finger into her mouth.

"Champagne?" he asked, holding up the bottle.

Kathleen shook her head. "You forgot. I don't drink."

He grinned, then lifted the lid on the second platter. "Your Diet Coke, my dear." He handed her the tall paper cup, complete with plastic lid and straw. "Hope this is more to your liking."

"You remembered."

"I never forget a thing." He shoved the bottle of champagne back into its holder, picked up the second cup of Diet Coke, took a drink, and cringed.

"Damn. This is awful. How can you drink this stuff?"

"An acquired taste."

"I prefer Molson."

"You should have brought one along."

"But you told me I drink too much."

"You listened to me?"

"You and my housekeeper. Wonderful old lady but a bit of a busybody. She's been harping at me, too."

"I'm glad you've got someone who cares enough to keep you on the straight and narrow."

"She's also stuffing me with junk food. I've been on a health kick for so many years I forgot what grease, white flour, and sugar tasted like."

"And you like it?"

"Love it." He smiled, munching a mouthful of hamburger.

"You told me you couldn't start over at forty-nine, yet now you're telling me you've switched diets, you've given up beer . . ."

"No. That, my dear, is something I'll never give up. Someone told me once that good things must be done in moderation lest they become boring and routine."

"All good things?" she asked, peering over the top of her soda.

He thought about her question a moment, wiggled his eyebrows and grinned. "Not all, I suppose. Some things should be done excessively."

"I think we'd better change the subject," Kathleen said, licking the oozing secret sauce from the side of her burger, never taking her eyes from Mac's. How is it possible that one man can look so good? she wondered. Roses, Big Macs, Diet Coke. How could I be so lucky?

She watched him sipping his soda, entranced by the way his lips formed around the straw—sweet, sensuous, made-to-be-kissed lips. She wanted to speak, but couldn't think of anything to say. Something personal? No. Stick with business.

"I met with my advertising exec—"

"Wait a minute. I thought we weren't going to mix business with pleasure."

"But you're here. I thought you might want to know what's going on."

"Listen, Kath. I'm here to have lunch with a beautiful woman, *not* with an employee. I don't want to talk about business when we're together."

"Why?"

He wiped his hands on the napkin, rose from his chair to take a place in front of the window. He looked out but saw only the reflection of the woman haunting his thoughts. He turned around, his hands digging deep into his pockets. "You know, I may sound like a pompous ass, *and* a chauvinist, but I decided a long time ago that the woman I'm involved with should be free to be with me. I want someone who can travel with me, be at my side at business luncheons and dinners. You can't do that and work, too."

"I didn't think we'd progressed that far."

"I've thought about it since I left you this morning. I like having a woman around. I especially like having *you* around."

She laughed. "But I work, and you seem to have forgotten I have a child. Sorry, Mac, but I can't be what you want." God, it hurt her to say those words. As much as she wanted him, she knew she couldn't be happy in that type of life.

"Ashley was here today. She still wants you. Maybe you should consider going back to her, since it's apparent she lives up to all your expectations."

He stiffened. "That's over." He walked to her side, not touching her, but stood only inches away. "Ashley's history."

"But she still cares." Kathleen looked up into eyes filled with emotion, trying to determine what he was feeling. Anger? Hate? Hurt? "I'd care if you said you didn't want me."

His expression softened. "I want you." He tenderly caressed her cheek. "I want the woman I was with last night. Warm. Soft. Sensual."

Kathleen drew in a deep breath, fighting for control of the senses he'd nearly destroyed by his touch and his words. "I'm the same today as I was last night."

He moved closer, so close she could feel heat radiating from his body. "Are you?" His fingers grazed her hairline and slipped into her disheveled bun. "I liked looking at your skin, and your legs. I liked your hair hanging down." He found the clips that held her hair in place, pulled them out one by one, then released the band that gathered her hair into a ponytail. He let it fall, splaying his fingers through the thick waves, spreading her hair down around her shoulders.

She reached behind her to pull his hands away. "Don't. Please," she begged, but he captured her hands in his, brought them to his lips, and kissed the backs of her fingers.

"You're driving me mad," he whispered, his breath so hot, so near to her ear that she shuddered from the nearness of him.

"Slow down, Mac."

"I don't want to."

Kathleen pulled out of his grasp, sliding out of the chair, quickly moving across the room where he couldn't touch her, couldn't make her tremble anymore, couldn't send feelings of warmth and desire coursing through her. She had wanted this for years, but suddenly she felt smothered, trapped and rushed. She wasn't ready for his advances. "You don't want *me*, Mac. You want what you want me to be, and I can't be that woman one hundred percent of the time."

He threw his hands up in the air. "This is crazy, Kath. I don't know why I thought we could ever get along. I'd take you away from all this if you'd just say the word. I'd take care of all your needs. But you argue with everything. You won't make concessions. You don't want to compromise."

"I have nothing to compromise. Everything I do I do because I have to do it. I'm not rich like you. I can't give up my job for a man who could be here today and gone tomorrow. I can dress differently, if that will make you happy. But I won't give up my job, and I won't be kept." She paused, took a deep breath, and continued, her face filled with hurt. "That's an insult, Mac. I could have dealt with everything else, but you're treating me like I can be bought. God knows you can afford it. But I never wanted your money. I only wanted you. And all of a sudden I don't think I even want that."

He closed the distance between them, then put his hands on her arms, not wanting her to move away again. "That's not true. You want me just as much as I want you."

"I don't. You *are* pompous. You *are* a chauvinist." She tried to pull away, but he held on tight. Her eyes blazed. "Why don't we pretend last night and this lunch never happened?"

His jaw tensed. His eyes burned into hers. "You're angry, and I can't reason with anger."

She pushed his hands away. "You've made it perfectly clear what you want from me. Well, I think I made myself clear, too. I want to be at the top in this company. It's something I've wanted for years, and I won't give up that dream.

If you want me, you'll have to make some concessions."

"Oh, I want you, all right. But what about you? What concessions are you willing to make?"

"At present . . ." She gave herself a moment, assuring herself she wasn't making a mistake in her choice of words. "I'm not willing to make any concessions."

"Then it's over, Kath." Slowly, defeated, he crossed to her door, pulled it open, then turned, wanting to memorize the features of the woman he already regretted giving up, trying to compose his nerves so he could make it out of the room. But the face he saw wasn't the one he wanted to remember; not the face streaked with tears. Real tears, not like Ashley's. He couldn't walk out on her now, not yet, not while she was crying.

He closed the door and leaned against it, trying to decide what to do next. Should he go to her? Should he leave and let her cry alone? Standing so close was pure torture. She hadn't bothered to turn around, hadn't tried to hide her tears. Hell! He'd just told her they were through, he couldn't comfort her now.

Damn! He couldn't reason with himself any longer, he just let his passion take hold of his senses. She was in his arms before he realized he'd moved. He shoved his hands into her hair, clutched the back of her head, and pulled her mouth forcefully to his. She struggled, but for only a moment, and then his lips overpowered her.

She wanted to hold back but couldn't. She wanted to hate him, to push him away. Instead, she found herself responding to his kiss, opening her lips to run her tongue across his teeth to savor his taste, to let her tongue mingle with his. She relaxed in his arms. His lips left hers and trailed down her neck, to the sensitive spot below her ear. He nibbled on her lobe, ran a big hand down her back, grabbed her bottom, and pulled her closer. She felt his desire, craved it, wished they were back at the Plaza in the room where their passion could have soared.

Her legs nearly buckled when the warmth of his breath surrounded her ear, when his lips trailed across her cheek and once again took possession of her mouth. Softly, gently, while his thumbs caressed her face, he wiped the escaped tears from her eyes, then he pushed her away, holding her at arm's length. His smoky blue eyes darkened, burning into hers. His breath was ragged. She didn't know what to say, didn't know what to do.

He backed away, straightened his tie. He smoothed back the hair that had fallen onto his forehead, opened the door, and looked back at Kathleen, his eyes filled with a mixture of anger, frustration, and overpowering desire. "I can't pretend last night didn't happen. I can't pretend this lunch didn't happen. I'm used to getting what I want, Kath, and the plain, simple truth is, I want you. Sometimes I have to make a few concessions, but it works both ways." He turned and stepped through the doorway, fully prepared to leave, but he turned to Kathleen one more time. "Let me know when you're ready to compromise."

CHAPTER

EIGHT

Kathleen stared at the empty room, gasping for breath, trying to regain her composure. Mac's kiss had unnerved her. His words flustered her. Why did their relationship have to become a contest of wills? She wanted him. God knows he wanted her. But it would be hell finding a common meeting ground.

Mac didn't call that afternoon. He didn't call the next day. Kathleen kept the door shut, forcing him out of her mind, concentrating only on the accounting figures that haunted her, the copy, the artwork, all the things adding up to disaster.

She picked up the phone and called her assistant. "Barb, I want to see everyone working on *Success* in the conference room. Now."

She picked up her papers and marched out of her office, down the corridor, and into the conference room on the left. She found it strange the way everyone stared, the whispers she heard. Maybe Mac had sent more flowers. No, that wasn't possible.

She paced the floor as her staff flowed in, one by one, taking their customary places at the table.

"Are you okay, Kathy?" Jon asked.

"I'm fine. In fact, I've made some decisions, but we'll talk about those later."

Kathleen continued to stand, looking from one staff member to another. Jon she trusted. In fact, she trusted them all, but something had definitely gone wrong.

"Wayne." She looked directly into the eyes of the long-haired aging hippie, who had disregarded her direction to change the female executive from gorgeous to professional. "What's the meaning of this?" She held up the artwork.

"You may be the boss, Kathleen," he said, "but McKenna O'Brien is still in charge. We're all aware that he doesn't like this magazine, and we're just trying to make a few changes to please him."

"Let me get this straight, Wayne." Kathleen paced the length of the conference room, hands folded behind her back. She liked to have their eyes follow her, liked having their attention. "We've spent months laying out a plan for this magazine, and after one meeting with Mr. O'Brien you determine it's best to go against my word?"

"Not everything," Wayne said. "He liked that piece. I didn't think it would hurt to keep it in its original form."

She went back to her place at the table and picked up piece after piece of art copy. "What about the rest of this?"

"We decided to rework a few of the details, make it less liberal, more feminine."

"What? Another *Woman's Day*? *Family Circle*?" Again she walked around the table, stopping behind Wayne so he had to turn around in his chair to see her eyes, which blazed with fury.

"We thought it would work better."

"Let me ask you this, Mr. Smith. Who is this *we* you keep referring to?"

She watched him glance around the room, watched the eyes of all her staff look everywhere but at her. "I see."

She went back to the head of the table and sat down, picked up a pencil, and chewed on the end, glaring from one person to the next, listening to the silence that permeated the room.

"Do you make a habit of making changes without discussing them with other managing editors? Was it that difficult to come to me and tell me how you felt? How many staff meetings have we had in the last two weeks? Two? Three? What have you been doing? Artwork and articles you thought I wanted, and another set that you felt would please Mr. O'Brien?"

Only Wayne had the nerve to speak. "We knew your mind was already set, and you've never been a good listener when this magazine's been discussed. The changes haven't been just to satisfy Mr. O'Brien, they've been made to help you out."

Kathleen leaned forward, observing the various degrees of discomfort each staff member displayed. "The only help I need on this magazine is for you, all of you, to do the work we've discussed. If you value your jobs, you'll work night and day to reconstruct our original plans. I'm in charge, not McKenna O'Brien. You *will* do it the way we originally discussed or you won't do it at all. Do I make myself clear?"

"Have you discussed this with Mr. O'Brien?" Wayne asked.

She refrained from slamming the pencil down on the table. "What I have or haven't discussed with Mr. O'Brien has nothing to do with what we're discussing here. This magazine is under my direction, not his."

"I suppose you've got him under your thumb now that that picture was printed in the paper," Wayne sneered.

What picture? Oh, God. The ones from the Plaza. Why did they have to turn up now?

She stared at Wayne, wishing he weren't the best art director in town, wishing she could fire him and get him out of her sight. But she couldn't resort to tactics like that. She needed their respect, and she was determined to have it.

"You're a fantastic art director, Wayne. I'd hate to see you fall into the trap of assuming the worst of people when you don't have your facts straight. We're running a magazine here, not a rumor mill." She looked at the rest of her staff. Individually they were tops in their field; collectively they couldn't be beat. "We all have work to do. It's not going to be easy getting back on the right path, but that's what I want you to do. If you have any more questions, remember, I'm the managing editor, not McKenna O'Brien, and I'd appreciate your coming to me with any questions or changes you think should be made."

She wasted no time at all leaving the conference room, Jon following closely on her heels.

"Great job, Kathy."

"They probably hate me."

She stopped suddenly. "Have you seen the picture Wayne mentioned?"

"No."

"Well, don't die of shock when you do. Mac and I spent some time together, and we got caught leaving the Plaza."

Jon grinned and she smacked his arm. "Don't jump to conclusions. We talked. That's it." Kathleen resumed her rapid pace toward her office and Jon tried his hardest to catch up with his very stubborn and very long-legged boss.

"I didn't say a word."

"No, but you thought it."

"I know you, Kathy."

Again she halted and Jon nearly smacked into her back. "What's that supposed to mean?" She turned to face him, her expression somewhere between outrage and embarrassment. "That I'm too stiff and liberated to hop into bed with a man? Is that what you think? If it is, you're not the first one to guess incorrectly."

Jon laughed. "You're losing it." He wrapped an arm around his friend's shoulders. "Let's go to your office and close the door."

The late-afternoon sun poured through her window, and Kathleen shut the blinds and collapsed into her chair.

Jon sat across from her, crossed his legs and leaned back to the point where the chair nearly toppled over. "Want to tell me about it?"

"No," she stated. She didn't want to talk about it. She didn't want to think about it. Why did everyone assume that just because she loved her job and loved to work that she was a feminist? Sure she believed in equal pay for equal work. Sure she felt more women should be at the top in major corporations, but that would come in time. More and more women were rising to the top. Soon things would be on a more even keel. But why did some men think a woman couldn't hold a responsible job and be a wife, a mother, or a lover at the same time?

"You've got that faraway look on your face again," Jon said. "If I didn't know better, I'd swear that crush you used to have on Mac never disappeared."

"No, but it should have."

Jon leaned forward, the chair once again touching on all fours, and rested his forearms on Kathleen's desk. "Why?"

"He's insufferable, unforgiving, unbending."

"Sounds like love to me."

"Hate is more like it."

Jon tried his hardest not to laugh. "You hate the man who sent you a fortune in roses? My God, Kathy. What did he do?"

"You want the truth, I'll tell you the truth." Kathleen pushed out of her chair and tried to escape the overpowering fragrance of the roses which only reminded her of Mac, but there was nowhere in her small, cluttered office to run. So she stood by her bookcase, pulled one long-stemmed yellow rose from its vase and absently plucked its petals.

"Where should I begin?" she asked, talking to herself more than to Jon. "Okay. Let's dispense with the problems he has with my attire and my hairstyle and get straight to the biggest problem of all. He wants me to quit my job so I can be at his beck and call whenever he wants me."

Kathleen turned around, looked at Jon's smug smile, and came to the conclusion her friend and confidant wasn't much different from Mac. But she needed someone to dump her frustrations on, and Jon was in the right place at the right time.

"The man likes to pretend that he's not a chauvinist. He puts on a big show by putting women in top positions in this company, but when it comes down to *his* woman, he wants some subservient, ditsy female who'll peel his grapes and fetch his slippers. Well, I'm not that woman." She tried to keep her tear-streaked face hidden from Jon, but the room was too small, and she knew he could see. She tried to wipe them away with the back of her hand, but the darn things continued to flow from her eyes.

Jon went to her side, gripped her arms and pulled her close. "No one ever said love is easy."

"I'll get over it." She pushed away from Jon and went back to her desk and pulled out the notes she had made the night before when she couldn't sleep.

"I've got some ideas for our advertising problems." She kept her eyes down and flipped through the loose pile of tearstained papers while Jon once again took his seat across from her. With a Kleenex pulled from a nearly empty box, she wiped her eyes, took a deep breath, and regained her composure. She sat straighter in her chair, leaned over the desk, and highlighted her ideas.

"I want a mass mailing to go out within two weeks. I want the picture of that woman in the limo in every mailbox in every major city."

"That's easy enough. But, Kathy, Mac was right about the woman. She did look good. I think you should leave it alone."

She shook her head. "Absolutely not. The skirt's too short, the hair's too wild. Stick some glasses on her, lengthen the skirt an inch or two, straighten the hair. Work with Wayne on it and show me what you come up with. She's too flamboyant."

"I take it you don't want orthopedic shoes?"

"No, but not three inch spikes, either." She grinned. "Then I want you to get a mailing list of all female executives—federal government, state government, big corporations and small corporations. I want the names of doctors, lawyers—"

"You're forgetting the woman at home."

"No. Get a list from the Literary Guild. I want women who like to read. The ones who buy books buy magazines, too."

"And what am I going to do with this list?"

"Send a premier issue to each of them—free. I want it in their mailboxes the day before it hits the street."

"This is going to cost a bundle."

"If McKenna O'Brien wants to make money, he's going to spend money. Lots of it."

"Okay, what's next?"

"I want *Success* to have a position right next to *People* on supermarket counters."

"That's impossible."

"Improbable, yes. Impossible, no. Get hold of the distributors and find out how we can do it."

"You might have to sell your soul for that one."

"I'll sell just about anything to make this work."

*   *   *

Ashley stared at the photo in *The Tattler* which had mysteriously showed up on her doorstep, the picture circled with a broad red felt-tip marker. *McKenna O'Brien and unknown beauty. Reliable sources say they checked into the penthouse suite of the Plaza after meeting for the first time in the lounge. They were not seen again until 5:30 A.M. O'Brien, the publishing tycoon, recently ended his long-term relationship with socialite Ashley Tate.*

Ashley threw down the paper and fumed. How dare Mac let himself get caught by those cutthroat photographers, and how dare they mention that he and I called it quits. How did they even know?

She didn't know which angered her the most—the reference to her and Mac, or the fact that he was with *that* woman. How could he possibly settle for someone like her after spending ten years with me? she wondered. In Ashley's opinion, he couldn't compare the two. She would win, hands down.

It took only a matter of minutes for Ashley to reach Mac's apartment. She hated standing at his door, knocking like a common person instead of someone who had every right to come and go at will. How could he possibly have asked someone else to retrieve the key to his apartment? His secretary, of all people. Didn't he have the guts to ask for it himself? Remembering that enflamed her wrath. She pushed the buzzer over and over again, then pounded her fist on the door. When she heard the click of the lock, she turned the knob and pushed, not caring at all that she might injure the person standing on the other side. She wouldn't give that funny old woman another chance to keep her out. It didn't surprise her to see the housekeeper barring her way, standing firm, fists on hips, just inside the door.

"I have to see Mac."

"My, my, my. Aren't we in a rush."

"Out of my way. I know where to find him."

"He's in the kitchen eating lunch." Merry's warmth disappeared with the appearance of Ashley. Her words came out cool, short, and very unfriendly.

"Don't give me that. He doesn't eat at this time of the day. I'll find him in the exercise room."

"Suit yourself," Merry said, moving to let Ashley by. "You'll only waste time by looking there."

Ashley stormed down the hallway and threw open the door to the well-equipped room. Not a trace of Mac. She turned around, only to be confronted by the strange-looking woman.

"Where is he?" Ashley hissed.

"I believe I already told you."

Ashley pushed the older woman aside in her rush to the kitchen. *What the hell is he doing in the kitchen? He doesn't know how to cook. Besides, kitchens are for servants.*

Her eyes widened when she found him, munching away on a plateful of cookies, a tall glass of milk in one hand to wash down the sugary Christmas-cookie icing.

"Want a cookie?" he asked, holding up the plate with a grin.

"Since when do you eat cookies?" Ashley stood with her arms crossed, staring directly into the eyes of the big man seated at the table.

"Since the day I broke up with you. And, you know what? I've never been happier." He silently toasted her with his glass, tipped it upright, and drank half the glass of milk in one continuous gulp.

"You're disgusting," Ashley screeched, grabbing up the plate of cookies. She looked around the room, obviously trying to decide what to do with the plate now that she held it in her hand. She didn't know the first thing about cooking or cleaning, but she did know a thing or two about modern kitchen conveniences. She spied the trash compactor, pulled it open, tossed in the cookies, plate and all, shoved it closed with her foot and turned the knob. She listened to the whirring crunch, then sneered at Mac. "That's what I think of you and your cookies. Now," she yelled, throwing the paper on the table in front of him. "What is the meaning of this?"

He didn't look annoyed. In fact, he ignored her rampage, got up from the table, and walked out of the room, paper in hand. Ashley ran after him, furious that he could so coldly turn his back and walk away.

She stared at his retreating back, taking in his appearance. His casual attire usually consisted of slacks, shirt, tie, and sweater—but not today. Ashley cringed at the faded blue jeans and, worse yet, a red-and-blue plaid cowboy shirt with pearlized snaps.

She ran in front of him, putting her hands on his chest to stop him from moving any farther. "What's going on, Mac? Why did you end our relationship? Why are you having an affair with Kathleen?" She tugged on his shirt. "Why are you dressed like this?"

"Stop yelling," he demanded in a low, soothing voice. He took her hands in his and led her to the couch where he forced her to sit.

"Are you ready to talk calmly?"

She took several deep breaths. "Possibly."

"First off," Mac said, "our relationship ended a long time ago. You know that, don't you?"

She pouted. "I thought we had a good relationship."

"Good? Mediocre is more like it." He sat in the chair across from her, folded his hands and leaned forward, his elbows resting on his knees. "Look, Ash. I don't want to do or say anything to hurt you, but it's over."

"Not to me." She forced a lone tear from her eye.

"It takes two to have a relationship, and neither one of us was interested in making ours work. We just kept going on. We didn't move forward, in fact, we seemed to regress."

"But how could you go from me to someone like . . . her?"

"That's not open for discussion."

"Why? If you just want someone to sleep with, you can get it a lot cheaper on the streets. You'd better wake up and realize she's out for your money."

Mac laughed and shook his head. Ashley stared. She didn't find it funny.

"No, Ash. I don't just want someone to sleep with. If that's what I wanted, you and I would have been history years ago. And no, she's not after my money. As for my relationship with Kathleen, well, my dear, that's strictly between her and me."

She wiped another tear from her eye. "Don't yell at me, Mac. I love you. I've always loved you."

"Stop acting, Ash, and please, stop the tears. After ten years they don't work any longer."

Her face burned red, and she took a swing at Mac. He caught her wrist and held it.

"Why don't you go home?"

"I don't want to go home. I need to stay here and talk some sense into you."

"No. You need to go home and make some sense out of your own life. I'm doing fine on my own."

"Are you going to keep on seeing her? Be careful, darling. Pictures with someone like her can be damaging to your image."

"I've never worried about my image. You have, but not me. And I told you already, I don't want to discuss my personal life."

Ashley eyed him suspiciously. "You're not in love with her, are you?"

He hesitated a moment too long. "No."

"You're lying. I can read you like a book."

"Then you know I'm serious when I tell you it's over between us. Let's get on with our lives."

"I'll try, but I'm concerned about you. I can't understand this sudden change in lifestyle. Cookies? Milk? And, my God, Mac. Cowboy clothes? How could you?"

"You'd never understand."

She didn't understand, and even if he had explained, she wouldn't have listened. She had made up her mind the moment she saw the picture in the paper what she was going to do. Ashley Tate planned to get even.

CHAPTER

NINE

Kathleen tried to ignore the pictures that appeared in *The Tattler* but found it hard to shove them completely out of her brain. They depicted her climbing into the taxi, great expanses of bare leg and thigh showing below Mac's coat, which just barely covered her backside. Mac stood beside her, sneering at the photographers, a hand placed squarely on her bottom. The headlines told all, at least from the columnist's point of view: *The Prince of Publishing and his latest flame—what was hiding under the big man's coat, and why was he looking so guilty?*

She tried to concentrate, to focus her attention on the pressing matters of the day. Unfortunately, she could only think of Mac's hand on her bottom, the touch of his lips, the warmth of his mouth, the smoothness of his teeth, the hardness of his body pressed against hers. God, how she wanted him. Years of dreaming had been nothing compared to five minutes of tasting, feeling, touching.

She wanted him still, in spite of that stupid argument. She knew he'd come back. She also knew she wouldn't give in. She couldn't give in. She might be able to bend a little. But why should she? He didn't want to bend at all.

She had tried not to think about him, but nothing seemed to work. If he had at least come into the office, maybe they could have talked, tried to iron out their differences, reach a compromise. But it had been three days since their argument, and three days since he'd been to work. Grace kept her posted, but even she heard little, except the early-morning call saying he wouldn't be in.

Unable to focus her attention on the pile of articles await-ing her approval, she grabbed her purse and walked out of her office. Since she couldn't concentrate, maybe a walk in the park would clear her mind.

The elevator doors opened at the lobby, and Kathleen stepped out, almost running head-on into Ashley.

"Why, hello, Kathleen. You're just the person I wanted to see."

Such a sickeningly sweet voice, Kathleen thought, and not an ounce of sincerity.

"I've had the most exhausting morning, and I'm just dying to have lunch. I remembered you telling me how busy you always are, and I thought maybe I could drag you away from all this for a while."

"Thanks for the thought. But I really can't get away today." What she wanted to say was she'd rather have lunch with a rattlesnake.

"Nonsense. Of course you have time for lunch."

"No, really. I have to get back to work."

"Please?"

What was Ashley's hidden agenda? Was something devi-ous lurking behind her false words and actions? What if she was sincere? The woman couldn't possibly have any friends. "Maybe we could get a Coke and hot dog in the park."

"Hot dog? No, that wouldn't do at all. I was thinking a nice crisp salad at my club."

Kathleen surveyed Ashley's cool appearance—the yellow sundress, white heels, and matching purse. Then she remem-bered how she had looked when she last peeked into a mirror. The day's humidity had played havoc with her hair, and much more than curly wisps had fallen out of her bun. In fact, she looked as if she'd been caught in a tornado. She had absently worn a wool suit instead of a linen one, and she had popped a button on her blouse just an hour before. Standing next to Ashley she felt drab, and hot. Looking at Ashley, she decided the blonde had never shed a drop of sweat.

"I'm not exactly dressed for your club."

Ashley looked Kathleen up and down, then waved off the statement. "Don't worry. No one will even know you're there. We'll just sit and chat."

She grabbed Kathleen's arm, pulled her through the lunchtime crowd, maneuvering toward the curb outside. She nudged an older man out of the way and pushed Kathleen into the backseat of a waiting taxi, following close behind.

"Club Anton," she snapped at the driver, then settled comfortably into the seat next to Kathleen.

"Have you got a date yet?"

"A date?" Kathleen wondered what Ashley was talking about, but more than that, she wondered how she had managed to get dragged into the taxi. What happened to her nice, pleasant walk in the park to clear her mind? Having lunch with Ashley would surely be a disaster, and not the least mind-clearing.

The ride in the taxi proved uneventful, discounting the dirty looks the driver tossed in Ashley's direction. She complained about his driving, the smell in the backseat, the outrageous prices, and told him she refused to give lazy good-for-nothing taxi drivers a tip. Kathleen prayed they would make it to Club Anton in one piece, knowing if Ashley had been alone, the driver might dump her in the worst part of town and speed away without bothering to look back.

Arriving at Club Anton, Kathleen smiled weakly at the driver, then placed a five-dollar tip into his hand as Ashley walked away.

She didn't expect the club's warmth and charm, the soothing floral wallpaper, or the soft blue-and-rose damask curtains and upholstery. When she envisioned Ashley's club, she had thought of gilt-framed landscapes and ostentatious furnishings.

Ashley brushed kisses across the cheeks of nearly every woman in the room as they walked to their table. Gossip flowed from her mouth, little tidbits shared with this one and that one as they passed by, and Kathleen wanted to fade into oblivion when she took a seat at their table. She didn't like gossip, and she despised showy displays of false affection.

"You seem to know everyone here," Kathleen said, as she attempted to control an errant strand of hair that refused to stay behind her ear.

"Of course I do. I've been coming here for years and years. These are my dearest and closest friends." Ashley blew a kiss to someone across the room, looking totally in her element and absolutely content. Kathleen wished she felt the same.

The waiter arrived and Ashley ordered wine, not giving a thought to what Kathleen might prefer.

"Now," Ashley began, "tell me all about yourself."

"There's not much—"

"Oh, look," Ashley interrupted. "There's Constance O'Brien, Mac's mother. But, of course, I'm sure you already know her."

"No. We've never met," Kathleen admitted. She dreaded the thought of meeting Mac's mom.

"Well, you've just got to meet her. She's a wonderful woman." Ashley waved to the older lady, beckoning her to the table.

Tall, regal, and still a stunning beauty at seventy-six, Constance O'Brien could have been royalty the way she commanded attention as she walked toward their table. A true aristocrat, all eyes in the room followed the woman whose short, stylish hair was as white as the pearls in her ears, and who looked like she'd just stepped out of *Town and Country* in her impeccable Wedgwood blue silk suit with a white silk scarf draped over her right shoulder. Ashley stood to greet her. Kathleen stood in awe.

"Hello, Ashley. How nice to see you here today," Constance O'Brien said, her voice and expression reminiscent of Mac's. Cool, composed; sophisticated and elegant. Mac's mother, like Mac himself, reeked of money and breeding. Kathleen studied Mrs. O'Brien's face and saw, hidden behind the aloof exterior, tenderness and compassion sparkling in her smoky blue eyes. Mac's eyes.

"I knew you'd be here today, Constance. That's why I came." Ashley's voice dripped with sweetness as she tossed an arrogant smile at Kathleen. "I knew you'd want to meet Kathleen Flannigan. Of course, you'd know her better as the woman in all those pictures with Mac."

Kathleen wanted to die. Instead, she threw back her shoulders and stuck her chin higher in the air. It felt wonderful. Mrs. O'Brien equaled her in height, and the two women looked straight into each other's eyes. Kathleen liked what she saw.

Mrs. O'Brien clasped Kathleen's hand in a firm, friendly grasp. "What a pleasure to meet you."

Kathleen had expected a snide comment, a cold handshake. "Thank you." She attempted to pull her hand away but found it trapped in Mrs. O'Brien's grip.

"I wasn't expecting to meet anyone today. I apologize—"

"Oh, no, dear. The first rule in society is never apologize, especially when you've done nothing wrong."

"Excuse me," Ashley butted in, positioning herself between Kathleen and Mrs. O'Brien.

"Oh, Ashley, dear. I'd almost forgotten you were here." Mrs. O'Brien gave Ashley a practiced smile.

"Those pictures of Mac were absolutely horrible, weren't they, Constance?"

"Horrible? Well, now that you mention it, Mac did have that tight-lipped frown on his face. I absolutely despise that look of his. He has such a wonderful smile. Don't you agree, Kathleen?" Mrs. O'Brien's frozen expression warmed as she turned to Kathleen.

"Yes. It is." Kathleen saw more than Mac's smile. She saw his lips lowering to hers, and she tasted them again in her memory.

Mrs. O'Brien tossed a wink at Kathleen. "Such a silly photo. And those captions. Annabella Adams is definitely slipping in her old age. She used to write the most wonderful gossip column. Made my day reading those stories about my husband and the quote-unquote women he was secretly seeing. It still amazes me how people believe that trash."

"Well, *I* thought they were awful," Ashley interrupted. "How embarrassing for Mac."

Constance frowned. "You've always given too much credit to the gossip columns. Anyone who's anyone wouldn't give them any credence."

"But this is different. These were so trashy. She wasn't fully clothed, and Mac hardly knows her. Don't forget, those pictures insinuated they were together in that hotel room."

Kathleen gasped in horror. How could Ashley be so cruel?

"You were together, weren't you?" Ashley asked, glaring at Kathleen.

"Well, yes, but—"

"Kathleen, my dear," Mrs. O'Brien interrupted, patting Kathleen's hand. "Remember what I said about apologizing."

Mrs. O'Brien turned to Ashley. "Thank you for bringing Kathleen to meet me." Then to Kathleen. "You *are* coming to our anniversary ball?"

"She *is* an employee, Constance. She has to make an appearance."

Mrs. O'Brien took Kathleen's hands in hers and squeezed them tightly. "Why don't you plan on staying the weekend?"

Ashley's eyes widened, but the other two women didn't see her shock.

"Oh, no. I couldn't," Kathleen said.

"None of that. Of course you can stay. I insist."

"Well, I guess—"

"Good. That's settled."

"I suppose I could change my plans and stay, too, Constance."

"No, Ashley. I couldn't ask you to do that. Besides, we've spent enough time together over the years."

"I could never spend too much time with you."

"Oh, but you could, my dear." Mrs. O'Brien's frozen smile returned as she looked into Ashley's bewildered eyes.

Kathleen couldn't tell if Ashley understood the meaning of Mrs. O'Brien's words, but Ashley continued to smile as if she hadn't been rebuffed. And then the tension eased when a high-pitched voice beckoned to Mrs. O'Brien.

"Oh, Constance." A petite, blue-haired woman in a ruffled fuchsia dress waved from across the room.

"It was lovely meeting you, my dear, but I really must go. My friends Eloise, Linda, and Nan don't like to be ignored." Mrs. O'Brien waved back at her companions. "Be right there."

Kathleen liked Mrs. O'Brien. All her life she'd thought rich society types would be stuffy snobs. But not Constance O'Brien. Just the opposite had to be said about her.

"I look forward to seeing you this weekend, my dear. Goodbye, Ashley."

Mrs. O'Brien disappeared, and the waiter instantly helped Ashley with her chair and poured the wine for her approval.

Without a thought, she swirled the wine in the crystal stem-ware, then tasted the sample. "This is awful. Where did you get it? California?"

"I'm sorry, Miss Tate."

"Just get me something else."

"Could I bring you something?" he asked Kathleen.

"No. But thank you very much."

Ashley jealously watched the exchange between Kathleen and the smiling waiter. She sipped on her water until the waiter left, then launched into Kathleen.

"I brought you here as *my* guest. How dare you monopolize the conversation. If I'd known you were going to throw yourself at Constance, I never would have introduced you."

Kathleen didn't utter a word. Never, never apologize. Instead, she grinned and watched Ashley's composure melt.

"You'll just have to think of a reason not to spend the weekend. What would Mac think? He didn't invite you. He wouldn't. Not to his mother's house."

The waiter returned with a fresh bottle of chardonnay, popped the cork, and started to pour. "Just fill it up and get out of here."

"The help is horrible around here lately." Ashley took a sip of wine, then another, and glared again into Kathleen's eyes. "It's absolutely ridiculous for you to spend the weekend. I mean, what would you wear? Surely not the stuff you wear to the office."

Kathleen couldn't help herself. She had to say something. "I don't think she invited me so she could check out my wardrobe."

"Then why? I just don't understand."

Kathleen couldn't answer. Instead, she stared at the woman heading straight for their table. Short, round, she appeared to be in a world of her own, staring at the luscious dessert on the plate she carried. She hummed something that sounded to Kathleen like a Christmas carol, but she couldn't place the song.

Kathleen didn't know when the woman's movements switched to slow motion, but she clearly saw her stumble. The plate sailed out of the old lady's hands and propelled through the air just as Ashley looked up from her glass of wine. It seemed to hover above Ashley's head, looking for the perfect position. And then it happened. The dessert slipped off the dish, an oozing concoction of brownie, vanilla ice cream, hot fudge, whipped cream, nuts, and a cherry. It settled on top of Ashley's blonde hair, each portion choosing its own course for sliding down her head. The gooey fudge streaked one cheek, the whipped cream another. The brownie slipped into her lap, and the plump, red cherry settled perfectly at the tip of her nose.

Kathleen laughed. She couldn't help herself. The women at surrounding tables laughed. But not Ashley. Her face turned crimson, ready to explode. She pushed away from the table, upsetting a water goblet and her glass of wine. The two liquids flowed together over the edge of the table, and Ashley stood in a dripping skirt, the brownie choosing to slither down the yellow silk, leaving behind a zigzag pattern of chocolate brown.

Ashley incoherently shrieked obscenities as she attempted to brush the brownie off her skirt, but ended up with more of a mess and a sticky brown blob in her hands. She straightened, her back stiff, glared at Kathleen with all the hate she could muster, and thundered from the dining room.

Kathleen caught Mrs. O'Brien's eye. Mac's mother winked while her companions laughed quietly amongst themselves. Kathleen searched the room for the woman who had lost her balance, and her dessert. She hoped she hadn't hurt herself when she tripped, and she secretly wanted to thank the lady for brightening her day. But the woman had vanished.

CHAPTER
TEN

"Good morning, Mother." Mac planted a firm, loving kiss on the ageless woman's brow.

He sat down in the chair the butler had pulled out for him and stared at the sliced melon and steaming black coffee. "Excuse me, George. Could you possibly find me something more substantial for breakfast? Hash browns, sausage. You know, a big country breakfast?"

George eyed him skeptically. "Would you prefer biscuits and gravy, sir?"

"I think you've got the right idea."

Mac picked up the newspaper lying next to his plate and quickly scanned the front page.

"I hope you didn't forget you're breakfasting with me this morning," he heard his mother say. "You can read the paper when you're alone, but this morning you're here at my invitation."

Mac eyed his mother over the top of the paper. She looked pretty good for seventy-six, and right now she looked as if she had a million things to discuss with the son she saw only once or twice a month.

He folded the paper and laid it back on the table. "Your roses look beautiful this morning," he said, surveying the expansive lawn bordered by roses of every hue. Their fragrance caught in the light breeze, and drifted toward the patio. He always loved spring and summer at McKenna House. At times he wished he lived here again, instead of in the city. He enjoyed looking at the garden, his mother's pride and joy. He remembered the feel of the dew on the freshly mown grass that he ran through, barefooted, as a child. And he loved and missed conversations with his mother, and his father, when meals were served outside in the clean, fresh air.

"You're off in never-never land, Mac."

"Sorry. Just reminiscing."

"Well, I didn't ask you here to talk about roses, or to talk about old times. I want to talk about Kathleen Flannigan."

Mac scowled. "How on earth do you know about Kathleen?"

"Besides the fact that your picture was plastered across the front of *The Tattler*, your old friend Ashley introduced her to me."

The frown lines deepened in his forehead. "When?"

"Yesterday. They were having lunch together at the club."

"That's not possible. Ashley despises Kathleen."

"Possible or not, they were together." Mrs. O'Brien took a sip of orange juice and studied her son's face. "Kathleen's charming, not a bit like the other women you've known."

"No. She's much different." Much, much different, he thought. "So what do you want to know about her?"

"Everything. She's spending the weekend with me, and I want to make sure we have plenty to talk about."

Mac choked on his coffee. "Did I hear you correctly?"

"Yes."

"What weekend?"

"This weekend, of course. After the ball."

"No, Mother. Kathleen is *not* spending *this* weekend here. I'm staying here and you know it."

Constance folded her hands in her lap and smiled sweetly at her son. "Yes, darling. Kathleen *will* be here for the entire weekend because I invited her. She's *my* guest, not yours. Now, will you please tell me what I should know about her, and why it is that you don't want her here?"

Mac stared at the plate of over-easy eggs and biscuits and gravy that had just been placed in front of him. His stomach churned. His appetite disappeared.

"I don't want her here because, well . . ." He couldn't think of a reason.

"Go on, Mac. I'm waiting."

What could he possibly say to his mother to make her change her mind about having Kathleen stay at McKenna House? In nearly fifty years, he couldn't remember his mother backing down on a decision. As much as he begged and pleaded, she had never changed her mind.

Cutting into the thick, creamy gravy and biscuit, he started to take a bite then paused, aiming the fork and his determined eyes at his mother. "I have no intention of seeing her again on a personal basis, and I think you should leave well enough alone."

"But I like her, son. You must, too. Why else would you spend the night together?"

"We didn't spend the night together," he fired back.

"Then why was that picture in the paper?"

He shrugged. "It's a long story."

"Did you or did you not spend the night together?"

"Am I on trial?"

"Yes, young man, you are."

Mac put down his fork and ignoring years of etiquette training, rested his chin in his hand, closed his eyes, and shook his head. His mother was the most relentless woman he'd ever known. Why did strong women seem to dominate his life?

"Yes, we spent the night together. No, I didn't sleep with her. And . . ." He looked up at his mother, hoping for sympathy and understanding. "She works for me."

"I see." Constance offered only an indulgent smile. "Broke your number-one rule about romance in the workplace, didn't you?"

"Don't make it worse. That night was an accident. I thought I was meeting someone else."

"And what happened to that someone else?"

"That doesn't matter."

"She's very pretty."

"Yes, she's very pretty."

"And you like her?"

"Yes." He envisioned her buttery lips, her bare feet, her generous smile.

"I'm not getting any younger, McKenna. I'd like a grandchild or two."

His brow furrowed once again. "She's not the marrying kind."

"And why not?"

Mac leaned back and thought of numerous reasons why Kathleen wasn't the marrying kind. Discounting those old rumors, there were dozens of other reasons. "Well, for starters, she's stubborn . . . opinionated. We don't get along away from the office and we sure as hell don't see eye-to-eye at work. Would you believe she told me she wants to eventually run McKenna Publishing?"

"She'd have to be a member of the family to do that," Constance stated.

"Oh, I'm sure she's perfectly aware of that. But what she seems to forget is that she can't have both."

Constance frowned. "I don't quite understand. What do you mean by both?"

"She can't be married and run the company, too."

Constance laughed. She pushed her chair away from the table. Apparently she'd had enough of her son's excuses. She

picked up a wicker basket and shears from a table at the edge
of the patio, and walked across the lawn to her rose garden.
Pulling on a pair of gloves, she delicately touched the bud at
the end of a long-stemmed yellow rose and inhaled its sweet
perfume, then started to clip her favorite flowers to fill the
many vases inside.

Mac watched his mother and knew that when he did get
married, he wanted a wife just like her, someone who loved
her family and home, someone perfectly content with only
those things as a career.

He strolled across the lawn, took the basket out of his
mother's hands and walked at her side.

"You should have married years ago, McKenna," she said,
her eyes still on her cutting.

"I never found the right woman."

"Maybe you have. Maybe you're just too picky."

"She has to be perfect."

"Then you'll look forever. Perfect doesn't exist."

"I thought your marriage was perfect."

Constance stopped and looked into her son's eyes. "Your
father was far from perfect, my dear."

"But you were happy."

"I loved him, with all his faults."

"The faults I can live with. I just don't want my wife to
work. I want her at home, and I want to come first. Always."

"Ah, the selfish little boy returns."

"Is it wrong wanting to be first?"

"You've always been first. Maybe Kathleen's never been
at the top. Maybe she needs to see what it's like and then
decide if that's where she wants to be. If she doesn't get that
chance, she'll always regret not knowing."

"It's more than just the career," Mac whispered.

Constance stopped, tucked her hand around Mac's arm,
and led him back to the patio. "Then what is it?"

"She has a child."

"She's divorced?" Constance questioned.

"No. She's never been married."

Constance laughed.

"What the hell are you laughing about?"

"You, my dear. You're such a conservative bore, and now you're making one excuse after another to stay away from the lady. What is it now? She's committed some kind of sin? You don't want a ready-made family?"

"I never should have mentioned it. You're just as liberal as she is."

"Not liberal, darling. Just wise. I think your feelings are stronger than you want to admit. Maybe you should make some concessions. I never saw your eyes light up when you talked about Ashley, but there's a spark there every time you mention Kathleen."

Why did his mother have to be so perceptive? Yes, his whole life lit up when he thought about Kathleen. But, damn. She just didn't fit into his mold. "I suppose I can't convince you she shouldn't spend the weekend?"

"No."

"Then you'll get a chance to see just how stubborn and pigheaded she is."

"But, sweetheart. You're stubborn and pigheaded, and I still love you."

CHAPTER
ELEVEN

"Mmm, look what I have for you, Mr. O'Brien," Merry said, pushing open the door to Mac's study with her generous round bottom. She turned to face him, holding a silver tray laden with plates of warm gingerbread topped with fresh whipped cream, and mugs of steaming cocoa.

"I said I didn't want to be disturbed."

"Yes, you did say that, didn't you?"

Mac looked up from the papers on his desk and scowled.

"Now, now, now. None of that, young man. I don't exactly call it disturbing when you've done nothing but stare at that same old paper for the last three hours."

"I'm thinking. And I'm not hungry."

"Nothing like a little warm gingerbread to get the brain churning." She set the tray down on the table and, pushing the papers aside, placed a plate and cup in front of Mac. He didn't fuss, just leaned back and stretched.

Merry settled into a chair beside the desk, took the remaining plate, and spooned a generous portion of gingerbread and whipped cream into her mouth. "My, my, my. This certainly beats paperwork."

"Did you have something you wanted to discuss?" Mac questioned, drawing designs in the whipped cream with his fork.

"Of course I do. Why else would I be in here?"

"To pester me, I suppose."

"Oh, I don't pester. I just tell it like it is."

"And what is it you want to tell me?"

"Every since you had that fight with Kathleen—"

"I didn't have a fight with Kathleen."

"Suit yourself, but the last time you saw her, you came home spittin' and sputterin' about liberated women. I know the signs. If you ask me—"

"I didn't ask you, Merry."

"Don't interrupt, McKenna. As I was saying, it's plain as the nose on your face that Kathleen Flannigan is driving you crazy."

"I won't dispute that."

"Then, I suggest you do something about it."

"Such as?"

"Well, in my day—that was a long time ago, of course—the men asked the ladies out."

"I asked her. She turned me down."

"Send her flowers."

"Did that, too. Listen, Merry. The lady just isn't interested."

"And you are?"

"Hell if I know why. But yes."

"Have you tried kissing her?"

"Now you're getting personal."

Merry's eyebrows lifted. "Of course I am. We have to examine this problem from every angle. Now, have you kissed her?"

"Yes."

"And?"

"And what?"

"My, my, my, Mr. O'Brien. You're not making this very easy. Did she enjoy it?"

"How the hell should I know?"

Merry's eyes narrowed. "You know my feelings about swearing, young man."

"Excuse me."

"Now, did she swoon?"

Mac laughed. "Of course she didn't swoon."

"Did she smile?"

His voice lowered. "Once. The first time."

"What about the second time?"

"I don't know."

"You don't know? You were there, weren't you?"

"I kissed her and left. I never looked at her face." Mac pushed away from the desk and went to the fireplace, warming his hands. He still couldn't get used to the unusually cold temperature in his apartment, and no matter how he adjusted the thermostat, it stayed a constant sixty degrees.

Merry patted her mouth with a lacy napkin, stood, and silently walked to Mac's side. "I'm not going to lecture you on kissing and leaving. Mind you, now, if my Nicky had done that to me, you'd better believe he wouldn't have me around to keep him warm on cold winter nights."

"So, you're telling me I should forget her?"

"Heavens, no. But you'd better get off your duff and quit waiting for her to make the first move."

"I can't go knocking on her door."

"And why not?"

"She'd slam it in my face."

"Then make her come to you."

"And how do you propose I do that?"

"My, my, my, Mr. O'Brien. You're not thinking." Merry went back to the desk and picked up the plates and cups.

"I suppose I could tell her I want to discuss work."

The rosiness deepened in Merry's cheeks, and her eyes twinkled with delight. "I suppose you could, at that."

* * *

Kathleen hesitated at Mac's office door, seething inside. How dare he call so late at night, expecting her to drop everything and run back to the office? Why couldn't he discuss the magazine during normal hours? How dare he call and not apologize for running out on her? That hurt, and it maddened her that he hadn't suffered in the same way.

She raised her hand to knock, and as her knuckles struck the mahogany door, it opened. Mac stood just inches away.

"I'm glad you decided to come."

"I said I would."

"Not very convincingly."

"It's late. What do you want?" Kathleen edged her way around him. He didn't move an inch. Her hand brushed against his. She smelled his cologne. She heard his breathing. Could he read her thoughts? Did he know she wanted him to kiss her again? Did he really want to discuss the magazine, or did he have something else in mind? If he only wanted to talk business, did that mean the possibility of a relationship no longer existed? Oh, God, she thought. I'm losing my mind.

"Have a seat," Mac said, interrupting her thoughts. He stood beside the buckskin leather sofa, his eyes never leaving hers as she gripped her briefcase handle and walked across the room.

She sat on the couch. Trying to avoid his stare, she allowed her eyes to peruse his body. He had on a long-sleeved white shirt, the cuffs unbuttoned and rolled up on his forearms. He wore fawn-colored suede boots and Levi's that hugged his hips and thighs. Men of twenty would kill for his body, she thought, letting her eyes roam slowly up his stomach and chest. She looked at his face, into his eyes. His lips didn't smile, but she saw a glimmer of amusement in his eyes. Was she blushing? She felt the heat rise up her neck, up to her cheeks. He knows he's making me nervous, she thought, and he's enjoying every second.

"Could I offer you something to drink? A Diet Coke?"

"Yes, thank you." She nearly strangled on her words. His calm voice unnerved her.

He came back to the sofa with a can and a glass of ice, set them on the table, and sat on the couch across from her.

Kathleen rarely found conversation difficult, but this new, unknown relationship with Mac made her uneasy. His crossed arms and all-knowing expression didn't help.

"I understand there's some dissension on your staff."

"Nothing I can't handle."

"I've been told they want to change the magazine's format."

"That's already under control. May I ask who told you this?"

"I don't divulge confidences."

"No, of course. I appreciate that." Kathleen poured the soda into the glass. Too much, too fast. The foam poured over the top, slid down the sides of the glass, and onto the table. Mac went to the bar and came back with extra napkins to wipe up the mess, took the glass from her hand, and cleaned the sides, then handed it back to her. She wrapped her fingers around the smooth surface. He didn't let go. Instead, he caressed her thumb with his, circled the inside of her palm. He touched her wrist. She stared at his hand, so close to hers, lightly sprinkled with blond hairs against tanned skin. She felt his warmth. Her stomach tightened.

She drew back. Why did his touch turn her to mush? Think business, she told herself. Don't let him see how vulnerable you are.

She leaned back, making herself comfortable on the couch. "I'd like to tell you what my staff had in mind."

"Please do." Mac stretched his arms out across the back of the couch and crossed his legs.

"The original premise was to put together a magazine for successful women and women who want to be successful."

"Your idea, as I recall."

Kathleen ignored his remark. "But my staff, knowing you don't approve, decided to make some last-minute changes."

"Such as?"

"How the little woman can save time during the week by cooking all weekend and freezing meals ahead of time. How she can clean a little bit each night so she has more time for cooking on the weekends. They even decided on a regular feature of hints from the happy little homemaker."

Mac grinned. "I take it you didn't approve."

"Approve? Hell! They wanted to change the entire concept."

"So you told them to do it your way, or else?"

"Yes, as a matter of fact, I did."

"Good."

Her eyes widened. "You approve?"

"It's your magazine. You have to do what you feel is right. I'm sure if their ideas had merit, you would have listened."

"But they didn't. They wanted to make changes because they were afraid of what you might say."

"You don't have those same fears?"

"I've never been afraid of you." That was a lie. She was afraid of him right now. Afraid he might kiss her again. Afraid he might not. She took a sip of Diet Coke and stared at him over the top of the glass. His expression said little. He appeared to be contemplating her words.

"This magazine isn't geared to just one aspect of the female population. It isn't necessarily for feminists or liberated women. But it definitely isn't geared directly to women who are perfectly content at being housewives. The articles in *Success* tell women it's okay not being the perfect wife or perfect mother, especially when you're also a busy working woman. It's okay not to feel guilty about buying TV dinners and expecting husbands and children to fend for themselves. *Success* says it's okay to be selfish, to take time for yourself."

"You sound as though you believe in these principles."

"I do."

"In other words, you don't think women should be wives and mothers?"

"That's not what I said. But women need to understand that they don't have to be perfect at everything. This magazine is geared toward making women feel good about themselves and their life. And once they accept that they don't have to be perfect, success, or greater success, will come naturally and easily."

"And you expect this theory to sell well?"

"I know it will. In fact, we hit the streets with the first issue on July twentieth. And we have a press conference set for next Monday to announce its release."

"What about advertising?"

Kathleen reached into her briefcase and pulled out several magazines. "Full-page ads in *Fortune*, *Women's Day*, *Family Circle*, *Ms.*, *Cosmopolitan*, *Working Woman*, *People*. Just to name a few."

"You're spending a lot of my money."

"I intend to make you even more money. We're doing a segment on *Oprah* about working women whose husbands just don't understand, and something similar on *Donahue*."

"You'll look great on TV."

Oh, how she loved it when his voice was only a whisper, so sexy and seductive she felt a tingle in the pit of her stomach. "Actually, Lynn Miller in PR's doing that. They'll love her."

"What about the press conference?"

"She's handling most of that, too. But I'll be there, along with several female executives who've seen the mock-up and love the concept."

"You're enjoying this, aren't you?"

"Every moment."

"You'll never give it up, will you?"

Kathleen thought a moment about his question. "I hope I'm never faced with a choice. Getting the TV slots wasn't easy. People haven't wanted to place advertising, either. I've begged and pleaded in the last couple of days."

Mac went to the refrigerator and came back with a bottle of beer. "May I change the subject?"

Kathleen laughed. "I knew you wouldn't stick to business."

"We could, if that's what you want."

"No." She quickly glanced at her watch. "It's late and maybe I could use a break."

"Okay, then. First off, can we call a truce?"

She smiled and the tension eased in her neck and shoulders. "I'd like that."

"Good." He sat down beside her. "You know, Kath, in the old days we always talked about work. I don't want to do that again. I want to know about you." He absently wound a strand of her hair around his finger. "Why did you leave Montana and come to New York?"

"The truth?"

He nodded.

"I wanted to work for you." She watched Mac's eyes widen.

"You didn't even know me."

"But I did. I read an article about you in *Fortune*." Her face became wistful. "That seems like ages ago. I was in college, majoring in journalism. I always thought I'd write for our local paper. Maybe freelance a bit. And then I read that article, and I was hooked." Kathleen squinted, deep in thought. "What was that quote? Let's see. You said you liked to give new talent a chance. You said, 'New—' "

" 'New ideas are what make publishing companies strong. You've got to be gutsy and creative to keep one step ahead of the competition.' " Mac completed the quote.

"You remembered."

"Some of the best words I ever uttered."

"Did you really feel that way?"

"I did then and I still do. Remember, I'm the one who hired you, a brash kid from the middle of nowhere."

"I knew I had talent, and my head was swimming with ideas."

"Like the *Urban Cowboy* magazine?" Mac laughed.

"It was a hot topic at the time." Kathleen frowned. "But it failed miserably."

"I didn't lose faith in you, though."

"I appreciate that."

"But . . ." Mac hesitated, taking a drink of beer.

"But what?"

"You were a thorn in my side. I don't think you've ever agreed with me on anything."

"I'm a born arguer."

"And I like to win."

"Me, too."

Mac ran his fingers through his hair, that look of contemplation returning to his face. "You've put together a good magazine, Kath. I may not agree with everything, but I looked at the latest mock-up and the advertising program you've put together, and, well, congratulations are in order."

She smiled with delight. "Once this one's launched, I've got other ideas you might be interested in."

"Personally, I'd like to put our professional relationship on hold and work on you and me."

Her heart skipped a beat. She didn't want to discuss the two of them. Their personal discussions always led to disaster. She found it much easier to avoid topics such as sex and desire. She put the magazines back into her briefcase and looked at her watch. "It's getting late."

"I'll take you home, but you can't evade me forever."

She didn't want to evade him. She wanted to push him down into the soft leather of the couch, comb her fingers through his hair, and kiss him until daybreak. Instead, she stood up and walked to the door, knowing Mac followed behind. He cupped his hand on her shoulder and pulled her back against his hard chest, his fingers slipping down to her elbows, caressing her bare arms. She exhaled deeply and relaxed against him.

"I'd like you to go to the anniversary ball with me."

She closed her eyes and smiled. "I was hoping you'd ask."

His hands moved up her arms, tenderly circling her neck, his fingers delving into the silky length of her hair. "I like your hair this way. Will you wear it down for me on Friday?"

She nodded, much too overwhelmed to speak.

His fingertips traced the line of her jaw. She drew in a deep breath at the tightening in her chest, at the weakness in her knees. Why did she have to crumble every time he touched her? She couldn't see his face, but felt his lips as he breathed her name into her ear.

"Kath?"

"Yes." Her voice was little more than a whisper.

"I meant it when I said I want you."

What words could she use to tell him the same thing? I need you? I'm yours? She turned her face to meet his and captured his lips. She found she didn't need words.

CHAPTER
TWELVE

"Merry!"

"You don't have to yell, young man. I'm standing right behind you."

"Where did you put my shoes?"

"They're all right there in the closet. My, my, my. Never seen a man with so many shoes."

Mac's crisply pressed white shirt hung out of the black dress slacks. The thin black tie hung loose around his neck. He held his socks in one hand and sorted through the neatly placed rows of shoes.

"But the shoes I always wear with my tux—they're not here."

"Oh, *those* shoes."

"Yes, Merry, *those* shoes."

"They were getting a bit worn on the bottom so I sent them out to be repaired."

"You what!"

"Repaired. But don't worry that head of yours, I got you a brand new pair for tonight."

"Where?"

"Don't be so impatient. They're in that box up there," she said, pointing to a shelf at the top of the closet.

Mac pulled down the box and pulled out shiny, black leather boots. "Cowboy boots?"

"You look disappointed. I thought you'd like them."

"No, no, no." Oh, God, he thought. Now I'm starting to talk like her.

He watched Merry putter around the room, picking up odds and ends of clothing he had tossed about. "Thanks, Merry," he said, sitting on the edge of the bed, pulling on his socks and the new pair of boots. He wiggled his toes. He stood before the mirror and admired the way they looked with the bottom half of his tux. "They're perfect."

"I've never yet picked the wrong thing. You should know by now that I have a habit of matching people with things that suit them perfectly."

Mac grinned, then slowly walked toward Merry, bent over, and kissed her tenderly on the cheek. "I have you to thank for so many things. I hope you'll never leave."

Merry looked up, her hands on her hips. "I'll stay as long as I'm needed, young man." She turned away, but not before Mac saw the tears beneath her funny little glasses.

Mac maneuvered through traffic, checking both sides of the street as he drove, looking for anything that might resemble a jewelry store. It was a last-minute thought. He didn't want to arrive at Kathleen's empty-handed. The flowers he sent earlier weren't enough. Tiffany's, and all the other stores he had frequented with Ashley, were closed early for the Independence Day celebration. But, surely, something must still be open.

He turned off Broadway to avoid the onslaught of cars, hoping he might find something on the side street. It was nothing but an alley, he realized, and regretted leaving Broadway. And then he saw it, Holly's, where the deserted alleyway came to a dead end. He parked the Mercedes at the curb and stared at the shop. Twinkling Christmas lights framed the windows, and holly draped around the door. This isn't real, he thought, but he didn't have time to question what he saw.

Inside, an elderly white-bearded gentleman stood behind the counter. He looked up and gave Mac a cheery smile. "Doing a little last-minute shopping?" he asked.

"Yes. How did you know?"

"I've seen that look hundreds of times. Forgot the wife's birthday. A gift to say I'm sorry. Yes, son, I've heard them all. In my line of work, people are always asking for something special."

"That's what I need. Something special."

"Of course you do. Let's see what we have in here."

He laid a purple velvet cloth on the counter and removed a tray of sparkling jewelry from the display case. "Ah, this is a rather special diamond necklace," he said, holding up the diamond choker for Mac's inspection.

"No," Mac said. Ashley might have liked something like that. Ashley loved diamonds, lots of them. But he had the feeling Kathleen would rather have something simple, understated, but beautiful nonetheless.

"No, no, no. I see that necklace won't do at all. I'll save it for someone who really deserves such a unique piece of craftsmanship." The white-haired gentleman placed it carefully back into the case. "How about a ring? Earrings?" He laid out piece after piece, all shiny and gold, sparkling with diamonds, emeralds, and sapphires.

"No. None of those are right." Mac pushed aside the velvet and peered into the case. His eyes lit when he saw the bracelet tucked away in the far corner of the cabinet. "May I see the bracelet?"

"Ah, the pearls. You've got good taste, son."

Mac held the triple strand of perfectly matched pearls up to the light. "They're beautiful. I've never seen any quite like them."

"They're rather unique. White as snow, they are. Come from oysters in the North Sea."

Mac's eyebrows knit together. North Sea? He had no idea there were oysters in the North Sea.

"Is there a problem, young man?"

"No," Mac shook his head. "Not at all. It's perfect. Could you wrap it?"

"Why, of course, young man. Be right back."

The man left the room just long enough for Mac to glance at his surroundings. Christmas tree in the corner, a wreath on the door. The smell of cinnamon and hot apple cider. Merry, he thought with a smile. And the old man, dressed in plaid shirt and suspenders. And the words he used. *No, no, no. Young man.* No. Couldn't be. He tossed the notion aside, roaming the room while he waited.

He picked up a teddy bear with a torn ear from a pile of what appeared to be discarded toys. He had had one just like it over forty years ago. A gift from Santa Claus. He laughed, and, for some strange reason, decided to purchase it, too. Lots of memories could be recalled sorting through the items in this store, he thought. An old paint-bare toboggan. He and his dad had sailed down the hills around McKenna House on one just like it. He ran his fingers over the wood, then he saw the silver aluminum Christmas tree in a far corner, with a multicolored light wheel on the floor below. Mac grinned, recalling his father's horrified face when his mother had purchased a tree just like it one Christmas in the sixties. Those were wonderful times, all those Christmases when his father was alive.

Mac felt a lump in his throat, remembering how he had walked into his father's study that last Christmas afternoon and found his dad in his big, rawhide leather chair, his head bent as if reading the book in his lap. But he wasn't reading. His glasses had slipped to the end of his nose, and one arm hung at the side of his chair. And he wasn't sleeping. The doctor said it was quick, that he must have fallen asleep and died peacefully.

He missed his father terribly, but he had so many wonderful memories, and the best centered on their Christmases together. How could he have forgotten? Mac wondered.

Again, he looked around the room, until he found a bookshelf, rather dark and dusty, filled with picture frames.

"Excuse me, son," the old man said, interrupting Mac's thoughts. "Your present's ready."

Mac walked to the counter, paid for the bracelet and teddy bear, then stared again at the bookcase.

"I don't sell many of those," the man said.

"Why?"

"There's not much of a market for dusty, tarnished old picture frames. Only very special people take those home."

"I think my father bought one here."

"Last one I sold was years ago. Nice man, he was. Looking for something special for his wife, if I recall. But then he found the frame. Said he wanted to give it to his son. I believe it was a Christmas present. Yes, that's right."

"My dad gave me a tarnished frame one Christmas. I still have it."

"And maybe one day you'll pass it on to your son?"

"If I ever have a son."

"My, my, my. Don't fret about that. Good things come to good people. Be patient, my boy."

Mac studied the man's face, the redness of his chubby cheeks, the whiteness of his beard. His eyes twinkled and he wore strange little glasses. No, Mac thought. No. It's not possible.

"Thanks for your help, sir." Mac tucked the box into his inside coat pocket, the teddy bear stuck under his arm.

"My pleasure, son," the old man said as he placed his hand

on Mac's shoulder. "Run along now. Don't keep your young lady waiting."

Mac looked at his watch as he ran out the door. He stood by his car and turned around to wave good-bye to the proprietor. The lights had gone out inside Holly's, and the decorations outside clouded over in his vision. He shook his head, blinked his eyes, then heard the mirthful laughter of the man inside.

He jumped into his gold sedan, turned the car around, and headed back toward the busy street. Looking in his rearview mirror he saw the alleyway he had just driven through. It was blocked with crates and Dumpsters. There wasn't a trace of a brightly lit shop called Holly's. But his face glowed, and his heart seemed to swell. He didn't believe in miracles, but his life seemed to be full of them lately. His normally routine existence had turned topsy-turvy when Merry entered his life. Was it a dream? Was it enchantment? He didn't know and he didn't care, as long as Kathleen was real.

He patted the gift box in his breast pocket to make sure it existed, then drove on.

Kathleen stared at the suitcase sitting beside the door. Inside the bag she had folded an array of expensive clothing purchased just for this weekend. She must be crazy, she thought, to spend so much just to impress Mac's mother. What had she told Ashley? "She didn't invite me to check out my wardrobe." Proper words to express in a moment of anger, but after careful consideration, Kathleen knew she wanted to look her best.

How many times in the last hour had she stood before the full-length mirror, looking at the image of a woman she had not known until just a few weeks ago? When had the businesswoman in navy blue been replaced by this elegant being? She felt like Cinderella going to the ball. Would everything disappear at the stroke of midnight? The high neckline of her ivory silk gown hid her cleavage, a precaution for the benefit of Mrs. O'Brien, yet the bodice fit like a glove. A little distraction for Mac's benefit. Long, tight sleeves, and a skirt that hugged her hips. From her thighs down, yards of fabric hung to the floor in gentle folds that swirled about her when she turned. She wore only a pair of pearl earrings to accent the dress, and let her hair fall in masses of auburn waves about her shoulders.

For the tenth time that day she smelled the roses Mac had sent. She took a deep breath and looked at the clock. Nearly six, and she had nothing left to do but wait, and think. Does Mac know I'm spending the weekend? Will he be staying there, too? Will he like my gown? Will he kiss me again? How long before we start arguing?

The ringing bell startled her back to reality. Oh, God, he's here.

She wanted to run into the bathroom to recheck her makeup and hair, but even more, she wanted to see Mac. She slid the safety chain off the door, unlocked the dead bolt, and tentatively put her hand on the knob. Running her tongue across her lips, she slowly opened the door.

Their eyes met. Hers sparkled. His admired the view.

He reached out, brushing his thumbs lightly across her cheeks. His fingers tilted her chin toward him, and he gently caressed her neck as he brought his lips down to meet hers. They touched, for only a moment, then he stood back and smiled. "You look beautiful."

"Thank you."

Taking his hand, she pulled him into the apartment, closing the door behind them.

She followed his eyes as they roamed over every curve of her body. She basked in the pleasure she saw in his face, knowing his desire must match her own. He looked spectacular, and it had nothing to do with his tux. She didn't remember his shoulders ever appearing so broad, his face so handsome. The hair at his temples seemed a little whiter; he stood a little taller. If she had to find one word to define him, she couldn't. No one word stood alone.

"Could I offer you a drink before we leave?"

"No. If we stay any longer, I might not want to leave."

"Oh," Kathleen said, looking down at his feet, not wanting to meet his eyes.

She grinned. "Cowboy boots?"

"You noticed."

"Nice touch."

"My housekeeper's idea, actually."

"She picks out your clothes?"

"No. But she seems to know what I want, long before I do."

"Sounds like a very interesting woman."

"That she is."

He took her hand, brought it to his mouth, and pressed his lips to her knuckles. Closing his eyes, he inhaled the fragrance of her perfume, capturing another memory. "I have something for you."

He pulled the box from the pocket of his coat, holding the red-and-white-wrapped package out to her. "I hope you like it."

"It looks like a Christmas present."

"I haven't wanted anything to do with Christmas for a long time. You've helped change my mind."

Her face lit with delight at his words, and at the fun of opening a gift. She carefully removed the bow, then the paper, and lifted the lid. Tears nearly sprang to her eyes. She found it difficult to breathe. "Oh, Mac."

"You do like it, don't you?"

"Oh, Mac."

"I take it that means yes."

She held the box and her wrist out to him, and with awkward fingers, he fastened the delicate bracelet, kissing her palm when he finished.

"I love it."

"May I have a thank-you kiss?"

She slid her fingers up his arms, over his shoulders, and pressed them lightly to his cheeks. She stood on tiptoes and kissed his lips, his nose, his eyes. Never had anyone felt so wonderful.

He managed to find her hands while he still had some control and gently pushed her away. "You'd better save some of your thanks for later. As much as I hate to say it, we have to go."

And then she remembered what she didn't want to tell him. "I . . . I'm spending the weekend with your mother."

"I know." He grinned. "I am, too."

Her eyes widened. She had thought that might be a possibility, but now that she was faced with it, she didn't know how to react. "You're not mad?"

"Mad? Hell, no. I can't think of anyone I'd rather spend the weekend with." A twinkle came to his eyes at the fright in her face. "Don't worry. If I know my mother, you'll be on one floor and I'll be on another."

"What about chaperones?"

"That's a possibility, too."

CHAPTER

THIRTEEN

They drove north through the Bronx and out of the city into Westchester County. The congestion of buildings and people transformed into the peaceful serenity of green parkland and stately old homes, glimpsed on occasion through the foliage of a thousand spreading trees.

"Sunnyside is just down the road," Mac said, pointing to his left.

Kathleen looked out his window for a better view. "Sunnyside?"

"Washington Irving's home."

Of course. Everyone knows Sunnyside. Hah! I've never heard of it, Kathleen thought.

Mac's love for the valley became obvious the moment they left Yonkers. He drove slowly, pointing out landmarks, and she listened, enthralled.

"That's Lyndhurst," he said, directing her attention to the gothic spires above the treetops.

She leaned against him to look out the window, her breast brushing against his arm. She wasn't about to ask who owned Lyndhurst.

"I'll take you riding through here someday. There's trails and streams and ponds scattered everywhere. I can't remember the last time I got on a horse."

Someday, Kathleen thought, overjoyed to hear him speak

as though they definitely had a future together.

She settled back into her seat, caught up in the beauty of the drive and the essence of the man who sat at her side.

Sunnyside. Lyndhurst. She had come a long way from the struggling ranch in Montana to be in the company of one of the richest men in the nation. Not that the money mattered. If it had, she would have quit her job at a moment's notice and let him take care of her for the rest of her life. What mattered the most was being at his side, the man she had idolized for so many years. The man from the cover of *Fortune* who had given a rancher's daughter inspiration, and the chance to fulfill a dream when he hired her fresh from college, brash, inexperienced, and starry-eyed.

From the corner of her eye she watched him, his eyes on the road, one hand on the wheel, the other leaning on the armrest. She sensed a quiver deep inside her, a quickening of her heartbeat, as his head turned. Those smoky blue eyes filled with more emotion than she had seen in years, caught hers in a flash of desire before he looked back at the road. His white dinner jacket, his fair hair against a golden tan, he had to be the most stunning man on the face of the planet. She closed her eyes and smelled his cologne, its intoxicating fragrance filling her senses.

"What are you wearing?" she asked.

"What?"

"Your cologne."

He laughed. "Old Spice. Inexpensive and not very original. You like it?"

"Mmm." She closed her eyes, leaned back against the headrest, and breathed deeply. "Smells wonderful."

Mac groaned, then suddenly pulled the car over to the side of the road, hit the brakes, and stopped under the shade of the trees.

"Why are you stopping?"

He rolled down the window and a warm, summery breeze blew inside. "Do you have any idea what you're doing to me?"

Bewildered, Kathleen shook her head. "No."

"That dress is a problem."

"You don't like it?"

"Oh, I like it. And I like what's in it. That's the problem. It leaves little to the imagination, and ever since you opened your door, I've been imagining what's under it."

"I hoped you'd like it." She put her cool hand against his warm cheek.

"Damn." He took her hand, sliding her fingers to his lips. "You're driving me mad."

"I don't mean to," she said in innocence.

"It doesn't matter what you do. You can yell at me, kiss me, ignore me. You just seem to have gotten into my head, and I think you're there to stay."

"Do you want me out of your head?"

"No. I forced you out of my thoughts once before. I won't do it again."

"I hope you don't. I couldn't take it again."

"Did it really matter to you before?"

"Matter? I think I cried every night for a week. And then I realized there'd never been anything real between us, that I had a crush on you and you already had Ashley. Then I told myself you couldn't want someone as young and unsophisticated as me. But I still don't know why you went away, or why you despised me so much when you came back."

He brushed his fingers across her cheek, gently circling her lips with his thumb. "If we talk about this now, we'll end up in a fight, and I don't want that. Not this weekend."

"We have to talk about it sometime. It's standing between us."

"Can't we just forget it?"

"For tonight, yes. But not forever."

She rested her hand on his leg, trying to read the expression on his face. But it was impossible. He squeezed her hand, turned the key in the ignition, and drove back onto the road.

Nearly five minutes passed in silence before he turned left down an elm-lined lane. Again he pulled to the side of the road, knowing he had to say something more.

"I'm not an easy man to live with. I'm stubborn and opinionated, and I've been that way for a very long time. I like to have things my way."

"I know all that."

"Hush," he said, placing a finger to her lips. "I want to take you away somewhere, just you and me. No work, no family, no phones. Just you and me, and I won't take no for an answer."

"Will you talk to me then?"

"I'll try."

"When?"

"Next weekend."

"But Julie's coming home on Sunday."

"Then we have all day Saturday."

He looked so sweet and innocent when he said the words, but Kathleen knew there was nothing the least bit sweet and innocent about the weekend he would plan. She didn't care. It's what she wanted. What she needed.

"Mac?"

"Yes."

"We're going to be late."

He looked at his watch. His mother would kill him if he showed up after the guests began to arrive.

"We're almost there. Just a little farther," he said, once again driving down the road.

And then she saw it, looming magnificently in the clearing

ahead. Three stories, all of stone. The Georgian mansion stood regally before them at the base of a circular drive. Stone planter boxes lined the walk leading to the stairs of the massive entry. They spilled over with red and white geraniums, and blue delphiniums. Bush roses of every possible hue rimmed the circular drive.

She didn't move when the car came to a stop. She sat breathless, taking a mental picture of Mac's home. "It's beautiful."

He wrapped a strand of her hair around his finger and leaned toward her, gently kissing her lips. "Yes, very beautiful."

A host of attendants filed out of the front door, stopping in two columns at the base of the steps. Their attire resembled the black-and-white livery worn one hundred years before by the servants in the homes of New York's elite. Two men came to the car, one on each side, opening the doors in unison, and helped Kathleen and Mac from the sedan. He walked to her side, took her arm, and led her up the steps.

"Don't be nervous," he said, squeezing her hand.

How did he know? Throughout the hour-long trip, not once had she mentioned her anxiety. She could handle crucial business meetings, speeches before crowds, but she felt lost in the face of grand society and elegance.

A doorman stood stiff and proud on each side of the entry. Mac led Kathleen into the spacious hall, watching the many expressions passing across her face as she looked from the crystal chandelier hanging at the center of the three-story-high room, to the mahogany circular staircases on either side.

She wanted to hide, but instead she moved closer to Mac and whispered in his ear.

"I don't belong here."

Gallant and handsome and so obviously a part of his

surroundings, he pulled her to him and kissed her nose. "I'm here, and you belong with me. Come on, let's find my mother."

They walked through the open double doors leading into the ballroom. Light from the fading sun shone through the floor-to-ceiling windows, its beams bouncing off the mirror-polished hardwood floors. She pulled him to a stop as they entered the room. She stood in awe, counting the number of windows. Ten—each one about fifteen feet high and three feet wide. If grandeur had described the entry hall, then opulence characterized this room. Richly carved mahogany paneling lined the walls. White lace drapes swagged at the windows. Round dining tables covered in white linen and lace, surrounded by white-brocade-cushioned Chippendale chairs, circled the room, leaving an area for dancing in the center. A chamber orchestra readied their instruments behind the black grand piano, set on a dais at the far end of the room. Tall, shimmering crystal vases filled with red and white long-stemmed roses sat atop each table. Kathleen had never seen such splendor.

Constance O'Brien gracefully entered the room dressed elegantly in black and white. A simple strand of pearls hung at her neck, with delicate pearls encircled by brilliant diamonds at her ears. "McKenna. Kathleen." Mac bent over and kissed his mother, who absently adjusted that lock of hair that continually fell across his brow. She stood back and inspected the woman on her son's arm. "Stunning, my dear. Absolutely stunning."

"Thank you. You have a beautiful home, Mrs. O'Brien."

Constance smiled. "Yes, I do. Tomorrow I'll give you the grand tour."

She linked arms with Kathleen and Mac. "We have a while before the other guests arrive. Why don't we go into the library and have a drink."

Kathleen couldn't disguise her excitement as Mrs. O'Brien led them to the entry hall and through one of the doors on the right. The library was all and more than Kathleen had imagined. Dark wood, walls lined in book-filled shelves, overstuffed couches and easy chairs in the center, with two additional chairs in front of the massive fireplace. Aubusson carpets pulled each furniture grouping together. Oh, how easily she could curl up on one of those couches, Kathleen thought, and let life pass by.

"What would you like?" Constance asked, standing before a sparkling array of crystal decanters and glasses.

"Nothing for me, thank you," Kathleen said.

Mac followed Kathleen's lead. "I'll hold off, too."

Constance O'Brien looked amazed. "Not even a beer?"

"I'm reforming."

"I hope this is your doing, Kathleen. I've always thought my son drank too much beer."

"He's switched to Big Macs and Diet Coke. I don't know if the change is for the better."

"Excuse me, ladies," Mac interrupted. "I believe we could find something more interesting to discuss than my eating habits."

"Ah, but darling. You're such an interesting topic of conversation." Mrs. O'Brien laughed, then poured herself a brandy, her smile turning to a pensive frown.

"We may have a problem tonight."

"What kind of problem?" Mac asked.

"Ashley."

Kathleen watched Mac's lighthearted demeanor disappear. She tried to stay calm, but her churning insides betrayed her misery, and something wicked reached inside and clenched her heart.

"Is she here?" Mac looked toward his mother, praying the answer was no.

"She's been here all day. She called early this morning and told George to send a car for her. The nerve of that woman—and now she's talking to the caterers."

"Talking?" Mac's eyebrows raised, and for some reason which Kathleen couldn't understand, his voice was tinged with amusement.

"Not exactly. I seem to recall her telling them the shrimp wasn't right."

"Poor man. What else has she found wrong?"

"Oh, just little things here and there. But, darling, we shouldn't make light of this. There's more involved than her thinking this is her party and that I'm not capable of managing alone."

"Then what's the real problem?"

"She was expecting you earlier, and she doesn't know you've brought Kathleen."

"You didn't tell her?" Kathleen stared at Mac, stunned by this latest obstacle in their relationship.

"I didn't see the need to." Not one shred of comfort appeared on Mac's face as he looked at Kathleen. "I told her before it's over between us."

"You may have told her, darling, but that doesn't mean she listened, or understood," Constance added.

"I just assumed she wouldn't show up. My mind was on other matters." He winked at Kathleen, but she couldn't see his gesture, her eyes had already lowered to stare at her hands.

"Maybe I should leave," she said, not wanting to get caught in a threesome.

"No!" Mac slipped his hand around her waist and pulled her close to his side. "I want you here. I'll deal with Ashley."

"I wish you'd done that earlier." Her face revealed little emotion as she looked into his eyes. "I don't know what went on between the two of you all those years, but I do know if I were Ashley, I wouldn't give you up easily." She pulled away from Mac and walked across the room.

Mac started to follow when the door opened and Ashley breezed in.

"Mac, darling. You're finally here." Ashley floated into the room in a Victorian gown of blue taffeta trimmed in white lace with a red, white, and blue bow decorating the bustle. She went straight to Mac, standing on tiptoes to kiss his lips.

"You look wonderful," she said, twirling around to give him a better view of her entire dress. "What do you think? My dressmaker laughed when I told her what I wanted, but it's perfect, isn't it?"

"Charming." Mac turned away, looking toward Kathleen, trying to catch her eye, wanting her to understand, hoping she wouldn't leave.

Ashley followed his gaze. She glared at Kathleen. "You're a little early. The invitation said eight o'clock."

"She came with me," Mac blurted out. He crossed the room and possessively pulled Kathleen back to his side.

"But, darling," Ashley mewed. "I go to every party with you."

"Kathleen, dear." Following Mac's lead, Constance joined her son and Kathleen. She slipped her hand around the younger woman's arm, and gave Kathleen a comforting squeeze. "Why don't we go into the ballroom and talk to the orchestra about tonight's music."

"I've already taken care of the music," Ashley stated.

"Thank you, Ashley. But I have a few personal selections I'd like them to play. Come along, Kathleen."

Mrs. O'Brien led Kathleen out of the room. Mac's eyes followed. He didn't want to be left alone with Ashley. He knew anything he said would lead to disaster. He felt all sense of warmth leave the room, and he was left standing in the cold, facing a woman he had long ago failed to understand. "Why are you here?"

"I thought you'd be with me tonight," Ashley said, wiping the corner of her eye with a lace handkerchief she took from her blue taffeta bag.

"Have you forgotten our last two conversations? We're history."

"But—"

"Listen, Ash. Ten years is a long time. I understand that, and I know it's hard to change."

"I have no intention of changing. You'll get over this thing you have for that woman, and I'll be waiting."

Mac's eyes blazed as he desperately tried to stay composed. "Don't wait."

Ashley smirked. "You'll get tired of her."

"Whether I tire of her or not doesn't matter. What matters is that I don't want you any longer."

As if Ashley had heard none of his words, her hands began a slow, calculated slide up to his shoulders. "Don't my feelings enter into it?"

Mac stepped away, out of Ashley's reach, and with saddened eyes thought again of all their wasted years.

"Your feelings have been at the forefront for the last ten years, Ash. I've wanted to keep this civil, but kind words are useless. You didn't want to share my life. You wanted me to be part of yours. No give-and-take whatsoever. That's over. I'm not giving in any longer. I'm doing what I want this time."

"Think about what you're saying."

Mac ran his fingers through his hair. "It's over. We're not going to pick up where we left off. We're not going to get back together. In fact, I think you should leave."

"But everyone expects the two of us to be together."

"The hell with everyone. Kathleen and I are together. Not

you and me. Not tonight. Not ever again."

Mac crossed the room, opened the door, and slammed it behind him. He stood on the other side, took several deep breaths, then thought about the words he had just said. *"You wanted me to be a part of your life. No give-and-take whatsoever."* As much as he hated to admit it, he had treated Kathleen the same way Ashley had treated him for the past ten years. And he knew it was wrong.

He went to the ballroom in search of Kathleen and his mother, hoping Ashley would leave, hoping Kathleen wouldn't.

And there they were. His mother so regal and elegant. And Kathleen—he found no words to describe her. Perfection in every sense of the word. Eyes that smiled at everyone. He had even seen the way she smiled at the doormen, and the way they smiled back.

He stopped behind his mother, put his hands on her shoulders, and kissed her cheek. "Hope you asked them to play some of my favorites."

"You mean that fifties stuff you insist on listening to?"

"Give me Elvis any day." Taking Kathleen's hand, he twirled her around, then pulled her to him and danced slow, close, to the music in his head.

"If I knew the song, I might be able to follow better," she whispered.

"Um, let's see." He hummed a few bars of the first song that came to his mind, then sang softly into her ear. " 'Some enchanted evening . . .' "

"Mm, *South Pacific.* One of my favorites."

"Perfect for waltzing." For nearly a minute they circled the floor while Mac hummed, their bodies close, their steps perfectly in tune.

"I'm sorry about Ashley," he whispered.

"Is everything okay?"

"I don't know, Kath. She doesn't want to give up. But please believe me. It's over between us."

Kathleen tenderly kissed his cheek. It was the only thing she could do at the moment to tell him she believed him, to tell him she understood. Words alone wouldn't work.

"Excuse me," Mrs. O'Brien interrupted. "I believe our guests are arriving."

Mac stopped in front of his mother, keeping Kathleen close at his side, her hand gripped tightly in his. "Guess I have to be a good host and say hello, at least to some of them. Will you join me?"

"I think I'd rather stand in the background somewhere."

"You could keep my mother company," Mrs. O'Brien suggested.

"Great idea. Come on, Kath. I'll introduce you." He led her to an alcove just off the entry to the ballroom. Cozy, bright, and cheerful, the small sitting room decorated in floral chintz had a warm, homey atmosphere.

"It's about time you came to see me, young man. I hate sitting in here all by myself." A strong but aged voice filled the room. "Is this your new girl?"

"Hello, Grandmother." Mac bent over the old woman in the wheelchair. He kissed her forehead and wrinkled cheek. "You look beautiful tonight."

"Nonsense. I look old. And quit ignoring me. Is this your new girlfriend?"

"Kathleen Flannigan, this is my grandmother, Maureen McKenna O'Brien."

Kathleen took the older woman's hand. "Pleased to meet you, Mrs. O'Brien."

"Always hated that name. Call me Maureen."

"I have to greet the guests, Grandmother. Will you look after Kathleen?"

"You trust me?"

"With my life."

"Then run along. The sooner we get this shindig started, the sooner it will end."

Mac pulled a chair up for Kathleen, squeezed her shoulder, gave her a look that said, *I don't want to go*, and reluctantly left.

Maureen stared at Kathleen through squinted, all-knowing eyes. "Are you in love with my grandson?"

Kathleen's eyes widened at the old woman's question. "Pardon me?"

"I'm not getting any younger. Ninety-eight last month, and I want great-grandchildren. We need some good breeding stock in this family."

Kathleen couldn't believe her ears. "I believe that is a private matter between Mac and me."

"Hell. I can't leave a decision like that up to McKenna. That grandson of mine spent half a lifetime with that wishy-washy blonde. Marriages should be arranged, and you'd better believe I'm going to have my say in who he spends the rest of his lifetime with."

"And what kind of woman are you looking for?"

"Haven't decided yet. What kind of woman are you?"

Kathleen smiled at the feisty matriarch of the family. "The kind your grandson doesn't think he wants."

"So *you're* the one who works for him."

"You know about me?"

"I keep informed. Used to be my company, you know. Foolish old farts the men were in those days. Said a woman couldn't run a company like McKenna Publishing. Well, I showed them." Maureen wiped her lips with her lace-edged handkerchief.

"That grandson of mine thinks women aren't much good for anything but sex and having babies."

Kathleen's mouth dropped, stunned by Maureen's words.

"Close your mouth, girl. You stand up to him, you hear? Kick him in the butt a time or two."

"He's really a sweet man, Maureen."

Maureen snorted. "He's spoiled rotten. But I've got you pegged. If anyone can straighten him out, it's you. Now, roll me out of this room, will you? I want to see my guests."

"I'd be happy to." Kathleen stood behind the wheelchair, then felt the old lady's cool, thin hand on hers.

"I'm glad you're in love with my McKenna. I like you. But you've got to keep the upper hand. Take my advice. Don't give in to him. Make him respect you." She patted Kathleen's hand. "It's stuffy in here. Let's get on with this shindig while I'm still breathing."

Hah! Kathleen thought. The feisty old lady would probably outlive her by years.

Kathleen pushed the wheelchair out of the alcove as Mac and Mrs. O'Brien walked into the ballroom surrounded by friends, many of them faces Kathleen recognized. Senators. Congressmen. A prince and a princess. Even Annabella Adams, whose hand rested on Mac's arm as they leisurely crossed the room. She had a light, fluttery laugh that continued until they stood in front of Maureen and Kathleen.

"Hello, Maureen," Annabella Adams said in the same light, fluttery tone of voice.

"Ah, the gossip woman. Constance!" She turned to her daughter.

"Yes, Mother?"

"Get me a whiskey, and roll me over to the band. I need something to drown out the noise in this room."

Constance rolled her eyes and pushed the wheelchair away, leaving Kathleen to face Annabella Adams, who appeared to be full of questions.

"Mac, darling. I hope you're going to introduce me to this lovely creature."

"Annabella Adams, this is Kathleen Flannigan."

"I've been dying to meet you since that night at the Plaza."

"You have?"

"Why, of course. The gossip industry seems to be running out of interesting material these days. It's absolutely exhilarating to have some trash on one of our most pious and sanctimonious citizens."

"Don't listen to her, Kath."

"So, you think Mac is pious and sanctimonious?" Kathleen grinned, recognizing Mac's discomfort.

"Not really. But it's so much fun to paint a picture that the public wants to see. If the truth were told, life would be so damn dull."

"Excuse me, Annabella. I'd like to steal this lovely woman away from you for a while. She promised me a dance, and they're playing our song."

"It's a pleasure to meet you Kathleen. I'll find you later so we can talk. I'm dying to know what happened at the Plaza. And Mac, darling. I'm glad to see you finally found yourself a real woman."

Mac swept Kathleen away before Annabella Adams could utter another word. "Welcome to my world."

Hour after hour Kathleen danced, most of the time in Mac's arms, circling the beautiful ballroom to the strains of Beethoven, Mozart, and Brahms, a little Rodgers and Hammerstein, and a lot of Presley.

"You seem to be having a good time." Mac cut in, stealing Kathleen away from Senator Hill, who seemed to have trouble keeping his feet off her toes.

"I didn't think I was cut out for a party like this. But it's wonderful. Everyone's so nice, even Annabella."

"She trapped you?"

"Of course. She's had her eye on me most of the night. She wants to know if it's true what they say about men with big hands."

"She what!"

Kathleen wiggled her eyebrows, teasing him over his indignation. "My goodness, Mac. Isn't it bad enough just being pious and sanctimonious, without being a prude, too?"

"I'm not pious, I'm not sanctimonious, and I'm definitely not a prude. Here, I'll prove it." The dance floor was crowded, and no one paid any attention to the couple towering over everyone else in the room. His hands slipped down her back, to her waist, slowly, ever so slowly, until they found the firm contour of her bottom. He lowered his lips to her ear. "Whatever you do, don't pull away from me now," he whispered and pulled her close, so close she could feel the first stirrings of his manhood.

"Tell me I'm not a prude."

"You're not a prude."

"And is it true what they say about men with big hands?" he teased, then led her deeper into the crowd on the ballroom floor.

"I don't know, but if you keep this up, I'm sure I'll find out."

"Do you want to find out?"

"Yes."

"Tonight?"

"No." Breathing had become difficult, and speech nearly impossible. "Not tonight. Next weekend, when you take me away."

"Do we have to wait so long?"

"You have to tell me everything first."

"Why?"

"Because until you do, I can't give you my soul."

His hands moved again to her back, tracing her spine with

his fingers, until they found the base of her neck. He allowed himself room to breathe, but couldn't resist the temptation of her lips. He tilted her face to his, seeking the sweetness of her mouth, softly, tenderly. He tried to read the look in her eyes and hoped she could read what was in his. God, he needed her. Never in his life had he wanted anything so badly.

They danced on, until Mac was pulled away by old friends who wanted and deserved their turns with him on the dance floor. Kathleen mingled with other guests, sharing stories with retirees long since gone from McKenna Publishing. She laughed with family friends who told tales of Mac as a youngster, listened in awe to stories of Maureen's iron fist during the Depression, a woman in a man's world, faced with a tough job. How Mac's father had run the company like a family, against the better judgment of Maureen, but increased profits by branching into new ventures, things Maureen had never dreamed possible.

Back again in Mac's arms, Kathleen rested her hands on his shoulders and gazed into his sparkling eyes as they circled the room. "So many people miss your father. I didn't know it was possible for one person to be loved by so many."

"He was rather special."

Her eyes brightened as she remembered the big Irishman. "I miss his smile . . . his laughter. He was the most gentle man I've ever known." Tears formed in her eyes but her smile never left. "You used to be just like him. I thought I'd never see that gentleness in you again, but I was wrong."

Mac tenderly wiped away an escaping tear, then pulled her close and captured her mouth. Never before had he experienced a kiss like this, and he knew, for the first time in his life, he'd found a woman he truly loved. With all his heart he wanted her—the hell with the rumors. Deep down he'd never believed them anyway. Next weekend he'd tell her the truth, tell her his suspicions; he only hoped she wouldn't push him away when he admitted why he'd ignored her for so many years.

"You bring out the best in me. Think you can stand to stick by my side?"

Kathleen buried her face into his neck, kissing him until her lips reached his ear. "There's no place I'd rather be."

The music seemed to play louder, something beautiful, melodious, and Mac swept Kathleen around the room singing so only she could hear. " 'If I loved you, time and again I would try to say . . .' " Kathleen closed her eyes and pictured Gordon McCrea singing those words to Shirley Jones in *Carousel*. Oh how she loved that music, oh how she loved being in Mac's arms. He couldn't sing like Gordon McCrea, but he was real, and alive, and in her arms, and she never wanted him to leave.

She heard no one but Mac. She saw nothing but the joy in his face as they moved with the music. And then, suddenly, she was ripped out of her dream. Something sharp dug into her arm. Fingernails. Ashley's fingernails.

"How dare you kiss him in front of me," Ashley hissed. Mac pried Ashley's hand from Kathleen's arm and maneuvered Kathleen behind him. "I thought you went home."

"I didn't want to go. I belong here, not her." Her voice was calm, quiet, and very calculated.

"Let's talk about this outside."

Ashley pulled her arm out of Mac's grasp. "Fine. I don't want to make a scene in front of my friends."

Mac looked at Kathleen, hoping to see some sign of understanding or sympathy. And he found what he sought. "Stay here."

"No, Mac. This is my fight, too."

They retreated through the ballroom and into the gardens, away from the eyes and ears of the other guests.

"Okay, Ash. What is it now?"

"It's simple. She's playing you for a fool. I watched that display in there. How dare you put on such a vulgar spectacle in front of your guests. You wouldn't have done that with me. She's leading you astray."

"I wouldn't have done it with you because you would have slapped my face."

Ashley glared at Kathleen. "He thinks you can take my place, but you can't. You don't know how to dress. You don't know how to entertain guests. You're just a small-town hick, and he knows it."

"Knock it off, Ash. She doesn't deserve this treatment from you."

"She's a tramp, Mac. I told you that years ago. Don't fall for her again."

Kathleen's eyes narrowed in a confused frown. She grabbed Mac's arm. "What's she talking about? What did she tell you years ago?"

Ashley grinned. Oh, how she enjoyed making them suffer.

"It's nothing, Kath."

"Don't push it aside, Mac. I want to know. What did she say?"

He turned to the woman he suddenly despised. "Go home, Ash."

"I'll leave this time, but you're not getting rid of me. I'll be back, and I fully intend to make your life miserable."

They watched her walk away, back to the guest-filled hall, wishing she would walk out of their lives for good, but maybe that would be wanting too much.

The soft music from inside wafted toward them on the light warm breeze, and Mac took Kathleen's hand, leading her farther into the garden to a white gazebo draped in banners of red, white, and blue. He leaned against a post, shoved his hands into his pockets, and fixed his eyes on Kathleen as she sat on a bench across from him. So graceful. So beautiful. God, he hated the thought of losing her.

Kathleen sensed his unease. "Is what she told you the reason you went to Europe?"

"Couldn't we discuss this next weekend when we're alone?"

Kathleen shook her head. "Do it now, Mac."

His shoulders slumped as he rested his head against the whitewashed post. "I'm afraid you'll run away."

"I won't run away, Mac, but I need to know why you did."

Knowing he couldn't hide the truth any longer, he swallowed his pride, but he couldn't swallow his fear. "Before we went to Europe, Ashley told me I was making a fool of myself over you."

Her eyes narrowed as if she didn't understand. "And what was that supposed to mean? We talked about work, that's all."

"But that's not all, Kath. I couldn't get you out of my mind. I can't begin to tell you how much I loved our sparring matches when we were together, and I guess I talked about you too much around Ashley. I don't think she appreciated it."

Kathleen felt her cheeks burning. She never blushed, but this may have been a first. "I'm flattered."

"Well, Ashley wasn't. The thought of you and I having anything more than a business relationship never really entered my mind. At least I didn't think it had. I liked you, and I sure as hell liked looking at you, but I didn't see anything more to it. I guess Ashley did, though, and she dug in her claws. She'd laugh and tell me I was too old for you, that you were playing up to me because you wanted my money."

"Did you really think I wanted your money?"

"Hell, no. If that had bothered me, I would have dumped Ashley the day I met her."

"Then what did bother you?"

He laughed. "Realizing just how much I did care for you . . . and that you were too young," he stammered. "Ashley made me see just how ridiculous it would look if the two of us got together."

"That's crazy!"

"I know that now. But along with being stubborn and opinionated, I'm pretty vain, too."

"I've known that for a long time."

"Damn it, Kath. Do you have to be so honest?"

"Yes. Now I want you to be honest with me."

"I have been."

"You haven't told me everything, Mac. I still don't know why you went to Europe or why you ignored me when you came back."

Mac rolled his eyes heavenward, took a deep, steadying breath, then found the courage to look back at Kathleen.

"Okay. I thought I loved Ashley, even when you were constantly on my mind. She promised if I took her to Europe for a year, we'd get married and have a family when we got back. Why the hell I ever believed that line, I'll never know."

"Sometimes love is blind."

"Well, I regained my vision pretty fast in Europe. She didn't want me. She just wanted the things I could give her. Clothes, jewels, endless partying. A whole year of it. I indulged her, Kath. I wanted to explore, see castles and the countryside. But she wanted to shop. It was a disaster."

"If it was so bad, why didn't you call it quits when you came home?"

He let out a deep sigh, all the pent-up frustration he'd felt for five long years. "I think she sensed I was going to.

She can be pretty conniving, Kath. She dropped subtle hints before we came home about you and an affair you were having."

Kathleen's eyes widened. "And who was I supposed to be having an affair with?"

Mac looked down at the floor of the gazebo. There was no way he could look into her eyes. "My father."

Silence. Deafening silence.

"Tell me you didn't believe that. Please tell me, Mac."

"No, I didn't believe it. I couldn't believe it. You knew my dad. He'd never have an affair with anyone."

Her voice was only a whisper. "But you believed it about me?"

He didn't look up. "Well . . ."

"Well, what?"

"I came back from Europe and you had a baby. What was I supposed to believe?"

"You weren't supposed to believe anything. Did you ever consider talking to me about it?"

"No." He paced across the wood plank floor, grabbed hold of one of the columns for support. He looked out into the dark night sky, afraid to look at the hurt in Kathleen's eyes. "I didn't want to know the truth. I just assumed you'd met someone, you'd gotten pregnant, and he didn't want to get married."

Now she was mad. "That does happen, Mac. Women do get pregnant, sometimes by accident, but there's always a man involved, or have you conveniently forgotten the man's role in conception?"

"Of course I haven't forgotten. I'm sorry, Kath. What can I say? Maybe I was jealous that I hadn't been the one sleeping with you while I was in Europe. God knows I thought about it enough."

Her head shot up and her eyes blazed. She took a deep

breath, and then another. He had a grin on his face. A stupid, insufferable-man type of grin.

"Is there anything else you want to tell me? I'm racking up a pretty long list of reasons why we should call it quits."

For some strange reason, the smirk didn't leave Mac's face. "No. I can only think of reasons why we should stay together."

"Such as?"

"I don't care what's happened in your past, but I care about our future."

Damn it. He could have said anything but that.

"You think we have a future after the way you've insulted me?"

He nodded, and his smirk turned into a smile. "All you have to do is forgive me."

"Forgive you? I'd rather lynch you for being such an insensitive, opinionated, self-righteous bastard. But . . ." Getting mad and staying mad at McKenna O'Brien would never be easy. She'd loved him way too long. "Fortunately, I don't think you're beyond redemption."

"And is it your plan to save my soul?"

"I can't take ten years of wanting you and throw it out the door. I guess if you can forgive me for my supposed indiscretion, I can forgive you for your archaic beliefs about right and wrong." But, she thought to herself, you're going to have to prove to me that you deserve to know the truth about Julie. I'm not going to tell you unless you ask. And when you find out, you're going to feel like an ass, and I hope you're miserable.

"Kath?"

Stop using that seductive, sexy voice on me, McKenna O'Brien. "What?"

"I meant it when I said I want you. I've damned my beliefs over and over because they kept me away from you far too long. My mother said I'm a conservative bore—"

"She's right."

"Perhaps. Conservative bore, insufferable pig, self-righteous bastard. Did I leave anything out?"

"Give me time to think. I'm sure I can come up with a much longer list."

He put a finger under her chin and turned her face to his. "Can you forgive me?"

Her angry eyes suddenly sparkled. "I'll think about it."

"We're a good match, Kath. A pious conservative and a tenacious liberal. We'll always have something to fight about." He brushed one of those beautiful strands of hair away from her face, never taking his eyes from hers, waiting for just a trace of emotion that said she felt the same. And then it came, that radiant smile that had captivated his heart, his mind, all his senses. He pulled her into his arms. He pressed his lips to her silky hair, inhaling her fragrance. But his lips wanted more. They sought and found the softness of hers, and he tasted heaven.

Boom!

They heard the soaring rockets and ran out of the gazebo to see the burst of a thousand exploding colors in the night sky. He stood next to her, gazing into her eyes, sparkling as never before. The thrill of Fourth of July made her smile, like a child, wide-eyed and innocent, gazing at Christmas-tree lights as they first came to life. He pulled her into his arms, tight, so very, very tight, her back pressed against his as they watched the glittering sky and dreamed of their own fireworks that were equally, if not more, exciting.

Together they stood, hand in hand, before the door to Kathleen's room. "Are you sure I can't convince you to stay with me tonight?" Mac asked.

Kathleen shook her head. "Shhh," she whispered, her index finger pressed to his lips. "You'll give people more to talk about."

"Let them talk."

He stepped closer, but Kathleen pushed open the door and escaped inside, away from his lips and the fear that she might want more than his kisses. "Good night."

Pushing his hand through the slim opening in the doorway, he marveled at how beautiful Kathleen still looked at three in the morning. More than anything, he wanted to wake at her side. He brushed a strand of hair away from her face and cupped her cool cheek in his warm hand. "Sweet dreams, Kath."

She took his hand and pulled his fingers to her lips, kissing the tips, and then his palm, letting her mouth linger as she inhaled his fragrance, something to hold on to until she saw him again. After one more taste of his skin, she gently squeezed his hand and lowered it to his side. She smiled as she closed the door.

Ashley stood in the gazebo and watched the lights going out throughout the house. It wasn't fair that she should be outside and that other woman was sleeping in the bed that she had slept in dozens of times before. Mac had no right to tell her to go. She swore several weeks before that she'd get even, and now was the time. But what could she do? She knew only one thing he wanted. A child. The idea repulsed her. Sex. Children. Living under the same roof with Mac, for all time.

She didn't want any of those things. She didn't even want Mac anymore. She wanted Kathleen to suffer as she had when Mac called it quits.

She crept across the lawn and through the service entrance. She knew the way to his room, she could find her way blindfolded. But dim lights burned throughout the house, lighting the way for guests who wouldn't feel comfortable walking in the dark. Up the stairs, down the hall. No one heard her. No one saw her. And then she was there. She turned the knob, quietly, and slipped inside.

She heard his deep breathing. She knew that sound so very well, the sound he made when nothing could disturb him. She unbuttoned the taffeta dress and let it fall to the floor, then slipped out of her stockings, panties, and bra. She stepped lightly across the room, cringed at the sound of his snoring. She hated that sound. Mac stirred when she neared the bed. He rolled to face her, and opened his arms.

Kathleen couldn't sleep. She tossed, turned, and finally climbed out of bed, pacing the floor. What the hell did she want from Mac? What did he want from her? She knew the answer. Her frustrations built every time he touched her. When he kissed her she felt her body quiver. Would he ever come to her? Could she go to him?

To hell with propriety, she thought. She removed the cotton pajamas she wore and slipped into the white satin robe she had bought "just in case." She hoped the floor didn't creak like the floors at home. She hadn't heard any noises when she went to her room with Mac. She had heard nothing but his words, his breathing, the light laughter in his voice.

The floors didn't make a sound. She heard only the deafening thump of her heart. Down the stairs. Which room was it? The third on the right? The fourth? Why hadn't she paid more attention when he laughingly pointed it out to her?

She put her fingers on the knob. Oh, please, God, let Mac be in this room.

Mac woke to the light steps crossing the floor. She had come to him after all. Even in the darkness he saw the flutter of silk dropping to the floor. He heard the familiar creak of the floorboard near his bed. He opened his arms, waiting for

Kathleen to come to him. And then the door opened again. A thin beam of light entered the room, illuminating the blonde hair of the woman near his bed.

Ashley's hair. And Kathleen stood in the doorway. He couldn't see her face, but knew full well the expression she wore. Less than a second had passed. He looked back at Ashley, seeing only her thin, naked back. He threw back the covers and stumbled from the bed, but the door had already slammed.

Ashley turned toward him and grinned. "Don't ever doubt me when I say I'm going to get even," she hissed.

Kathleen slammed Mac's door, tears flowing freely as she leaned against the wall, trying to compose her emotions before returning to her room. She took several deep breaths. Damn that woman. How dare she enter Mac's room! How dare she mess around with Mac when he belongs to me! She felt no anger toward Mac, only a burning rage that Ashley would again try to come between them.

She wiped her tears with the back of her hand and, without giving it any more thought, faced the door, turned the knob, and pushed it open so hard it slammed into the wall behind.

Ashley stood, *naked*, at the edge of the bed, grinning in victory.

Mac was just inches from the door, and Kathleen could almost hear his teeth grinding. She tossed him a quick smile, then pushed him out of her way. "Close the door, Mac. I have a few things to say to Miss Tate, and I don't want to wake the rest of your guests."

She slowly walked across the room, picking up pieces of Ashley's clothing as she neared the woman whose composure hadn't yet crumbled. She wanted to slap Ashley's smirking face. She even considered scratching her eyes out. But that meant stooping to Ashley's level. Words were a much better tool.

She held the gown in front of her. "I believe this is yours. It's not very attractive, but you look better in it than out."

Ashley snatched the dress away and covered her body. "I think you should direct your anger at Mac, not at me. I think he rather enjoys seeing me this way."

Kathleen glared into Ashley's eyes. "I think I know what Mac likes."

Mac hadn't moved an inch; he still stood by the door, watching the exchange. He hadn't expected Kathleen to come back into the room, hadn't expected her to fight for him. He expected to see her packing her bags to make a hasty retreat from McKenna House. But this was heaven, the way she spoke with her back stiff as she confronted Ashley. But most of all, he thrilled at the smile Kathleen wore on her face as she seductively sauntered toward him.

She pressed her palms against his bare chest, and lowered her eyes to his waist and the sheet he had hastily wrapped around his hips. Like a schoolboy, he blushed at her intense perusal of his anatomy, but he stood quite still, letting her touch him, letting her caress his body, forgetting that Ashley stood across the room staring in anger.

Kathleen's long, slender fingers slowly slid upward to his shoulders, to his neck, to his cheeks, and into his hair, then pulled his head down and she captured his lips. His body tingled at her touch. She was heaven. She was his, and he knew nothing, no one, especially Ashley, could ever separate them again.

Unable to keep his hands from her any longer, he slipped his arms around her soft, warm body, lifting her feet off the ground, insistent on taking all he could get. But then he felt resistance, felt Kathleen pulling away, and he couldn't stop her.

When he saw the look of victory on Kathleen's face, a look directed toward Ashley, he knew just what she was doing. Kathleen was staking a claim.

"That, my dear," Kathleen gloated, "is what Mac likes. He's mine. I don't have to be with him every moment. I trust him. I'll always trust him, just as he trusts me."

Ashley smirked. "If you think I'm giving up, you're wrong."

"Then you're going to have one hell of a fight on your hands. Don't waste your energy."

Kathleen ignored Ashley's sneer, her look that said she hadn't comprehended one thing that had just occurred. She turned back to Mac. "It's been a long day and I've got a terrible headache." She kissed her fingertips and touched them to his lips. "I'm going back to bed now. Would you mind terribly escorting Miss Tate back to New York?"

Mac pulled Kathleen back into his arms. He didn't want to let go. "I'd rather stay here with you."

Ashley began to struggle into her dress. "Take me home, Mac. We'll talk about this in the car."

"Yes, Mac." Kathleen pressed her palm to his cheek, lightly caressing it with her fingertips. "Take her home, then come back to me when you're sure we don't have to deal with her any longer."

"But, Kath—" Mac stammered.

But Kathleen had already pulled out of his arms and walked to the door. She turned around and smiled. "Good night, Mac. Good-bye, Ashley."

CHAPTER
FOURTEEN

"Would you *please* slow down!" Ashley yelled. "And roll up your window." Her words caught in the wind, blowing back into her face. Mac heard, but chose to ignore the woman in the passenger seat. Instead, he kept his eyes focused on the road and the scenery speeding by as the speedometer inched toward ninety. The Mercedes negotiated the road's twists and turns with little effort, and Mac enjoyed the reckless feel of his foot pressing the accelerator to the floor. Out of the corner of his eye he watched Ashley wrestling with her hair, trying, without success, to keep it in place. A smile crossed his face. Not because of Ashley's dilemma, but because he thought of Kathleen, of the way her long, wavy hair would be blowing if she occupied the seat and not Ashley. Kathleen wouldn't care about the wind, wouldn't care about tangled hair. She would smile and laugh in that carefree way that sank to the pit of his stomach and made him hunger for more than her smile. God, how he wanted her.

"Didn't you hear me?"

Mac glanced at Ashley, wanting to laugh at the way she wrapped her hands and arms about her head. Instead, he turned his eyes back to the road and addressed her in a stony voice. "I heard you. But to be perfectly honest, the wind feels good, and I have no intention of rolling up the window."

"You know I hate having the windows rolled down."

"I also know how much you hate sex, junk food, cold weather, snuggling in bed, children, and me. You've made it perfectly clear for years that you hate a lot of things, and for once, I really don't care. As far as I'm concerned, you can hate the world and everything in it."

"What's gotten into you?" Ashley leaned across Mac's lap, reaching for the window control, but Mac pushed her back.

"Leave it alone, Ash." His eyes narrowed. His jaw tensed. "I want the window open."

"This is crazy. Why are we fighting over something so silly as a window?"

"It's not the window and you know it. It's you and your total lack of conscience."

"What are you talking about?" She didn't look at Mac, just leaned forward in the seat, trying to find a place safe from the wind. She pulled a lipstick and mirror from her taffeta handbag and lined her lips in a dark blood red.

Mac took a deep breath. What could he say? "Why do you hate me so much?" He said it so low the words were nearly lost in the noise of a passing car.

Ashley turned her head and smiled. "I don't hate you, Mac. I *loathe* you. You can't expect to take ten years of my life and throw them away without batting an eye."

"I threw away ten years of my life, too. But I'm happier now than I was at any given moment during those ten years."

"Because of Kathleen?"

"Yes."

"It won't last forever." Ashley laughed. "You may have won this time, but there's always the next."

"You're wrong. She's mine in spite of you. Nothing you do can change that."

"Sorry, darling. But *you're* wrong. I have no intention of letting her have you."

Mac laughed, shaking his head as he pushed his fingers through his hair. "What do you plan to do? Follow me around day and night?"

"If that's what it takes."

Mac slowed the car, knowing what he needed was a miracle, he needed his prayers to be heard. They were in the city now, but he found a spot at the curb just big enough to squeeze the Mercedes in. He put the car in park and rolled up his window to keep his words from the ears of the passersby. "Don't do this, Ash. Don't take the good times we had and turn them into a bad memory."

"I have no bad memories. I think we made the perfect couple."

Mac looked into her expressionless eyes. When had she become obsessed? Had she always been that way? Had he been too blind to see? "You've destroyed every good memory I ever had about us, and you're trying to destroy what's between me and Kathleen. I want you out of my life."

He stared out the window at a couple walking by, arms linked, stealing kisses, not caring if anyone looked. That's what he wanted. That's what he needed.

"Once I get you home, I don't want to see you again."

"But you will."

"No, I won't. My lawyers will make sure of it."

Fifteen minutes later Mac pulled to a stop before Ashley's building. It had been the longest fifteen minutes in his life, listening to Ashley's threats to sue for palimony, her voice screeching in anger about his total lack of concern for her welfare, not to mention the contempt of her friends. He said not a word, fully intending to stand pat on his statement about bringing his lawyers in if necessary.

He popped the trunk so the doorman could get Ashley's bags, climbed out of the car, walked to the passenger side, and reached for the door handle.

"Excuse me, sir. Let me get that for you."

The voice had a familiar lilt to it, something Mac couldn't quite place. It wasn't the regular doorman who stepped in front of him to open Ashley's door. This man stood less than four feet tall, had twinkling eyes and a jaunty smile.

Mac stood back to watch the exchange between Ashley and the doorman as he tried to help her out of the car. Doormen, like secretaries, clerks, and waiters, didn't qualify in Ashley's mind as parts of the human race. Mac had always been aware of Ashley's treatment of those she considered beneath her. In the beginning he ignored it. Later he tried to change her. When he realized she saw nothing wrong with her behavior, he compensated those she spurned with a friendly smile, a handshake, warm conversation, or a job or loan for those in need. They respected him. They ignored Ashley. But this little man was different from all the rest. Ashley's abuse didn't sway him from his duty.

"Let me help you, ma'am," the little man reached for her hand, but she shook him off.

"Out of my way," Ashley snarled, her eyes glaring from the tips of his curl-toed shoes to his tiny turned-up nose. "You're not my regular man. Where is he?" Ashley demanded to know.

"His name's Harold."

"I don't care what his name is. Why isn't he here?"

"Does it really matter?"

Ashley threw up her hands. "I suppose one incompetent is just as good as another. Get my bags out of the car."

"I'd be happy to do that for you, ma'am."

"My name's Miss Tate, not ma'am."

"Wonderful, wonderful, wonderful." The little man beamed. "I've been waiting for you."

Ashley rolled her eyes. "I don't have all day. Just get my bags."

"But this is important."

"What is it?" she asked in exasperation. "I don't give out money. That's Mac's department. See him if you want something."

The little man winked at Mac, put his fists to his hips, and tilted his pointed chin toward Ashley's scowling face.

Mac crossed his arms and watched the interplay between Ashley and the strange man.

"No, no, no, Miss Tate. I don't want anything. Not anything at all. I want to *give* you something."

"What could *you* possibly give *me*?"

The little man pulled an oblong purple velvet box from his inside coat pocket. "I was asked to give you this," he said while lifting the lid. He held the box out to Ashley. "My, my, my. Isn't it the most beautiful necklace you've ever seen?"

Ashley's eyes widened as the sun's rays glinted off the three rows of brilliant diamonds studding the choker.

Mac's eyes widened also. Hadn't he seen that necklace before? At Holly's? And the little man and his choice of words. *My, my, my. No, no, no.* They were Merry's words. And the man at Holly's. He looked at the little man's strange shoes, his turned-up nose. He grinned, he laughed, and the little man turned to him with a wink. Mac leaned against the Mercedes. Could this little man be the miracle he had prayed for?

Ashley grabbed the box out of the little man's hand. "Did you steal this?"

"No, Miss Tate. I was told to give it to you. I was also told to give you a message."

She removed the necklace and dropped the box on the sidewalk. "What's the message?" she asked, holding the choker to her neck, ready to fasten the latch.

The little man touched his index finger to his chin and smiled up at Ashley. "I believe the necklace is enchanted."

Ashley laughed. "Nonsense. It's only a necklace."

"A beautiful necklace. One with a story behind it."

"What's the story?"

"They say the wearer of the necklace will fall madly in love with the first person to call her by name."

"You're insane."

"No, no, no. It's true."

"All right, then," Ashley said as she fastened the latch. "If you think it's enchanted, let's give it a try. Call me by my name."

"Oh, I couldn't do that, Miss Tate," he said, furiously shaking his head.

"And why not?"

The man looked at Mac with an impish grin, then back at Ashley. "I'm not particularly fond of you, Miss Tate. I'd rather have you fall in love with someone more your type."

"How rude. I don't believe a word of your story, and I have no intention of giving you back the necklace."

"I don't want it back, Miss Tate," he said. "You deserve that necklace. I'll get your bags now, but you be careful. I wouldn't want you to fall madly in love with the wrong person."

Mac watched Ashley lightly finger the surface of the diamonds, then bend to admire herself in the car's side mirror.

He felt a hand slap him on the back. "Well, Mac, old man." He recognized the loud, abrasive voice. Reginald Morgan, the "Prince of Porn." "What the hell are you doing here?"

"The question is, what are you doing here? Isn't this part of town a little out of your league?"

"Touché." Reginald quipped, leering at Ashley's bottom, at the way the red, white, and blue bow swayed with the movement of her hips. "Got to hand it to you, Mac. No one man should be fortunate enough to have a babe like that one *and* that long-legged creature I saw you with at the Plaza."

Mac ignored the comment. He didn't remember seeing Reginald Morgan at the Plaza and wanted to change the subject.

Ashley came to Mac's side, sliding her arm through his, but he unconsciously moved away, no longer liking the feel of her touch. He turned to look at the little man struggling with the luggage. He wanted to leave, to get away from Ashley, and now from that vile, disgusting creature who called himself a man.

Mac watched Reginald's eyes dart from Ashley's face, to her diamond choker, her small breasts, her tiny waist. He detested the man, hated his underhanded deals and the pornographic sleaze he published.

"Excuse me, sir." The doorman stood between two tweed Pullmans. "I'll take these up to the lady's apartment now."

"Thank you," Mac said, extending a hand and a warm smile. He reached into his pocket and pulled out several bills.

"No, no, no, sir. Give it to charity."

Mac nodded. The little man picked up the bags and started to walk away, then stopped, and turned around.

"Excuse me, Mr. O'Brien."

"Yes?" Mac said, and for only a brief moment wondered how the little man knew his name.

"May I make a suggestion, sir?"

"Please do."

"Why don't you introduce Mr. Morgan to your friend?" The little man winked and, with no further words, bustled up the stairs and through the revolving doors.

"Yes, darling. Why don't you introduce me?" Ashley purred.

Mac eyed Reginald Morgan, envisioning drool dripping out from between his fat lips and down his pockmarked chin. He looked at Ashley, at the necklace she wore. He thought about the story. He didn't want to say her name. What if the necklace *was* enchanted? What if the little man's story *was* true?

Mac saw Ashley staring at the large diamond rings Reginald Morgan wore on the stubby middle fingers of each hand. He looked at his shiny brow and saw beads of perspiration erupting from the pores at his hairline. His neck and numerous chins rolled over the top of his tightly buttoned collar, the pink shirt looking as sleazy as the man himself, not to mention the obnoxious gold medallion dangling from a thick gold chain around his neck.

He couldn't hesitate any longer. They stared at him as he fought for a way to introduce them.

"Reginald Morgan, this is an old friend of mine."

"Mac, darling, you know how I hate to be referred to as an *old* friend."

"Pretty insensitive of you, old man," Reginald snorted. "How could you call a gorgeous creature like this old? Why, she couldn't be a day over twenty."

"Thank you, Mr. Morgan." Ashley's voice dripped sweetness. Men who looked like Reginald Morgan repulsed Ashley, but she obviously made an exception for vile men who reeked of money.

"Mac can be pretty insensitive at times. I'm Ashley Tate," she said, stretching out a dainty hand.

Reginald Morgan took Ashley's hand and pressed a wet kiss to her knuckles. "It's *so* nice to meet you, Ashley Tate."

Mac stood perfectly still. A bolt of lightning shot through the cloudless blue sky, instantly followed by a loud, earth-shaking roll of thunder.

An odd expression crossed Ashley's face. She pulled her hand out of Reginald's as if she'd been shocked. She stared at Mac, a quick look of fear crossing her face, perhaps a moment of regret, and then she grinned. Her fingers found their way to Reginald Morgan's face, then slid through his oil-slicked hair. She slipped her other hand under his unbuttoned jacket, letting it glide over his sweat-dampened shirt up to his shoulder. She moved close, pulling his head down to capture his lips.

Mac couldn't move. He fought his senses which told him to pull them apart. As horrible as Ashley had been, did she really deserve someone like Reginald Morgan? He touched her shoulder, tried to pull her away. "Come on, Ash. Let's get out of here."

She slapped his hand. "Get away," she hissed and resumed her perusal of Reginald Morgan with her lips.

"God, you're a tiger," Reginald gasped as he came up for air.

"Marry me and I'm all yours," she whispered while her tongue darted around his ear.

"I have a place in Vegas," Reginald groaned. "We can be there in just a few hours."

She kissed his eyes, his nose. "I want a round bed, red velvet wallpaper, and mirrors—lots of mirrors."

"Anything, my sweet."

"Let's hurry," Ashley breathed. She wrapped her arms tightly around his neck as her mouth once again fought for total control of his lips and tongue.

A crowd gathered. People stared. Photographers came from nowhere, and Mac listened to the *click, click, click* of cameras. He moved to the driver's side of his car, pulled open the door, and started to step inside. He looked up to the building's revolving doors. The little man stood outside, smiling down at Mac. Again he winked, and then he disappeared into the crowd.

Mac looked heavenward. He closed his eyes. "Thank you, Lord."

CHAPTER
FIFTEEN

Kathleen opened her eyes as the light of late morning shot through the window. She had lain awake throughout the early morning thinking of Mac, about how she had wanted him all those years ago, and now he was hers. She closed her eyes and remembered their first meeting.

She stood at the door of his office. She had already interviewed with the senior copywriter and the hard-nosed editor of *Back Country* magazine; now she had to face the man whose *Fortune* magazine picture had been on her desk all through college as she dreamed of working for McKenna Publishing. But had it been McKenna Publishing she wanted to work for, or McKenna O'Brien?

She remembered knocking, the voice she heard, wanting to run. Instead, she had wiped her damp palms on her best navy blue skirt, pushed the door open, held her head high, and walked up to the man. He took her outstretched hand and shook it firmly. She stared into his eyes. Those same smoky blue eyes she had dreamed of for years.

"So, you want a job with McKenna Publishing?" he had asked.

"Yes, sir."

"They tell me you want to be a copywriter."

"No, sir. I want to be senior editor of my own magazine."

"I see. You want to start at the top."

"No, sir. I don't want your job, yet."

She smiled at the thought of those early days, and at the thought of all the pleasant things yet to come. But why did she have to feel so lousy now that her dreams were finally coming true?

She wiped perspiration from the back of her neck and pressed the heels of her hands against her temples, trying to squeeze out the throbbing headache. All the pleasant thoughts in the world couldn't wipe away her misery.

The light hitting her eyes added to the pain. She scooted down into the softness of the bed, pulled the covers over her head, and went back to sleep.

"My, my, my, Mr. O'Brien. You look absolutely awful," Merry declared when Mac walked through the door. He hadn't shaved, and he had slept only one hour in the last thirty-six. Not only did he look awful, he felt awful. The only thing that kept him going was the one thought that kept running through his mind—*I'm free of Ashley.*

"Can you get me something to eat?"

"Of course, Mr. O'Brien. Won't take me a moment, and I'll have something hot and delicious waiting for you on the kitchen table."

"Do you have any chocolate chip cookies?" he asked, slumping into a chair before the fireplace.

"Why, of course I do. You just sit and relax a spell. When the food's ready, we'll discuss what's troubling you."

"There's nothing troubling me, Merry. In fact, life couldn't be better."

Merry's eyes twinkled. "Well, my word, Mr. O'Brien. That's absolutely wonderful. You just close your eyes now and think pleasant thoughts." She bustled into the kitchen, humming a medley of Christmas tunes. Mac took a deep

breath and smelled cinnamon and apple cider. He'd grown to
love their scent. He closed his eyes, resting his head against
the back of the chair.

He thought about his first meeting with Kathleen, the way
she stood in the doorway of his office in that navy blue suit
with a misplaced gold button. He smiled at the thought of her
cool, damp palm, the only time he remembered her nervous
or at a loss for words. He remembered that moment as though
it had just happened, and he particularly remembered her
eyes, the way she looked up at him with a mixture of longing
and awe. And, in the next moment, spunk and intelligence.
Had that been the moment he'd fallen in love?

"Excuse me, Mr. O'Brien." Merry's hand rested on his
shoulder. "Your lunch is ready. You must not have heard
me calling."

"My thoughts were miles away."

"With the woman you left at McKenna House?"

Mac nodded, all his emotion clearly written on the smile
he wore. "Yes. I need to hurry back."

"Then you'd better run along and eat. I've got a piping hot
lunch on the table."

"Will you join me?"

"My, my, my, young man. I can't be by your side all
the time. I have dusting to do." She shooed him toward the
kitchen with her feather duster.

When Mac pushed open the swinging doors, the aroma
of fresh-baked bread and cookies assailed him. A bowl of
potato-cheese soup steamed on the table alongside a plate
of thickly sliced, crusty white bread and a cube of butter. A
glass of milk sat on the other side, and in the center of the
table lay a tray of chocolate chip cookies. A feast for a starving man, Mac thought. Starving for the love of Kathleen.

He sat down and dipped his soup spoon into the bowl,
blowing on the steaming potatoes and cream. His elbows

rested on the table, something he had never been allowed to do as a child at home. He tested his first mouthful, savoring the taste. Hot soup, warm buttered bread, chocolate chip cookies, and thoughts of Kathleen, things to soothe a man's soul.

He stared into his bowl while he ate and again thought back to days long since gone.

"Miss Tate and I are going to Europe for a year," he told her.

Kathleen had looked at him with those big blue eyes that made him melt every time she came near. He hadn't wanted to go to Europe, he hadn't wanted to leave Kathleen and the working relationship they had built over the years. But he had to. Ashley had accused him of being infatuated with the girl. She had hit it dead on the nose. But it had been more than infatuation. He and Kathleen argued about everything from politics to women's rights, to the color of the sky. If he said it was blue, she said it was azure. She made him come alive. And she still did.

He dug into the soup and anxiously anticipated seeing her again in just a few hours, longing to see once again those azure eyes.

Mac opened the door and peered into the darkened room. His mother had told him she had pulled the drapes earlier that afternoon when she peeked into the room and found Kathleen still asleep. It wasn't common practice for her guests to sleep so late. But she had heard the exchange between her son and the two women during the night, had watched her son drive away with Ashley, hoping she would never see that skinny blonde again. She was more than happy to let the feisty brunette sleep the day away.

He stepped into the room, instantly comforted by the quiet, the peace. Kathleen lay on the bed, the summer-weight comforter pulled up to her chest. Her hair fanned out over the lace-edged pillowcase, a few wisps lying over her nose and mouth. He gently moved the hair away from her face, listened to her soft breathing, watched the movement of her eyes beneath closed lids. He bent over and touched her lips with his own. She didn't stir, not an inch.

His eyelids grew heavy. The bed looked inviting, partially because he was drop-dead tired, partially because Kathleen slept in its midst. He slipped off his shoes and socks, removed his shirt, and lay down beside her on top of the comforter. Lifting her hair to make room for his head on the pillow, he caressed the silky strands that slipped through his fingers. Without waking, Kathleen rolled onto her side, facing away from him. With one arm under the pillow, he draped the other over her ribs, carefully avoiding the breasts he longed to touch. He breathed deeply, trying to recognize the scent in her hair, the remnants of perfume behind her ear. Oh, dear Lord, he whispered, let me always lay at her side. He moved as close to her as the bedclothes would allow, closed his eyes, and slept.

Kathleen woke to the soft, resonant breathing near her ear. A warm, heavy arm lay across her, the long, sturdy fingers sprinkled with light golden hair intertwined with hers. She turned her head to look into the face of the man who lay beside her. Her head pounded, her body ached, but at that moment, everything seemed perfect. She rolled over in his arms and felt his fingers tighten when she lightly kissed his eyelids. His eyes opened slowly. "I'm glad you're back," she whispered.

He pulled her closer, gently outlining her lips with the tips of his index and middle fingers. His lips lightly touched hers, and he sucked in his breath when he felt the warm softness of her skin. He abandoned her mouth and found her ear, nibbling on the smooth skin of her lobe. She was so hot, so close.

She wanted to push him away, to tell him she ached from head to toe, but she didn't want to break the spell, didn't want him to take his lips away from all those places on her body that burned, not only with fever, but with desire. Instead, she spread her fingers out across the muscles of his warm, smooth back, memorizing his shoulder blades, the indentation of his spine, a mole at his waist.

"I think we slept the day away," she whispered into his ear when he sat up and allowed her to move out of his grasp.

"Must have. Are you hungry?"

Kathleen's stomach churned. She sat up for only a moment, shook her head, then lay back against the cool pillows.

"Well, I'm starved. Mind if I get something to eat?"

"Go right ahead. But I have no intention of getting out of this bed."

"I'll raid the refrigerator and bring up a tray." He stole a parting kiss and bounded out of bed.

He took a quick look at himself in the mirror and smoothed back his hair. "God, I look awful."

Kathleen laughed. "That's supposed to be my line."

He glanced fondly at the woman lying in the bed. "Let me assure you, Kath. You're a feast for the eyes."

"Are you decent?" Mac asked, peeking around the door.

Kathleen sat cross-legged on the bed in an overly large chenille robe she had found hanging in the closet. "I think so," she answered.

"Damn. I was hoping you'd say no." He pushed through the door, then shoved it closed with his foot. In his hands he held a tray laden with goodies from the kitchen—fried chicken and chocolate cake, potato salad, milk, a Diet Coke, and cold shrimp and lobster left over from Friday night's celebration.

"Umm, doesn't this look wonderful." He set the tray on the bed, climbed up beside Kathleen, and grabbed a cold drumstick. "Maggie makes the best fried chicken. Care for a bite?" He held the drumstick out to Kathleen.

"No, thanks." She sighed, feeling as though she had turned ten shades of green.

"Is Ashley gone?" she asked.

He nodded and smiled.

"You're positive?"

"Positive."

Mac studied Kathleen's face. Her color had disappeared, the hair at her temples was damp and clung to her face. He put his palm to her forehead. "You're sick. Why didn't you tell me?"

"I hate to be sick. I don't like to be a burden."

He dropped the drumstick onto the tray, wiped his hands, and pulled her into his arms, smoothing the hair away from her face. "Do you want to go home?"

"Would you mind taking me? I know it's a long drive and you wanted to spend the weekend here."

"Shh." He placed his index finger to her lips and shook his head. "I'd do anything for you."

Kathleen slept from the time they left the grounds of McKenna House until Mac pulled to a stop in front of her building. He helped her out of the car and watched her lean against it while he got her suitcases out of the trunk. "Come on, sweetheart. Let's get you up to bed."

"I can make it on my own. I know you want to get home."

"I'm not leaving your side. Besides, who said I wanted to go home? I'd rather be with you."

"But I look awful."

"You look beautiful. Now, move. The sooner you're in bed, the better you'll feel."

Mac unlocked the outside door and ushered Kathleen into the lobby. He stopped before the elevator door, posted with an OUT OF ORDER sign.

"Damn!" He set the suitcases on the floor. "Which floor are you on?"

"Fifth."

"I haven't exercised in weeks, so bear with me and promise not to laugh if I have to stop a time or two to catch my breath."

"What are you talking about?" Kathleen asked, hanging on to his arm.

He didn't answer, just put one hand under her knees, the other around her back, and swung her into his arms. "You're a lightweight, kiddo, even if you are nearly six feet tall."

"Put me down."

"Not until we climb all five flights. I need to prove to myself that I'm not an old man."

"You're not an old man, okay? Now, put me down."

"Hush. I'll put you down in bed, not a second sooner."

"You're stubborn."

"You've been a great teacher. Now, close your eyes and be still while I huff and puff up the stairs."

Kathleen laid her head against his shoulder, her arms wrapped tightly around his neck. His heart beat rapidly as he neared the top. She lost count of the steps Mac had climbed when she reached forty-nine, one for each of his years. He's far from old, she thought, her fingers absently playing with the well-manicured hair at the back of his head. She listened to his breathing, slow, even, as though climbing the stairs with her in his arms came naturally.

He reached the fifth-floor landing, only a little out of breath. He liked the feel of holding her this way, caring for her. He wanted to do it forever.

They heard the *ding* of the elevator just as Mac stuck the key in the lock of her door. The elevator doors slid open and a repairman stepped into the lobby. "Hello, folks. Hope I didn't inconvenience you none. The elevator's been fixed for . . . let me see." He looked at his watch. "Geez, guess I've had it fixed for at least half an hour now. Forgot to take down the sign before I stopped off to visit a friend on the sixth floor. Well, I'll let you get inside. I'm just checking to make sure it stops on all the floors. Good night now," he said as the doors closed once again and they listened to the hum of the elevator's descent.

Mac looked at Kathleen with a grin. "Hell. I would have carried you anyway." He laughed as he flipped on the light switch just inside Kathleen's door.

"Which way to the bedroom?"

"I'm fine, Mac. Please let me down here."

"I told you I'm not letting go till you're in bed. No arguments. Which way?"

"Down the hall, second door on the right."

Mac closed the door and walked down the hall, turning the light on when he reached Kathleen's bedroom. "Now I see why you didn't want me in here."

"What?" Kathleen opened her eyes and saw the disaster she had left behind the day before. "I suppose I never told you I hate housecleaning."

"Never mentioned a word about it. Of course, I never would have guessed," he teased.

"Put me down, please."

"Well, ma'am. Guess I don't have much choice. I don't see a clean spot anywhere on that bed of yours."

In spite of her weakness, Kathleen managed to jab him in the chest with her elbow as he set her on the floor. "Stop teasing. I suppose you don't have any faults?"

"They're too numerous to mention." He removed his arm, which supported Kathleen, but no sooner had he let go than she wilted, her legs unable to support her. Mac gathered her against him in one arm, grabbed the edge of the bedspread with his free hand, and pulled it off the bed, along with the array of clothing scattered on top.

"I'm sorry."

"There's nothing to feel sorry about. You're sick, that's all." He lifted her onto the bed, removed her tennis shoes and socks, and reached for the button on her jeans.

Kathleen grabbed his hand, but she didn't have enough strength to squeeze.

Mac sat beside her and pressed a kiss to her blazing forehead. "I'm going to see you soon, anyway. Let me make you comfortable." He moved her hand, released the button, and opened the zipper. He carefully pulled down the jeans, holding her silk panties so they wouldn't slide down along with the denim. He had imagined for weeks what she looked like unclothed, and it was only the heat of her body that kept his thoughts in tow. He wanted to make her comfortable, wanted to cool her fever, wanted her well so he could remove her clothes again with other thoughts in mind.

She closed her eyes, no longer concerned that Mac's hands tugged at her jeans. His fingers cooled her skin as they brushed across her legs. She wanted him to press them to her face, to cool the burning that made her weak.

His fingers clumsily unfastened the buttons of her shirt and, sliding his hands under her shoulders, he lifted her gently so he could pull the fabric away. Her skin burned everywhere, quite similar, but oh, so different from the way he burned as he released the hooks of her bra. As much as he wanted to look, he tucked the sheet under her chin before he removed the lacy support. His fingers swept through her hair, pushing it off her neck.

His touch felt so good, so cool, She wanted him to keep his fingers at the back of her neck forever. And then he touched her cheeks, her eyes, with his lips. They, too, cooled her burning skin. She felt the shift of his body on the bed, felt him stand up.

"Don't go," he heard her whisper.

He looked down at her red, tired eyes. "I'm not going anywhere, sweetheart. Just close your eyes and try to sleep. I'm going to get a cool washcloth for your forehead. Maybe we can get this fever to go away."

Kathleen closed her eyes, and slept.

Buzz!

Kathleen rolled over and slapped the snooze button on her alarm clock. "Oh, God. I don't want to get up."

"You're not getting up even if you want."

Kathleen's eyes flew open. She sat up much too quickly, then grabbed her head at the dizziness she felt. Then she sensed Mac beside her, pushing her down, tucking the sheet beneath her chin.

She stared at the man who stood at her bedside with Julie's *Beauty and the Beast* beach towel wrapped around his hips. Sick as she was, she stared at his stomach, the stomach she had imagined touching so many times. Flat, muscular, just as she had dreamed. No—better than she dreamed.

His cool fingers touched her forehead. "You've been asleep almost twenty-four hours, but you've still got a fever. Do you feel up to eating? Maybe something to drink?"

Kathleen shook her head. A drop of water dripped down his chest from his shower-dampened hair. She followed it with her eyes as it raced between his ribs, over his stomach, and disappeared into the hollow of his navel. He smelled of her strawberry shampoo and soap, and she doubted any man could wear a *Beauty and the Beast* beach towel the way he did.

She turned her head to meet his eyes. He breathed deeply and seemed to hold his breath for an eternity, his jaw clenched, his eyes masked in a look she didn't understand.

"No one's ever looked at me that way," he whispered.

Kathleen allowed her eyes to wander again to the towel. Her look spoke volumes. She wanted him, plain and simple. Why did she have to be so sick? She wanted the towel to drop. She wanted Mac to join her in bed. But she could hardly lift her arms; how could she enjoy everything she wanted to feel the first time they made love?

"I like your wardrobe," she said with a weak grin.

He bent his reddened face and examined the towel he wore. "Is it the towel you like, or this dashing fellow holding the pretty bouquet?" he asked, pointing to the Beast.

"Umm. I much prefer the beast wearing the towel."

His eyes closed and he inhaled again, running his fingers through his hair. "God, Kathleen. Do you have any idea what you're doing to me?"

"Possibly the same thing you're doing to me. Here I am lying on my deathbed, and you have the nerve to parade around in front of me in a damp towel that leaves absolutely nothing to my imagination. No wonder I have a fever."

"Serves you right. How do you think I felt undressing you last night?"

"I didn't want you to undress me. Besides, you led me to believe you were being gallant and sympathetic. I had no idea you'd enjoy doing it."

Mac sat on the edge of the bed, bent over Kathleen, an elbow on each side of the pillow supporting her head. He kissed her warm forehead, the tip of her nose, her pale cheeks. "Let me tell you something," he whispered, gazing into eyes only inches from his. "Never in my life have I felt closer to anyone than I did last night. I'd like to tell you I felt nothing when I removed your clothes. But I did. I feel something every time I touch you, every time I see you."

Buzz!

"Damn that alarm clock," Mac cursed, pulling away from Kathleen to shut it off.

She laid her hand against his arm. "I have to get up."

"No. You have to stay in bed."

"But I have a press conference this morning."

"I'm doing the press conference."

Kathleen stared at him in disbelief. "You can't do my press conference."

"I can and I am. You're too sick to get out of bed."

Kathleen used his arm to pull herself up. "You hate *Success*. How can you possibly say one nice word?"

"It may be your magazine, but it's my company. Do you think I'd sabotage something that's going to make money?"

She smiled, ran her fingers around his neck, and laid her head on his chest. "Did you hear what you just said?"

"Of course. I said I wouldn't sabotage the magazine."

"No, that's not exactly what you said. First, you called it *my* magazine. Second, you said it's going to make money."

"A slip of the tongue," he teased.

"You *do* believe in it, don't you?"

"Believe in it? No." He took her shoulders and lowered her to the pillow. "I believe in you."

CHAPTER

SIXTEEN

Mac sat in his office with Kathleen's speech to the press before him. He penciled out words here and there, adding his own touches. He read it over and over, then wadded it up and tossed it into the trash can across the room.

He pressed a button on his telephone, and within moments the door to his office opened and Grace walked in.

"Are the press here yet?" Mac asked.

"Yes, sir. They're waiting in the boardroom."

He looked at his watch. "I still have fifteen minutes, don't I?"

"If you were Ms. Flannigan, sir, you'd have fifteen minutes. If they know you're speaking, they'll stay longer."

"Thanks, Grace. Ask Lynn Miller to start her presentation first, and tell the press I'll be making the closing statements."

"Yes, sir." She started for the door, then turned back to Mac. "Do you know what you're going to say?"

"I haven't the faintest idea."

"I have a portfolio Ms. Flannigan put together about the magazine. Perhaps it might help?"

"Something I haven't seen?"

"I'm not sure, sir. I told her I liked her ideas, and she asked me to take a look at what she had planned for the future."

"And what did you think about her plans?"

"They're wonderful, sir. She's very creative."

"Hmm. Bring me the portfolio and tell Lynn to get started. Tell her to stall till I get there."

"Yes, sir."

Mac walked into the boardroom as Lynn made her last announcement. For years he had let his public-relations people handle the press, preferring to stay in the background. But this press conference was different. He wanted to do it for Kathleen.

"Ladies and gentlemen," he addressed the assemblage from the elevated podium at the end of the room. "I know Ms. Miller has done an outstanding job filling you in on the ins and outs of *Success*. Now I'd like to tell you what you don't know.

"*Success*, like any other magazine, is a collaborative effort of many talented people. The staff of *Success* have put their heads together to bring to the public stories and features on today's hottest issues—women's issues, issues that are often overlooked in magazines directed to the successful people of this world.

"Most of you have known me for years. I rarely single out individuals, because I believe it's the contributions of all the individuals at McKenna Publishing who have made this company prosper. But the woman behind *Success* has put her heart and soul into its production. The innovative ideas of its creator, Kathleen Flannigan, will make *Success* prosper where other magazines of this type have failed, or merely survived.

"Ms. Flannigan fought me on several issues—things I knew would never work. Whoever heard of Saks Fifth Avenue advertising in the same magazine as WalMart? Well, Kathleen Flannigan made it work. Did you think Barbara Walters was the only one who could get an interview with Barbra Streisand? Wrong. Kathleen Flannigan brought Ms.

Streisand together with a group of acting students starving for success. The picture is on the premier issue. Read the article for yourself and hear Ms. Streisand's candid comments about the triumphs and tragedies of success.

"Putting together a successful magazine requires the talents of innovative editors, writers, artists, advertising execs, and the behind-the-scenes people who make sure the bills are paid, letters are typed, and appointments are made. But more than that, it needs the determination, perseverance, and enthusiasm of a person who believes in the magazine's concept and who can infect the entire staff with the same determination, perseverance, and enthusiasm.

"Ms. Flannigan is that type of person. Unfortunately, she couldn't be here today, or you would have been infected too. You've all been given advance copies of *Success*. Read them. Examine them. I'm anxious to see your reviews.

"Thank you for coming."

"Excuse me, Mr. O'Brien. Will you accept questions from the press?"

Mac looked into the eyes of Morris Anderson of *The Tattler*. A question from Morris could lead to trouble, but the rest of the press seemed anxious for a question-and-answer period. "All right, Morris. Fire away."

"Is Kathleen Flannigan the woman your picture was taken with at the Plaza, and is she the same woman you've been seen with on several occasions since?"

"Yes." Mac didn't feel the need to say anything more. He waited for the next question.

"Your speech touted Ms. Flannigan as a savior. Is it the magazine you like or Ms. Flannigan?"

Mac laughed, leaning over the podium toward the press. He didn't need the microphone. His voice came across deep and resonant. "You used to work for me, didn't you, Morris?"

"Yes, I did."

"Then you know I'm very verbal about my likes and dislikes. Yes, I like Kathleen Flannigan. That's a personal thing between her and me. As for the magazine, I'll go on record to say I did not like the idea, but Ms. Flannigan fought me every step of the way and I gave in because nearly every idea she has developed for this company in the past ten years has been a success. I read this magazine, cover to cover. It's good. It's damn good. I suggest you read it cover to cover, too."

"Mr. O'Brien," a voice called from the third row.

"Yes, Dorothy," Mac acknowledged the representative from *Womankind* magazine.

"Don't you feel the market is already saturated with women's magazines? And how are you going to make this one succeed when so many others are losing circulation?"

"Yes, the market is saturated," Mac stated, "but have you noticed where many of those magazines are found? On the bottom shelf, in the back row at the grocery store. Like I've said several times today, it takes perseverance and ingenuity to bring a magazine to the forefront. Ms. Flannigan has worked with our marketing people and secured a position for *Success* right next to *People*, *Woman's Day*, and *Family Circle*—right there at eye level at the checkout counters at the grocery stores. We've got full-page ads running in major magazines, and we've done a nationwide mailout seeking subscriptions. *Success* has the backing of McKenna Publishing, which has the respect of the industry, and I fully intend to make sure it succeeds.

"By the way, Dorothy. I've read your stuff. It's good. Really good. I could use your talents at McKenna. If you're interested, give me a call. I'll interview you personally.

"Are there any more questions?" Mac looked around the room. No hands appeared, but Dorothy had a grin on her face.

"Did you have another question, Dorothy?"

"I'll ask it during my interview."

Mac laughed. "Thanks, again, for coming today. Have a good afternoon."

"How did it go?" Kathleen asked when Mac walked through the door, arms laden with bags from the corner deli and a bouquet of fresh-cut flowers.

"You're awfully animated for a sick person." He dropped the bags on Kathleen's nightstand. "Do you have a vase I can put these in? Thought they might brighten up the room."

"In the kitchen, over the sink."

"Umm, the kitchen. Another disaster area."

"Mac!" she yelled, throwing a pillow at his back as he walked toward the bedroom door.

"Save your energy." He tossed the words over his shoulder.

"Why?"

Mac stopped in the doorway and turned around. "Because you have a magazine to run."

"Is that all?" Kathleen asked in her most seductive yet feverish voice.

"I want you out of bed so I can take you back to bed. And I have other games in mind besides nursemaid."

"Umm."

"I'm going to get a vase. I hope you put a nightgown on while I was gone. I'm getting awfully tired of pulling up that sheet."

"Get the vase, Mac. I'll show you what's under the sheet when you get back."

"Promises. Promises."

He rummaged through the shelf and found a tall, clear glass vase behind wicker baskets and a popcorn popper. He filled it with water, stuck in the bouquet, then surveyed the disaster Kathleen called a kitchen. What the hell, he laughed, and proceeded to fill the sink with hot water, dirty dishes, and detergent. I've got nothing better to do while Kath's on the mend, he laughed to himself. Might as well try my hand at dishwashing.

He whistled a tune as he went back to the bedroom, carrying the unarranged vase of flowers. "For you, my dear," he said with a bow.

"Why, thank you, my beast." She pressed her fingers to her aching head and lay back down on the pillow.

"Still not feeling well, are you?"

"No, unfortunately."

"Maybe you're just trying to avoid my advances?"

"When I feel better, you can have your way with me."

"I'll take you up on that. I've got our getaway weekend all planned."

"Don't forget I have to pick Julie up on Sunday."

"I haven't forgotten. Now, do you want to know about the press conference?"

"Yes. How did it go?"

"I told them you're my girl and they'd better say good things about your magazine."

"I don't believe you."

"Okay, I told them you're a better editor than you are a housekeeper. Do you know you have a pile of dirty dishes in that kitchen, some of them growing mold?"

Kathleen rolled her eyes. "I don't have a maid like some people I know. I have me, myself, and I, and I didn't plan on having you sleeping and eating here, or I would have cleaned house."

He sat on the bed, smoothing Kathleen's hair back from her face. "I'm teasing, sweetheart. I don't care about the dishes or the clothes on the floor. I'll get you a maid if you want one."

"Hush." She put a finger to his lips. "I don't want you to get me a maid. I'm perfectly happy the way things are. I'm just not in the mood for teasing. My head hurts, my muscles ache, and I really want to know what happened at the press conference today."

He kissed the backs of her fingers. "You have nothing to worry about. It went great."

"And the speech? I worked on it for ages. I hope you didn't have to make many changes."

"I didn't use your speech."

"*What?*" She closed her eyes and pulled her hand from his. "You didn't have time to write something new. What did you do? Go in there cold?"

Mac nodded. "Grace gave me a portfolio of yours."

"She didn't. That was private."

"It was wonderful stuff. I especially liked your notes about the arrogant male. I hope there's a happy ending to the story."

"You arrogant—"

He silenced her with his lips. He felt resistance at first, then she relaxed, giving in to his warmth and gentleness. It lasted only long enough to calm her, then he pulled away. "You're too sick to make love. Quit enticing me."

"Believe me, Mac, when I get well, I have every intention of getting even."

"I hope so. I truly hope so."

CHAPTER

SEVENTEEN

Mac's words had rung true about the press conference. It had gone great, and the word was out on the street that *Success* would be one of the top ten periodicals within the year. By Thursday, when Kathleen struggled to work, her calendar was filled with appointments for people wanting, begging, to see her, each hoping for a chance at a featured article in one of the initial issues. Advertisers sought space rather than being pursued. And the First Lady had invited her for lunch with a small group of other successful women.

Heaven couldn't be much better than this.

Or could it? In exactly five minutes McKenna O'Brien would knock on her door, and they would drive off to the little piece of paradise he had rented in the woods. That, she knew, was the epitome of bliss.

Nearly everything she would need for their short overnight trip was packed. He had wanted to leave Friday, but she couldn't pull herself away from the office—too many things demanded her attention. He settled for eight A.M. Saturday, and she knew from experience, if he said eight, he didn't mean eight-oh-one.

She gave the bathroom one last check and threw toothbrush, toothpaste, and other essentials into a bag. The *Beauty and the Beast* towel hung over a chrome bar, neatly folded, just as Mac had left it. Never before had her apartment looked so orderly. Those first two days, while she slept, he had cleaned. It amazed her to hear him whistling a tune, to see him with feather duster in hand, bustling around her apartment. It also lightened her heart, for in a matter of weeks the man she had longed for had suddenly become a man she could love.

From a box imprinted *Saks*, she lifted the delicate white satin negligee, hugging it to her chest before carefully laying it on top of the other items in her suitcase. Tonight would be special. Tonight would be magic. She longed to slip the gown over her body, to see Mac's eyes when she appeared before him, ready, desirous, willing to be his.

She heard his knock, put her hand to her chest, and felt the strong, erratic beat of her heart. Would there ever come a time when the mere thought of him wouldn't send her into a dizzying spin? Surely when they were old and gray and sitting side by side in rocking chairs her heart would calm, but she was positive even then she would desire him just as much as she did at this very moment.

She released the chain lock, the dead bolt, and turned the knob. He stood before her looking like a god—tall, masculine, and heaven-sent—and she knew as sure as the sun rises and falls that her eyes gave away every lusty thought in her head.

He looked at the woman before him, the tight blue jeans, a bit worn at the knees, the scuffed cowboy boots, the pink T-shirt, and he knew he'd never seen anyone so warm and generous and bright and—perfect. Not the ravishing beauty today that she had been the night of the ball, but an older, wiser version of the captivating and beguiling innocent he had longed for years ago. Once again he beheld the woman who had so thoroughly charmed him, and he never wanted that woman to leave.

"So, is this the woman the First Lady wants to meet?"

"Can you believe it?" Her voice raised an octave. "Me? Kathleen Flannigan. The rancher's daughter from Corvallis, Montana."

"Yes, you. The rancher's daughter from Corvallis, Montana, and you, the intelligent, successful creator of what's going to be the hottest magazine to hit the market since *People*."

"Do you mean it?"

"Yes, I mean it. But your head's starting to swell from all the attention. Let's grab your bag and leave civilization before you're too caught up in the excitement and forget to come back down to earth."

"You're happy with the way things have turned out, aren't you? You've seen what we've got so far. You do like it, don't you?"

Yes, he liked it. No, he didn't like the way things had turned out. How could he talk her into settling down now? How could he ask her to marry him and give up the glory she was so obviously reveling in? "Does my opinion matter that much?"

"Yours is the most important."

"More important than the press? The advertisers? The First Lady?"

"Well"—she grinned—"I am just a little bit excited about the First Lady's opinion."

"Actually, the most important opinion is your own. You feel good about what you've accomplished. That should stand on its own."

"It does."

"Then my opinion doesn't matter." And then he said words he didn't really mean. "I suppose we're going to have to discuss a promotion one of these days?"

She grabbed her jacket from the back of the couch, handed Mac her suitcase, and tucked her arm around his. "No talk of promotions today. No talk of business. My gift to you for taking care of me all week is a day of me being just plain old Kathleen, the rancher's daughter."

"Thank you. You'll never know how much I wanted to hear those words."

Three hours later they stopped in front of the cottage Mac hoped would be the perfect spot for their magical weekend alone. Merry said she had found the perfect spot for a getaway. No telephone poles, no electric wires, in fact, nothing seemed to connect the outside world to this dwelling, which looked like a Swiss chalet. Sitting behind the wheel of the Mercedes, he took a moment to survey the surroundings—pink and red geraniums in planter boxes and frilly white lace curtains adorned the windows. Painted cement deer stood in welcome amidst the wildflowers growing up in profusion along the cobblestone walk, which led from the gravel drive to the ivy-covered arch over the front door. Definitely not a man's house, but a place to capture the heart of a romantic woman.

Kathleen watched the many expressions crossing Mac's face as his hands gripped the steering wheel. What could he possibly be thinking? Maybe the same thing as she? Alone at last. No need to worry about interruptions or propriety, just the two of them. Time to talk, to share their feelings, and, perhaps, to explore the overwhelming emotional bond that surrounded them.

"It's beautiful." She lay a hand on his leg, feeling the tensing of his muscles at her touch. Since the morning he had stood before her in that damp, clinging towel, she had longed to touch his body, every inch of it. She hoped it wouldn't be long.

"Should we see if it looks as good inside as it does out?" she asked.

"Let's go."

They exited the vehicle and met at the cobblestone walk. Hand in hand, slowly, somewhat apprehensive, they walked to the entryway. He put the key in the lock, turned the knob, and pushed the door open to be greeted by a sight straight out of a storybook. A massive rock fireplace, with logs stacked inside as though a fire might be needed. Overstuffed chairs one could get lost in. Hand-carved wooden knickknacks painted with colorful scrolls, leaves, and hearts lined the shelves. An adult-size rocking horse stood in a corner, its face beckoning for a rider. And a ladder to the loft where a bed could be seen, piled with pillows and covered with a thick, downy comforter.

"Heaven has just gotten better," Kathleen whispered, her eyes wide and sparkling. "How did you find this?"

"My housekeeper. She seems to have a knack for such things."

"Oh, Mac. Thank her for me when you go home. This is wonderful."

"I may never go home," he said with a sly grin, then watched Kathleen roam the room, her slender fingers lightly touching the ceramic candlesticks on the table covered with a white linen cloth. She went to the mantel, picking up a small silver frame.

"Isn't this cute? Someone put a picture of Santa Claus in this one."

Mac chuckled. "Maybe he lives here."

She flashed him a hypnotic, laughing smile that caused his heart to race, made his manhood come alive. He needed fresh air, needed to escape before he threw her down on the floor and possessed her completely.

"I'll get the bags from the car while you explore." He nearly ran from the house, stood outside and took a deep breath, letting the aroma of pine fill his senses. Hell. He was acting

like a teenager, losing control at the site of a beautiful woman. He heard her humming inside the cottage, heard her boots
moving lightly across the hardwood floor. Would he ever get
enough of her? Would there ever come a time when he
wouldn't want to touch her, hold her, lay with her?

He went to the car, opened the trunk, and removed two
overnight bags and the wicker basket Merry had packed for
their weekend alone. He gave no thought at all to the contents
of the basket, but let his mind drift to what might be inside
Kathleen's case. Silk. Lace. He remembered the panties he
had tried so hard not to look at that night he removed her
clothes. Pale pink with lace edging. A woman of contrasts.
The hard exterior she presented at work. The unsophisticated
beauty in blue jeans and cowboy boots. The woman from the
Plaza. So very different, yet somehow the same. Oh, how
he longed to strip her of the clothes and hold in his arms
the alluring woman whose tantalizing smile and captivating
voice fascinated him, bewitched him.

Kathleen opened the door. Mac seemed to have been gone
for hours instead of just minutes, but she hated letting him out
of her sight. He walked toward her, arms laden with bags and
basket. A gust of wind stirred the pine needles, and a dark
shadow pushed away the sunlight that had streamed down on
the cottage. A drop of rain fell on her nose, then the clouds
let forth an unexpected burst of rain.

Mac ran for shelter, and Kathleen closed the door behind
them, barely escaping the downpour.

"Looks like we may get to take advantage of those logs
in the fireplace," Mac said, dropping the bags and carrying
the basket to the bar that separated the small kitchen from
the living area.

Kathleen walked up behind him, running a hand up his
back and resting it on his shoulder. "What kind of goodies
did your housekeeper pack?"

"Let's take a look." He opened the lid. "Mmm. Potato chips, chocolate chip cookies, fried chicken, potato salad."

"What's in the thermos?"

Mac unscrewed the lid. "Smells like hot apple cider."

"I don't see any wine or beer."

"She refuses to cater to my bad habits."

"Smart woman. Here," she said, moving in front of Mac. "Let me put this stuff away. Why don't you start the fire? It's getting rather chilly in here."

"I can warm you quite easily without a fire."

"I'm sure you can." Kathleen put her hands on his chest and gently pushed him away. "But you promised me a long, heart-to-heart talk this weekend, and I'm afraid if I rely on you to warm me up, we'll never have that talk."

"A man can try, can't he? Besides, I've already spilled my guts, and there's nothing left to talk about. I thought we could just wile away the hours making love."

She gave him her most beseeching look. "Start the fire, please."

He couldn't resist obeying her request.

She put the chicken and potato salad in the refrigerator, then rummaged through a cabinet and found a bowl for the chips and a plate for the cookies. Setting the cookies aside for the time being, she dumped the chips into the bowl and carried them into the living room, sat down on the couch, and watched Mac moving pieces of kindling around with the poker, his handsome, thought-filled face illuminated by the fire.

It was shortly after noon, but the sunshine had faded with the onslaught of clouds, and only the area around the fireplace was bathed in light. He put the poker back in its holder, stood, and held his hands out toward the heat of the flames, flexing his shoulders and the muscles across his back, unaware that Kathleen sat behind him, admiring the view.

He turned, slowly, looking toward the kitchen where he thought she would be. And then his eyes lowered, meeting hers, and he nearly blushed when he read the expression on her face. Desire. Need. Anticipation. All rolled into one.

"Help me with my boots?" she asked and stuck a leg toward him. He grasped the heel and pulled. She wiggled her toes as he held the boot in his hands, staring at her thick socks and jeans-covered leg. "The other one, please?"

Not even Coquette could have teased so effectively with stocking-covered feet. How the hell did she expect him to keep his hands off her when every movement she made sent his mind into erotic fantasy?

He pulled off the other boot, set them both on the floor at the end of the couch, and sat in a chair across from her.

"You don't want to sit beside me?"

"No. I'm perfectly fine right here." He reached for the bowl of potato chips and grabbed a handful. "Would you like some?"

"Later. Right now I want to talk." She curled her feet under her on the couch, the warmth of the fire finally reaching out to her.

"You look so serious." He munched on a potato chip.

"I am. I've been keeping something from you, something I should have told you that night in the gazebo."

His brows knit together. What could she tell him? He didn't want to know about Julie's father. He fought the lump in his throat. "I'm listening."

"I have to start by telling you how much you hurt me when you went to Europe."

"We already talked about that, Kath."

"I know." He moved to the couch where she sat and snugged up next to her. "I just want to reinforce it in your brain, because I don't want you to leave me again. And, now, I want to thank you for leaving."

"You're not making sense. Why do you want to thank me?"

"Because if you hadn't gone, I wouldn't have Julie."

He tensed. "Don't thank me for that, Kath. And you don't have to feel compelled to tell me what happened."

Kathleen laughed. "But I'm going to tell you anyway."

"I'm not the least bit interested in who you slept with."

"Shut up while you're ahead, Mac, and just listen. I never had an affair with your dad. I didn't have an affair with anyone. McKenna Publishing employees don't have time for extracurricular activities."

"I haven't forgotten the man's role in conception, Kath. Have you?" Mac teased, remembering her words to him.

"No. But maybe you've forgotten about adoption."

The grin on his face disappeared completely. "You mean you've let me believe all this time that—"

"I haven't *let* you believe anything. You never asked. Everyone else knew, even your precious Ashley. But you were too damn stubborn to take the time to learn the truth for yourself."

"Okay, I'll quit being stubborn."

"I doubt it."

Again he grinned. "Tell me about Julie. I want to know."

Mac wrapped an arm around Kathleen and she nestled her head into the comfort of his shoulder.

"Julie's mother was a friend from high school. She came here to live with me. She was a model and just getting successful when she found out she was pregnant. She didn't want to get married, and she didn't want a baby. We talked about all her choices, but too much time went by and her choices narrowed. I watched her getting bigger and bigger every day." Kathleen closed her eyes, remembering how she had wished she was the one carrying the baby. "I got so caught up in what was happening, the next thing I knew I was looking at baby clothes and furniture, and then I knew I wanted her child."

"Is she still in New York?"

"No. We didn't keep in touch."

"Does Julie know?"

"Yes."

Slowly he reached out for her hand, pulled it to his lips, and held it there for what seemed to Kathleen like an eternity. "It seems like I'm always asking you to forgive me."

"Promise you'll quit making assumptions."

"I'll try. I'd never purposefully hurt you. I love you too much."

Love. Oh, how long she had wanted to hear that word. "I love you, too."

She looked at him with those startling blue, tear-filled eyes that grabbed his soul. She was so headstrong and beautiful, and he doubted there would ever be a peaceful moment in their lives. But he had already wasted too many years of his life, and he wouldn't waste one more moment. He pulled her to him with all the strength and desire of a man long denied. But he held back. There was more, so much more he wanted from this woman than just making love. He wanted her completely—her heart, her soul, her life.

Taking her face in his hands, he looked into those azure eyes that had haunted him for so long. "Marry me, Kath. Marry me and I'll give you everything humanly possible."

She slid her fingers around his hands, clasping them tight, and pulled them to her heart. "What about Julie?"

"I've always wanted children. I'll just start with one a little older. She'll be my daughter—nothing less."

"I think she'll love you as much as I do."

"Does that mean you'll marry me?"

She nodded.

He swept her into his arms and brought his lips to hers. The heat of the blazing fire was nothing compared to his searing kiss. He slowly sank to his knees on the rug in front of the hearth, laid her down, and grabbed a pillow to place under her head. "The last time I undressed you I thought I would die from frustration. This time's going to be so much more pleasant."

"Then hurry, please." She lifted her arms, and he tugged the T-shirt out of her jeans and pulled it over her head. Her fingers found the snaps of his shirt and ripped them apart.

He knelt above her, his eyes ablaze with desire, his blood nearing the boiling point. He pulled the shirt out of his pants and removed it, tossing it to the back of the couch. Leaning over, balancing his body over hers with both arms, he bent toward her, slowly, until she reached out and clasped her hands around his neck and pulled his lips down to meet hers.

His kisses had always been heaven, but this kiss was sheer ecstasy. He didn't close his eyes, and she didn't want him to. She wanted to read each thought as it crossed his face. And she liked what she saw. Never in her life did she think she could be loved so well, yet McKenna O'Brien was giving her more than love, he was giving her himself.

Hot, ravishing kisses coursed from her lips to her neck, to the swelling above the lace of her bra. His fingers nimbly released the hook at the front, and he pulled it away. His head raised and he looked down at the woman he held. A picture of perfection, her skin pink from the heat of the fire and his love. With skillful fingers he traced her collarbone, letting them travel again to the swell of her breasts. He touched her. Soft, warm skin, so tender and smooth. He sucked in his breath, like a dying man begging for one last moment of life. And then his hands left her breasts, circled her arms, and he stood, pulling her with him.

Their mouths met, their lips opening, tasting one another, drinking in and savoring the beauty of the moment. As if in sync, their hands explored while their mouths feasted. Their fingers sought and found, and then released the clasps of the jeans covering their most sought-after and desired parts, and with little effort, they each stepped out of the last barrier to their lovemaking.

They stood back and looked at each other, their eyes moving from head to toe, perusing with delight the naked splendor of their partner.

She touched him, circling her hands over his chest, feeling the hard, fast beating of his heart that matched her own.

He touched her, a hand on the side of each breast, his fingers tracing the dark pink of her nipples. Oh, how good the softness of her skin felt on his hands.

They smiled at each other, at the joyful wonder of their love. And then he lowered her again to the floor, to the pillows where she could rest her head as he tasted her breasts. His tongue played with their peaks. He had nearly forgotten how good such a small part of foreplay could feel. His lips and tongue strayed lower until he felt her muscles tense. Pulling himself away from what he wanted so badly, he looked into her hesitant eyes. "I want every part of you Kath. Please. Don't deny me this."

She couldn't help the tensing of her muscles, but she let him delve into her innermost being. Never had anyone touched her this way, his tongue teasing, his lips and mouth tasting, seeking, sending her senses to the peak of rapture. She didn't want him to stop, wanted him to touch her this way forever. And then, as if he knew she couldn't take any more, he raised himself above her, looking down into her love-filled eyes when he entered her, filling her with his hot desire.

Tight. Warm. Oh, the heavenly feeling of being inside her. Deep, so very deep. He couldn't seem to get enough. He wanted to become one with her, to hold her this way until the end of time. More than passion, more than desire. He wanted to kiss her, but even more, he wanted to look into those beautiful, azure eyes as they traveled to heaven and beyond. He wanted to know that she loved him, loved him the same way he loved her. Together, perfectly matched, one in sync with the other, they reached the pinnacle of their love, and they rejoiced in their cries of fulfillment.

Lying side by side, he brushed wisps of dampened hair away from her face, kissed her temples, held her close, and in the light and warmth of the fire, they fell asleep.

CHAPTER
EIGHTEEN

"I'm starving."

"You're always hungry," Mac teased Kathleen, pulling on the socks he had found shoved in a corner of the couch.

"You've worn me out, McKenna O'Brien. And you haven't been gentleman enough to feed me in the last six hours."

"Oh, but you've fed me, my love, and nothing ever tasted so good."

She tossed a pillow from her sitting position on the floor and hit the side of his head, then covered her face when she thought he might throw it back. Instead, he stood before her, grinning his most wicked and lascivious grin, and managed to look just as wonderful partially clothed as he had stark naked.

"All right, I'll feed you. Don't leave."

He went into the kitchen, and Kathleen watched his every step. Oh, how she loved the man. Never in her life had she felt such wonderful abandonment as she had in his arms. Six hours of touching, exploring, tasting, finding sensitive spots, and trying out new and original ways to delight each other, until they pushed themselves to the brink and had to come up for air. The next time they came together, she planned to be in that satin-and-lace gown she had so carefully packed in her bag, but for now they needed to talk of things to come, their hopes, and their dreams.

"A penny for your thoughts?" He held a plate piled high with food and stared down into her eyes.

"It will take a lot more than a penny to make me divulge my secrets."

"How about a bite of chicken?"

"Mmm, you've won me over." She reached for the plate, but he pulled it away. "Oh, Mac. I'm hungry. Don't tease."

"I plan on feeding you, but I thought we could find a better place to eat than on the floor."

"At the table?"

"No. I thought I'd save that for later, in the middle of the night, when I'm tired of bed."

"Stop it!"

"Okay, how about the rocking horse?"

"You're out of your mind."

"I've been looking at it for hours. It's big enough for two."

"You *are* out of your mind. I'm not getting on that horse."

"Please?" He tried so hard to fight the laughter ready to burst from inside, and somehow managed to keep the little-boy look on his face.

"Oh, all right."

She started to climb on the horse when Mac stopped her. He shook his head. "The other way."

"You mean facing backward?"

"Of course. We'll face each other and share this wonderful plate of food."

"This is crazy, but I suppose if I'm going to get anything to eat . . ."

"That's my girl." He climbed on after her, pulling her legs over his thighs so she would lean back against the horse's neck. "Now, isn't that comfortable?"

She shook her head and laughed. "Can't we do anything without my legs being wrapped around you?"

"Hush." He picked up a chicken leg and held it to her mouth. She took a bite, and he took one after her, savoring the taste, and reveling in the feel of having her so near.

"Tell me about Julie."

"She's adorable. Long black hair, straight as can be, and big brown eyes. She's got a pudgy little face and dimples on both sides of her mouth. She likes Big Bird, Cookie Monster, and Beauty and the Beast. And I can't wait for her to come home tomorrow."

"You miss her?"

She nodded, taking the fork out of his hand and offering him a bite of potato salad. "My parents love her and I've often thought it would be a good idea to move back to Montana. She'd have a much better life growing up there than in New York."

"Why do you think that?"

"Cleaner air. More room to run and play."

"Now she'll have McKenna House. And if you want, we'll get a place in Montana, too."

She leaned forward and kissed him, the horse rocking slowly beneath her legs. "I'd like that."

"You know what I'd like?"

"What?"

"To dance with you."

She laughed and he nearly melted into her eyes, her smile.

"Are you tired of the horse already?"

"No, I just felt this strange compulsion to hold you in my arms and waltz around this room."

"Did you see that old gramophone?"

"Where do you think I got the idea? How about if I crank it up while you change into something, um, more comfortable?"

"I thought you'd never ask."

He climbed off the horse and helped her down. She found her suitcase and went to the door of the small bathroom, turned, and looked back at the man she was hopelessly in love with. "I'll only be a moment."

"Make sure it's only one moment. I don't think I could stand it if you were gone much longer."

She closed the door behind her, and Mac went to the gramophone. He'd never used one before, but had seen them operated in many old movies. Turn the crank and put the needle on the record. Please work, he begged the machine. He turned the crank over and over again, and when he heard the door to the bathroom opening, he put the needle on the record.

He heard only scratching noises coming from the antique machine as he turned to look at his bride-to-be. The silky white fabric of her long, slim gown was more beautiful than the dress she had worn at the Plaza, more intoxicating than what she had worn to the ball. Both of those times he had thought she was the most ravishing woman on earth. Now he knew no one could equal her.

The scratching stopped and a mellow voice filled the room. He walked to the woman whose long auburn hair fell over her shoulders and curled at the rise of her breasts. He took her in his arms and kissed her lips, waltzing around the room to Bing Crosby's *White Christmas*, and all thoughts of disliking the holiday left forever. He would remember this moment for the rest of his days, the happiness he felt holding her close. He even thought it would be nice to celebrate Christmas every day of the year, if all of those days could be like this.

Except for their breathing and the strains of the song, all was quiet. Their eyes met and held, and when they neared the window, Mac looked out into the dark night sky and saw the light snow falling to the ground. "Look," he said, pulling her to a stop before the window.

"How odd. Snow in July."

He laughed. "My guardian angels at work."

"Oh, I think I like your guardian angels. Do they perform other miracles?"

"They brought us together."

"No. We were always meant to be."

Mac rolled over in the overstuffed mattress and pulled Kathleen into his arms. She opened her eyes and he moved a strand of hair away from her lips. "It's morning, sleepy-head."

She stretched and yawned. "I don't think I've ever slept in a bed so nice and warm and comfy."

"Maybe my being in the bed had something to do with that."

"Oh, maybe just a tiny bit."

He rolled onto his back and pulled her on top of him. "I like you this way."

"We do fit together rather well, don't we?"

"In every way imaginable. And I think we tried them all last night." He put his hands around her neck and pulled her mouth to his. "You taste wonderful, even in the morning."

"Good. I expect you to feel that way every morning for the rest of your life." She sat up, straddling his hips, and stared down at his unshaven face. "But for now, I hate to put an end to this, but we have to get back to the city."

"And interrupt what you just started?"

She looked at him questioningly, then felt the stirrings at his groin. "Mmm, maybe I can give you five more minutes."

He pulled her back to his chest, kissing her lips, teasing her tongue as he rolled over on top of her. "I have every intention of taking full advantage of those five minutes."

*   *   *

"So, what do you think about living at McKenna House? I've always thought it would be great to live there again."

They were halfway back to the city, driving along in the warm summer morning air. When they stepped out of the cottage, it was as though there had never been any rain, or any snow. Maybe they had imagined it all, but the cold, stormy weather had only enhanced their night. On their drive to the cottage, Kathleen had spent her time admiring the scenery. Now she only had eyes for the man behind the wheel.

She thought about living at McKenna House. It would be wonderful, especially for Julie. Fresh air, plenty of room to play. A grandmother close at hand. But it was a long drive from the city, and her job. "Maybe on weekends. I don't want to commute every day to work."

"Did you forget we're getting married?"

"Of course not."

"You don't plan on working once we're married, do you?"

She hadn't expected to hear those words. "Do you have a problem with that?"

"I just assumed . . ." He pulled over to the side of the road and stopped the car. "Look, let's not talk about it now. Let's not spoil the day."

But a damper replaced her lighthearted spirit. Mac didn't want her to work, he never had, he probably never would, and deep inside she had known he would ask her to quit. How could she have gotten so caught up in his love that she forgot this major problem? How could she ignore it now? Earlier, her thoughts had cried out an unconditional love, and she did love him. But she loved her work, too.

"Kath?" He lifted her chin with his fingers, letting his thumb trace her lips. Looking into her eyes he saw the hurt—the hurt he had caused, but all he wanted in life was a wife and children, someone to come home to at night. He'd given up so many things with Ashley, he didn't want to give them up again. "I told you I'm a selfish man. I don't want you to work. I want you at home. Can you understand my feelings?"

"No." She shook her head. "I can't understand your feelings any more than you can understand mine." She looked out the passenger window at the bright, sunny sky, but her day had been darkened.

"I want to understand. But I thought you'd enjoy staying home with Julie."

"I've tried to explain my feelings before. I love my work."

"What about Julie? What about me? Do you love us?"

"How can you ask that?"

"Because I want to know."

"I love Julie very much. We've done okay by ourselves for the last five years. She doesn't mind me working, in fact, I think it makes me a better mother. And I love you, too. But . . ." Tears ran slowly down her cheeks and she did nothing to stop them. "I've already proved to myself I can live without you. I don't want to, but I got by before, I can do it again."

"We don't have the same relationship now that we did back then. I don't want you to live without me. I don't want to live without you." He turned her face to his and saw the streaming tears. "I love you."

"I know. But I think we'd better rethink our plans to get married. I don't think it would work." She looked into his eyes, at the sorrow, at the tears at each corner. "Take me home, please."

It was a long, quiet drive back to New York. Mac pulled the car to a stop in front of Kathleen's building, grabbed her bag from the backseat, and started to open his door.

"Please, Mac. Don't come up with me. Let's end this here."

"Damn it, Kath. I don't want to end it."

"But I do. Please, let me have my way, just this once."

He listened to her words, but he didn't want any part of what he heard. He wouldn't let it end.

"Let me take you to pick up Julie."

She shook her head. "Listen to me, please. Last night was special and I'll never forget it. Can't we just say good-bye now, before we end up hating each other?"

"We'll never hate each other, and we can't say good-bye. You promised to marry me."

"I didn't promise to give up my job, and you told me once before you wouldn't compromise." She wiped the tears away from her face. "I'm not going to marry you. I'm going back to my old life. Just me and Julie."

"Are you saying there's no room left in your heart for me?"

She grabbed her bag and opened the door. "You'll always be in my heart. Always." She slammed the door, ran up the stairs and into her building, and Mac sat alone, lost, and the tears that had swelled in his eyes ran freely down his cheeks.

CHAPTER

NINETEEN

Mac entered his apartment, surprised at its warmth, its darkness. He switched on the lights and found it emptied of Merry's personal touches. The rocking chair was gone. So were the crocheted doilies, the afghans, the pictures of children.

A red envelope had been propped up on the mantel next to a photo of Mac's dad. With shaky hands, he opened the end and pulled out the letter.

My dearest McKenna, it read. *I leave with sadness, my child, for I have grown to love you as a son. Yet, there is joy in my heart, knowing you have found the woman of your dreams. True love is a rare and tender thing. It must be nurtured, and, above all, you must give of yourself and ask nothing in return. I will miss you, young man, but you will always be near to my heart. Merry.*

He paced the floor, reading and rereading Merry's note. *Ask nothing in return.* Those words reverberated in his head. He agonized over them.

He went to the kitchen and poured himself a glass of milk and carried it and the cookie jar back to the living room, and slouched in a big, cold leather chair. Where had he gone wrong? He wanted to marry Kathleen and give her everything—a beautiful home in the country where she would feel comfortable raising Julie; the time to enjoy Julie without the pressures of working. What more could he give?

But Merry's words weren't about what he could give. They said, *Ask nothing in return.* And he had. He had asked that she give up her job.

He thought about that. How would he feel if someone asked him to give up his job? It didn't take long for him to agonize over that possibility. He would give it up in a moment if he could have a wife and child. But he didn't love his work. It didn't give him joy and fulfillment. Not the way it did Kathleen. The First Lady wanted to have lunch with her. He couldn't forget the excitement in her eyes, the thrill of knowing she had accomplished a great feat and was to be rewarded with accolades from someone she respected. That meant the world to her.

She didn't complain about not having enough time with Julie. She didn't complain about anything, except that he wanted her to give up her job. She must be a good mother in spite of working probably sixty or seventy hours a week. He remembered the pictures on the refrigerator. Crayon drawings of a mother and her little girl in the park, swinging on swings, and they all said, *I love you, Mommy.* Magical words—I love you.

Hell! He wouldn't give up now, not when he had come so far. He would have Kathleen, and he would have Julie. But what could he do so everyone would be a winner?

Kathleen anxiously watched the passengers exiting from the ramp that connected the jet to the terminal, her eyes bloodshot and swollen from hours of crying for the love she had lost. Yet when the stewardess escorted the dark-haired little girl into the waiting arms of her mother, Kathleen beamed with joy. She grabbed Julie and swung her around in her arms, kissing her hair, her cheeks, and her forehead, then held her tight and wept with happiness.

"I missed you, Mommy."

"I missed you, too, sweetheart. My goodness. You look like you've grown a foot."

"Hello."

Kathleen spun around at the sound of Mac's voice, and tears instantly appeared at the corners of her eyes. "Hello."

"Mommy?" Julie put her little hands to her mother's face and whispered up close. "Who's that man?"

"My boss."

"A very dear friend," Mac corrected. "I'm McKenna O'Brien," he said, taking Julie's hand and gallantly kissing the backs of her fingers. "But you can call me Mac."

"Mommy says that's not polite. I'll call you Mr. O'Brien." She looked away from Mac and back to her mother. "Can we go home now?"

"Of course we can, sweetheart."

"I've got a limo outside. I thought it would be more comfortable than a taxi."

"Thank you, but we can get home on our own."

"I want to ride in a limo." Julie wiggled out of her mother's arms, and Kathleen stood her on the floor.

"Let's get your luggage," Mac said, taking Julie's hand. He looked at Kathleen, who stared back with saddened eyes. Julie tugged and Mac followed, heading swiftly to the baggage-claim area.

Kathleen walked behind, watching the big man and her tiny daughter strolling through the terminal, hand in hand, as though they had known each other forever, as though they belonged together. Maybe she should give up her work, for Julie, for Mac. A bond seemed to have formed the instant the two touched fingers, quite the same way it had when she had first seen his picture. Could she be selfish and keep them from sharing a happiness that may have been meant to be?

They retrieved the luggage and walked out of the bustling

terminal to the traffic-jammed street. The limo driver met them at the door and took the bags from Mac, and Kathleen watched as Julie instantly grabbed Mac's empty hand. They were linked together, a threesome, and Mac maneuvered them through buses and taxis to the waiting white limousine parked not far away.

They climbed through the open door into the back of the car, and Julie's eyes lit up. "There's a TV in here, Mommy. May I watch it?"

Kathleen looked at Mac for an answer.

"Of course. Here, let's see if we can find something good to watch." He picked up the remote control. "Do you know how to use this?"

Julie turned her head from side to side, examining the controller. "It's different from the one I have at home."

"Here, let me show you." He took it in his hand and, holding her index finger, pointed out the different buttons. "This says Volume, and this arrow turns the sound up, this one turns the sound down. And this says Channel. You can push this button until you find something you want to watch."

"Thank you, Mr. O'Brien."

Kathleen couldn't help but smile. "You seem to have a way with children."

"I'm much better with children than I am with adults."

"That's not true."

He reached out a hand and with his thumb wiped a tear from her cheek. "May I take you to lunch?"

She started to say no, then looked at Julie. She needed a father, and Mac wanted a child so badly. In less than a week *Success* would be on the newsstands. She would have had her moment of glory, her lunch with the First Lady. Maybe that was all she needed. Maybe she could turn the magazine over to someone new, let someone else continue her work. It hurt to think about that. But it also hurt to think about not spending the rest of her life with Mac.

"Lunch would be nice." She avoided his eyes, finding it much safer to look at Julie, to gather the little girl into her arms and hold her close.

"I'm going to take you and your mommy to lunch," he said to Julie. "Is there someplace you'd like to go?"

"Can we go to our special place?" she asked her mother.

"Oh, honey. I don't know if Mr. O'Brien would like it."

"I'll love it. Just tell me where."

"The zoo. Mommy takes me all the time, and we have hot dogs and cotton candy."

"Do you feed the animals, too?"

"No. They don't like hot dogs. Do you like the zoo?"

"I haven't been in a very long time. Will you show me around?"

"Sure. I like the tigers the best. But I'll show you the elephants and zebras and giraffes."

Kathleen interrupted. "Let's just make it a short trip today, honey. Mr. O'Brien had a very late night, and he'll probably want to get home early." Kathleen looked beseechingly at Mac.

He smiled. "Your mother's right, Julie. We'll have hot dogs and cotton candy, then take a quick peek at the tigers. Then I'd better head for home."

"Okay, Mr. O'Brien."

Julie turned back to the television while Mac asked the driver to take them to the zoo.

He reached out and took Kathleen's hand, holding it tight, but he felt nothing in return. Dear Lord, please, don't let me lose her now.

At the zoo Kathleen watched Julie lead Mac from the hot-dog stand to the tigers, then to a vendor selling ice cream. For the first time in ages, she didn't feel like eating, but watched Mac down several hot dogs and wipe mustard off

Julie's face with his napkin. He looked as though he were cut out for fatherhood. His face beamed as her little girl pointed out one delight after another, totally ignoring the idea about seeing only the tigers.

Four hours later Mac held Julie in his arms, her head resting on his shoulder, her eyes closed in sleep. "Maybe we'd better go home now," he said, looking sheepishly at Kathleen.

She swallowed the lump in her throat. How could she give up this man?

They rode quietly back to Kathleen's building, and Mac carried Julie until they reached her bedroom, the driver and Kathleen following behind with her luggage. Mac laid her down gently on the bed, removed her shoes and socks, and pulled the lightweight blanket up to her chin. Bending his large body, he leaned over and kissed her on the forehead.

Kathleen stood in the doorway and watched. Such a big man, and so tender. Just what Julie needed in her life. Just what she needed in hers.

He walked back into the living room and pulled Kathleen into his arms. "Don't worry. I don't plan to stay. I know you want to be alone." He kissed her forehead, just as he had kissed Julie's, only his lips lingered longer, and Kathleen felt the strong beat of his heart, the heavy, labored breathing.

"Could we have dinner tomorrow night? You, me, Julie?"

She shook her head. "I have to work late tomorrow. Maybe Tuesday?"

He smiled. It was a breakthrough. She did still want to see him. "Is Tuesday your lunch with the First Lady?"

She nodded. "So, don't expect me to be my normal, calm, highly in-control self."

"I prefer you out of control. Like last night. Remember?"

"I remember." She led him to the door, opened it, and he stepped just outside.

"Who's taking care of Julie tomorrow?"

"The sitter. She lives just down the hall."

"Oh. I thought maybe I could take her out for the day."

She laughed. "What would you do with a five-year-old?"

"I don't know. Wing it, maybe."

"What about work?"

"I'm the boss. I don't have to be there. That's why I hired people like you."

"I almost forgot." She leaned her head against the door-jamb and gazed into Mac's eyes, a wistful look on her face.

"What about tomorrow?" he asked.

"Oh, I don't know. She likes going to the sitter's."

"Maybe she'd like going out with me. I always thought I was a lot of fun to be with." He wiggled his eyebrows. "Think about it. I'll call you in the morning."

He kissed his finger and touched it to her nose. "I love you." He turned to walk away.

"Mac?"

He looked back. "Yes?"

"I love you, too."

He took a deep breath. Thank you, Lord.

Kathleen hesitated only a moment when Mac called the next morning. His voice sounded so imploring she couldn't say no to his request to take Julie out for the day. When she posed the question to Julie, the little girl beamed.

"The whole day with Mr. O'Brien?"

"Uh-huh. Would you like that?"

"Can he buy me ice cream?"

"Oh, sweetheart, I'm sure if you want ice cream, Mr. O'Brien will buy it for you."

"I like him, Mommy. Is he going to be my daddy?"

Julie's question took her by surprise. Oh, the innocence of

youth, whose eyes see so much more than adults could ever imagine. "I don't know, honey."

Mac arrived and whisked Julie away in his limousine while Kathleen insisted on taking the bus, as usual, to work. He didn't argue, just gave Kathleen a list of phone numbers for his mother, his attorney, and his doctor, "just in case."

"Well, young lady," Mac said, flipping through channels on the television. "How about a little *Sesame Street* to start off the morning?"

"Okay. Do you like Big Bird?"

"Of course. And Cookie Monster, too." He'd seen pictures of the characters, but didn't have the faintest idea what they were all about. But an hour later he was an avid fan, as the limousine drove around town, killing time until Mac was ready to stop for brunch.

They dined on Egg McMuffins and orange juice, then went window-shopping until they found a toy store to browse in. He tried out Super Nintendo. He was all thumbs, but Julie's skills amazed him. He purchased the video game to hook up at home, although he didn't own a television, then found Big Bird and Cookie Monster stuffed animals which he couldn't resist buying.

For lunch they had pizza with the works, except anchovies, which Julie absolutely refused, saying they were much too salty and not good for his health. They found an electronics store, and Mac bought a large-screen TV, a VCR, and a camcorder. At a video store he stocked up on a large assortment of old Disney movies, the Muppets, *The Little Mermaid*, and, of course, *Beauty and the Beast*.

They went to the zoo for ice cream, and Mac took movies on his new toy while Julie fed peanuts to the elephants.

He was in absolute heaven and didn't want the day to end, but forced himself to deliver Julie to her mother at precisely seven o'clock, just as he had promised.

"You don't look the least bit worn out," Kathleen said, then was assaulted with Julie's description of the day.

"Mac bought me Big Bird and Cookie Monster, and took pictures of me at the zoo. And he wants me to spend the day with him again tomorrow. Can I, Mommy?"

What could she say? How could she break Julie's heart?

"If Mr. O'Brien doesn't mind."

"Oh, he doesn't mind." Julie wrapped her arms around Mac's legs, her face the picture of innocence. "Do you?"

"Not in the least." Mac absently caressed Julie's shiny black hair while concentrating on Kathleen. "I had fun. I never imagined there was so much to do away from the office."

"Mommy?" Julie said, looking up to her mother's face.

"Yes, honey?"

"We're still going to have dinner with Mr. O'Brien tomorrow, aren't we?"

"I plan on it. Why?" She picked Julie up and brushed a lock of black hair behind her ear.

"Because he's going to take us someplace really fancy."

Kathleen looked at Mac. "How fancy?"

"Real fancy."

"But—"

"I know what you're going to say." He mimicked what he expected to hear. " 'But I don't have anything to wear!' "

She laughed. "You're right."

"The dress you wore at the Plaza will do quite nicely, thank you. As for this one"—he took Julie into his arms and swung her up in the air—"we're going shopping for dresses tomorrow."

"I can't let you do that." She looked horrified.

"And why not?"

"It's too expensive."

He gave her an odd look and shook his head. "Kathleen,

darling. I know you're not aware of this fact, but I'm not penniless. I can afford a dress."

"I know, but you shouldn't. I mean . . ."

"Please?"

How could she resist? Her daughter looked at her with big, dark brown eyes as if the man who held her was Santa Claus come to life. And Mac looked at her, too, with those smoky blue eyes that she wanted to look into for the rest of her life. "Okay. But you have absolutely no idea how to go about buying little girls' clothes."

"You'd be amazed how well we did when we went shopping today. Wouldn't she, kiddo?"

Julie nodded, and a knot formed in Kathleen's throat at the word *kiddo,* the same endearment her father used when he spoke to her.

Mac stayed only a few minutes longer, saying he had things to do, when, in truth, he was dead on his feet. Julie was still going strong, but he needed to head for bed. He had big plans for Tuesday.

He brought breakfast with him when he came for Julie in the morning, and tried to stay out of Kathleen's way as she moved frantically around the apartment, trying to find a missing shoe to go with the new suit she had bought the day before. Thoughts of lunch with the First Lady had kept her awake half the night; the other half she had lain awake thinking about how charming and gentle Mac had been with Julie the day before. Perfect father material.

Mac dug under the sofa while Kathleen stuck her hair back in its usual bun. He found the shoe and presented it to Kathleen, along with a gentle kiss on the cheek and a hug for good luck. Then he pulled the pins out of her hair and let it fall about her shoulders. "This is the way you should meet the First Lady. Don't hide your beauty, Kath."

She took his hand and pulled it to her lips. "This isn't the kind of thing you want your wife to be doing, is it?"

"How many wives get to run off for lunch with the First Lady? I'm proud of you."

A tear formed at the corner of her eye, and she nearly melted into his arms when he brushed it away. "That means more to me than lunch."

His smile widened. "Tonight you can tell us all about your day, and we'll tell you about ours, and we'll see who had the best time."

"I don't think we can compare the two. They're both pretty special."

"I suppose it depends on whose eyes you're looking through."

She touched his cheek. "You're sweet."

"Are you sure? You haven't tasted me in two days. I may be turning sour."

"Or getting sweeter."

"Would you like to try me out?"

"Don't tempt me." She grabbed her purse from the tabletop, kissed Julie good-bye, and went to the door. "I'll see you at seven?"

"Seven, straight up. Don't worry about getting Julie ready. I'll take care of that. Just put on your fancy dress and we'll do the town. The boss says you can sleep late tomorrow."

"Oh, if only it were that easy." She rushed out the door, and Mac longingly watched her run down the hall.

"Why does Mommy cry when she looks at you?" Julie asked, standing behind Mac, clutching Big Bird and Cookie Monster.

"Does she?"

Julie nodded.

"Well, sometimes people cry when they're happy. I think your mommy was happy about having lunch with the First

Lady, and about us having dinner together tonight. She missed out on all the fun yesterday, and I think she's happy she gets to join us this time around."

"She was crying last night after you left. I thought maybe you made her sad."

He picked Julie up and cradled her in his arms. "The last thing on earth I ever want to do is make your mommy sad. Or you, either."

"You make me happy. I like being with you."

"Thank you, sweetheart. I like being with you, too."

They started the day at Neiman-Marcus, looking for that really special five-year-old-little-girl dress, with shoes and purse and undies to match. Mac had them throw in a few extra items that Julie seemed to like, and then they went looking at furniture.

"You haven't seen my house here in New York," he said to Julie as they browsed through sofas and chairs, lamps and tables, and aisle upon aisle of accessories.

"What does it look like?"

"Pretty awful. Lots of black-and-white leather. And chrome and glass. I never really thought it suited me. Maybe you could help me pick out some things that you and I would like, and maybe your mommy, too."

Three hours later they had managed to completely redo Mac's apartment, everything but the office he had never let Ashley touch. He did away with the leather, glass, and chrome, replacing it with warm woods, tweeds, and plaids in forest green and shades of blue and rose. He made sure everything would be delivered within the week, and then he took Julie to look at bedroom sets, just to get an idea of what she would like if she could furnish her own room, too.

In the late afternoon they stopped at Mac's before picking up Kathleen. Mac gave Julie the run of the place while he got into his tux. When he came out of his bedroom, he found her sitting on the couch in his office, the teddy bear from Holly's beside her, and an old photo album open in her lap.

"Did you find something interesting?"

"A picture album. Is this you when you were a little boy?"

He sat down beside her. "Looks like me."

"Are these your mommy and daddy?" she asked, pointing to the man and woman standing on either side.

"Yes. That was taken in front of McKenna House, where my mother and grandmother live."

"Where does your daddy live?" She looked up at him, her dark eyes wide, waiting for an answer.

"He died and went to heaven."

"A long time ago?"

"Not too long after you were born."

"Mommy says when someone dies, someone else is born to take their place. Do you think I took your daddy's place?"

Mac had to force back his tears. "Yes, I think you did take my daddy's place." He pulled her into his lap and hugged her, smoothing back her hair, pressing a kiss to her forehead.

"Come on, little one. I think we'd better get you dressed or we're going to be late, and I don't think your mommy would be too happy with us."

He ushered her into the bedroom and pulled out all the underclothes they had purchased, and the pretty dress. "I can get dressed by myself," she stated. "But you might have to button me up."

"Okay. I'll be just outside if you need me."

She came out of the room ten minutes later and turned around, presenting her back to Mac so he could fasten the tiny buttons. He clumsily tied the bow, turned her around, and inspected her attire. "Perfect." He held out his hand, and she grabbed hold. "Shall we go?"

Julie grinned. "I wish you were my daddy, Mr. O'Brien."

"I wish I were, too, sweetheart. I wish I were, too."

Kathleen opened the door, looking even more stunning than she had that night at the Plaza. Mac and Julie came inside. "Isn't my dress pretty, Mommy?"

"Very lovely. Did you pick it out all by yourself?"

"No. Mr. O'Brien helped. He said he liked me in pink. I wanted blue, but I figured I'd get the one he liked."

Mac laughed. "You didn't tell me you wanted blue."

"It's her favorite color, Mac," Kathleen offered. "You'll learn in time."

"I have something for you before we go."

"Oh, Mac. You've already done too much."

"Hush." He pulled a long velvet box out of his pocket and opened it for Kathleen to see.

Her eyes widened, and the tears that had been so prevalent of late crept into their corners. "They're beautiful."

"I tried to match the bracelet, but I couldn't find the store. It's the funniest thing. I thought for sure I knew which alley I turned down the last time. But the store wasn't there."

"But look, Mac. You couldn't have found a closer match."

He looked at the necklace in the box. A single strand of pearls with a diamond catch. Perfectly white, like the ones from the North Sea oysters that she wore on her wrist. He took it out of the box and held it to the light. This wasn't the same necklace he'd purchased. The other one wasn't as white, the pearls weren't as perfect. But what was one more miracle in a life filled with them?

Kathleen pulled her hair off her neck and stood before Mac. "Will you put it on?"

He brushed away a stray strand of Kathleen's hair, kissing her neck as he lay the necklace against her skin. The fragrance of her perfume filled his senses, along with the lingering scents of cinnamon and spice, peppermint and pine. His fingers shook as he fastened the catch and watched it twinkle, even in his shadow. He rested his hands on her shoulders, leaned over, and whispered in her ear. "They're beautiful, and so are you."

"Thank you, my beast," she breathed, so only he could hear.

The limousine waited at the curb, the driver holding the door for the stunning couple and the little girl. Julie chattered away about the day she had shared with Mac, and although they listened, Kathleen and Mac appeared to be lost in each other's eyes. They sat across from each other, afraid to touch, afraid of all the emotion they kept bottled inside.

The limousine stopped, and Mac stepped out first, wanting to see Kathleen's expression when she saw their destination. Her face lit up from the thousands of white twinkling lights outlining the yacht anchored in the harbor, and those lights reflected in her eyes. She looked at Mac and beamed; that smile he hadn't seen in days had returned. Oh, how he had missed that smile.

He escorted his favorite ladies to the boat, to the table set for three. The centerpiece of red roses contained three tall white candles, their flames flickering in the light breeze. A white baby grand stood in the corner, the pianist in white tie and tails lightly playing *Some Enchanted Evening* as the waiter seated them.

"Oh, Mac. This is wonderful."

"Only the best for you and Julie." He nodded to the waiter. Another waiter pushed out a tray of covered sterling silver platters. "And only your favorite foods for dinner."

The waiter uncovered the trays, revealing the same foods Kathleen had ordered at the Plaza—fettuccine Alfredo, lobster, shrimp, even chocolate éclairs.

The waiter filled their plates, then stood away, allowing them privacy.

"I'm waiting," Mac stated.

"For what?"

"Aren't you the least bit interested in telling me about your lunch at the White House?"

Her face nearly burst with excitement. "It was wonderful. She was so gracious and kind, and intelligent. She said she had always wanted to be a journalist and asked if she could write a story for *Success*. Of course I said yes, and I'm going to edit it for her."

"Sounds like you hit it off."

"I can't even begin to tell you how good I felt in her company."

"I can tell. It's written on your face. I saw it the moment we walked through your door tonight."

"That wasn't just the First Lady's influence."

"No?"

"Of course not. I was excited about seeing you, too."

"Why, thank you. I'm glad I rate right up there with the First Lady."

She laughed. "You know what she suggested?"

"What?"

"She said she absolutely loves decorating for Christmas, and asked if I'd like to do a special feature on Christmas at the White House."

"And I suppose you've already got a plan in mind."

"I've already got staff working on it. I can't slack off on an opportunity like this."

Mac smiled indulgently. He, too, had long ago had his day at the White House, but he wouldn't mention it. This was her day to revel in the glory. Kathleen described everything in detail while he listened to every word, but every once in a while he couldn't help but wonder why the First Lady had suggested a Christmas theme. It seemed as though Christmas constantly crept into every aspect of his life. He had even spent time with Grace discussing the office Christmas party and giving in to her pleas that he play Santa.

They ate and laughed and sang for hours. Mac swept Julie up into his arms and danced her around the deck, and Kathleen stood back and nearly cried. Never had she known such joy. Watching Mac and Julie together brought a lump to her throat, the emotion was so overwhelming.

The evening ended all too soon, and by midnight they had tucked Julie into bed, and Mac leaned against the doorjamb, wishing he could stay, but knowing it wouldn't happen.

"If you want to sleep in late tomorrow, I'll explain to the boss."

She laughed and combed her hand through her hair. "Can't. We've moved up the release date on *Success* to Friday."

"It's gone that well?"

"Yes. Of course, if you spent any time at the office, you'd know."

"I've had much more fun with Julie. But Kath, I'd really like to spend some time alone with you. Tomorrow, maybe?"

"No . . ."

"I know. Too much work. So, when?"

"Friday night?"

"Perfect. My place at eight, and I'll fix dinner. Do you think you could get someone to watch Julie all night?"

"And just what do you have in mind?"

"No definite plans. I just want nature to run its course, without any interference."

Kathleen stood at Mac's door, afraid to knock. She felt the same way she had felt ten years ago when she had stood at his office door for the first time. She wanted to see him, yet she was afraid she would turn to mush once she looked into his eyes.

She raised her fist, knocking lightly. The door opened and he stood before her, looking absolutely wonderful in a charcoal suit she wanted to remove, piece by piece.

He took her hand and pulled her inside, closing the door behind them. He hadn't seen her in three days, but it felt like years. He hadn't really kissed her in five days, but he hadn't forgotten the feel, the taste, the sensations that coursed through his body. He felt all that and more now, just looking at her. She wore a black silk sheath, short and strapless, quite similar to the white dress she had worn at the Plaza. Above-the-elbow black gloves, three-inch black heels, and, of course, her pearl necklace and bracelet.

"I know this phrase is getting rather worn out, but you look beautiful."

"Only for you."

He sighed, trying to keep his distance, his composure. It wasn't time to take her into his arms. He wanted to, but the time had to be perfect. This woman he loved more than life itself managed to be sensuous without even trying. She'd been that way in blue jeans. She'd been that way naked in his arms. And she was that way dressed like a million dollars.

"Is something wrong?"

"Wrong? No. Let me show you around."

He clutched her hand and led her into the living room. Her breath caught. She had expected something contemporary, a man's room. Instead, she saw their cottage. The gramophone. The rocking horse. She closed her eyes and opened them again, but it was all still there, just as she remembered. She picked up a picture frame and looked at the photo.

"That's me and my mom and dad," Mac said. "Julie found it in a photo album. It's funny how you put things like that away and forget about them." She picked up another, of Mac and Julie at the zoo. "We took that one yesterday. I still need one of you and me."

"Oh, Mac, it's all so wonderful. I didn't expect you to live in a place like this."

"It hasn't always been this way. Julie and I picked out everything on one of our excursions. That kid has great taste."

"Did she pick out the rocking horse?" she asked, walking to its side and lovingly touching the painted wood.

"No. That was my idea. She hasn't even seen it yet." He took her hand. "I invited you to dinner. You're hungry, I hope."

"Always."

"Good." He pulled her into the dining room, lit by a hundred candles. He watched her face, her smile illuminated by the fire's glow. The table was intimately set for just the two of them, white linen and lace, white bone china, delicate crystal stemware, sparkling sterling silver.

He pulled out her chair and pushed it in as she sat down. On her plate lay a single white rose and an envelope embossed with a gold *M*. She picked up the rose, closed her eyes, and inhaled its wonderful fragrance. She looked into his eyes, and no words of thanks were necessary. Their exchange said more than any words.

"Shall I open this now?"

He nodded and walked to his chair while she pulled out the card. *Congratulations on your Success. May all your future endeavors be such crowning achievements. All my love, Mac.*

"It is a success, isn't it?" She beamed.

"Yes."

"You're not upset? I mean, now you owe me a promotion."

"No, I'm not upset. And, yes, I'm going to give you a promotion."

"But—"

"Oh, hell." He got up from the table and threw his napkin back down in his plate.

Kathleen's eyes widened. "What's wrong?"

"Nothing, but I'm not hungry, not now, anyway." He took her hand and pulled her up out of the chair. "Come here."

"Where are we going?"

"To the living room. We have to talk." He led her to the couch and asked her to sit, then got down on bended knee before her. "Kathleen Flannigan?"

"Yes," she gulped.

"I've had more than my share of success in my lifetime. Everything I touch seems to turn to gold. I suppose you've heard that rumor? Well, it's pretty much true. But I haven't been too lucky in love, until I met you. You've turned my whole life around. You haven't asked me for anything. You've given me your love, and all I've done is ask things from you in return."

"Only one thing, and I've decided you're right."

He frowned. "What are you talking about?"

"I've decided to quit McKenna Publishing. I want to get married and live at McKenna House, and do charity work and eat watercress sandwiches."

"No, you don't," he quickly fired back.

"But I want you."

"I'm yours, but on my terms."

"Which are?"

"First, I'm retiring."

"You're what?"

"Retiring. I've had it up to here"—he waved his hand over the top of his head—"with going to work every day. I can do the stuff I need to do from home. I have accountants and

attorneys and vice presidents who can run things quite well.
I'm perfectly happy being chairman of the board. I don't need
to run the show, too."

"And what do you plan to do while you're retired? You'll
hate sitting around with nothing to do."

"I don't plan on just sitting around. Now, if you laugh, I
won't go on with the rest of my plan."

"I won't laugh."

"Okay. I'm going to buy a ranch in Montana and be a
part-time cowboy."

"Sounds like a wonderful idea to me. But Montana's a long
way from New York."

"Oh, I plan to stay here part time, too. In this apartment,
and at McKenna House."

"What about me and Julie? Do we fit into this picture
somewhere?"

"You're the biggest part of the picture. But let's start with
Julie. She's going to have a full-time father. You know,
carpools, room mother, that sort of thing."

She couldn't help herself, she had to laugh.

He grinned. "You think it's funny?"

"I think it's wonderful. But are you sure?"

"Kath, I loved every moment I spent with that child. I
know it won't always be perfect, but it's what I want. It
means more to me than running a company."

"Okay. But where do I come in?"

"Where you've wanted to be for ten years. Since I'm
retiring, McKenna Publishing needs a new president."

She didn't laugh this time, she just sat there staring, her
mouth open, her eyes wide.

He pulled out a long velvet box and handed it to her.
"Open it."

She lifted the lid. Before her in the box lay an etched gold-
plated door plaque. *Kathleen Flannigan O'Brien—Presi-*

dent. Her eyes filled with tears as she tilted her head up to look at Mac.

"You don't like it?"

She was speechless. Her tears said everything and more than her words could. She reached out her hands to his face and pulled him to her, kissing his lips. "This is the most wonderful present I've ever received."

"Probably the most expensive, too."

"Oh, Mac."

"I love it when you say 'oh, Mac.' But, sweetheart, there's a few conditions attached to this promotion."

She looked at him, waiting to hear the conditions.

"I'd like you to work halfway normal hours so you can spend your evenings with me and Julie."

She nodded. "I can do that."

"If you have to take any trips, I'm going with you. I have no intention of ever waking up in the morning without you beside me."

She continued nodding. "I don't want to be away from you, either."

"And last, but certainly not least, I'd like to have more children. I'll always love Julie, but I'd like a McKenna, Jr., too, and maybe a few more for good measure."

"Can we start tonight?"

"Why do you think I bought the rocking horse? We never got to fully try it out last weekend."

"Mac?"

"Yes?"

"You're on bended knee. Do you plan to propose again?"

"You turned down my last proposal. This one's binding. If you say yes, I'm holding you to it."

Kathleen took his hands in hers. "I'm waiting."

"Kathleen Flannigan, I give you my love, my life, and" —he laughed—"my job. I ask nothing from you in return, except that you love me for the rest of your life. Will you marry me?"

She nodded. "Yes," she whispered and slipped into the loving warmth of his arms.

He held her tight, closed his eyes, and said a prayer. "Thank you, Lord."

EPILOGUE

McKenna O'Brien stood at the window and watched the light snow falling outside. Snow had come late this year, but Christmas Eve morning had dawned with blue skies and sunshine, and a thick blanket of snow that had fallen during the night. They had used Julie's new toboggan for the first time, singing Christmas carols as they slid down the hill, Kathleen standing at the top, cheering them on, her voice also joining in the merry refrains.

Together they had strung popcorn and cranberries to hang on the massive tree that stood in the grand hallway of McKenna House. Even Mac's mother and grandmother had joined in on the fun. Oh, how they loved having a child around the house. He loved it, too. After five months he couldn't remember even one day where he had regretted his decision to step down as president.

He looked toward his bed, to the beautiful woman whose long auburn hair spread across his pillow. His wife, the mother of his unborn child, whose movements he had felt for the first time that night when they lay quietly in each other's arms. Kathleen had pressed his hand to her slightly rounded belly. He nearly cried when he felt the kick of the miracle they had created. The past six months had been nothing but miracles, and he felt truly blessed.

Outside, he heard the sound of bells, an odd, light tinkling noise. He looked again through the window but saw nothing, only the snow. Kathleen stirred in bed. He sat beside her and pulled the down comforter under her chin, and lovingly kissed her forehead. He heard the jingle again, then a tapping noise on the roof. A squirrel, maybe, hopping from the branch of a tree and scurrying across the shingles.

He started to climb back into bed, but listened intently to noises down below. Maybe Julie had gotten out of bed to take an early peek at her Christmas presents. He quietly went to the bedroom door, opened it, and went to the stairs. For a moment he could have sworn he saw a bright light flash around the tree, then up through the chimney. But it was only his imagination.

He crept down the stairs. The rocking chair moved slightly, back and forth. The tray of cookies on the table beside it was empty, the glass of milk only half-full. He looked around for Julie, or possibly his mother, placing some last-minute gifts under the tree. But he saw no one. Nothing except a red envelope sitting in the rocker.

Merry? Nicky? He smiled. He had never told Kathleen about his truly miraculous housekeeper. She probably would have believed his story, for she did believe in miracles. But he wanted to keep Merry to himself. A special woman who would always be close to his heart.

He picked up the envelope, lifted the flap, and pulled out the note. A tear came to his eye, along with a smile for the lady who had given him back his life. He read her words. *Keep Christmas in your heart, young man, and your life will be enchanted, and your dreams will surely come true.*